# THE TOURIST TOWN MURDERS

A Novel

by

M. C. Lemley

THE DALLES-WASCO COUNTY
PUBLIC LIBRARY
722 COURT ST.
THE DALLES, OREGON 97058

## DEDICATION and THANKS

This book is dedicated to my family and friends, whose support and encouragement helped my to realize my dream.

I thank my three children, Jeff, Audrey and Tony, for your gentle confidence in me and for your moral support. If you ever doubted your mother could write a book, you never let it show. I especially thank you, Audrey, for your many, many hours of patient editing and for your invaluable work on the cover.

To my sisters, Pam and Annette, I offer a great big thank you for your moral support.

Thank you, Mom, for your patience and foresight. It was your enthusiastic reaction to reading my manuscript that gave me the inspiration and the courage to publish it. May you rest in peace.

And, last but not least, I'd like to thank my many friends, whose belief in me means the world to me.

God bless you all.


Cover photos and design by Audrey Lemley

This book is a work of fiction. Any likeness to any real person, in name or description, is completely coincidental and unintended.

ISBN: 1-4348-5647-X

Copyright© 2010 M.C. LEMLEY

No part of this work may be copied without express written permission of M.C. Lemley

The Tourist Town Murders

Chapter 1

*Monday afternoon, June 15, 1987*

The 45-mile-an-hour west wind and 6-foot waves on the Columbia River had Matt Goodell fighting to keep control of his sailboard. With intense concentration, he played the wind and rocketed across the tips of the whitecaps. The impact of his board, pounding wave after wave, combined with the howl of the wind to create a deafening rhythmic pattern in his ears.

As he neared the Oregon shore, Matt shifted his weight slightly to slow his speed, unaware that his left foot had slipped free of the foot straps and balanced dangerously close to the edge of his board. He quickly moved his hands along the boom, pulling it toward him while deftly performing a boom-to-boom crossover as he leaned into the 180-degree turn. With a small, quick twist of his hips, he shifted his weight forward. His left foot slipped off the edge of his board and plunged into the cold river.

Matt went down onto his knee, but managed to stay on his board. Instinctively he sprang back into a standing position, fighting hard to regain his balance. In another quick maneuver, he re-shifted his weight and adjusted his faltering sail to catch the full force of the wind. The agility and strength gained from years of physical training enabled him to remain in control of his sailboard and not take an embarrassing and ungainly dive into the Columbia River.

A minute later, the small slip all but forgotten, he sailed out into the middle of the river, where the waves were eight feet high and the sailing was even more challenging.

After a few more runs across the river, Matt once again headed back toward the Washington shore. It had been a good day of sailing, but he was growing tired. His arms trembled slightly and his knees felt weak. He'd been on the river too long, and was now vulnerable to an accident, but Matt was young and felt invincible. Three months at the police academy and five years on the job should have taught him that no one was invincible, but he wasn't thinking about his invincibility or lack thereof. His concentration wavered.

When he left the Oregon shore and started across the water, he led a group of about fifteen to twenty windsurfers. As they neared the center of the river, unnoticed by him, the others turned back. Instead of focusing on his sailing, however, he started thinking about his future, which at this point in his life remained uncertain.

Now he realized he was alone on the water. *That's odd,* he thought, *where'd everybody go?* He looked up river, to the east. The river was clear. In the distance he could see the Hood River Bridge.

Suddenly five long, deep horn-blasts from an approaching tugboat exploded across the waves, a warning to all to clear the river. Startled, Matt almost slipped off his board again. Twisting his neck around in a contorted effort, he looked behind him, down river, and gasped at what he saw.

Bearing down on him were 15,000 tons of steal and wood, a tow of river-barges pushed by a tugboat traveling ten knots per hour. Matt was dead center in the path of that huge tow and had little chance of getting out of the way in time. His heart stopped for a second, and then almost leapt out of his chest, his breath caught in his throat. That priceless commodity, *time,* seemed to stop for him as he stared in shocked disbelief at the rapidly approaching barges.

Matt realized he'd made a terrible mistake. He'd let his focus waver from what he was doing. He would never make that mistake again.

The day had started out fine. It was a beautiful day to be sailing and he felt like a million dollars, physically.

His yearly vacation would begin in another week. His plans included spending most of the two weeks at his parents' ranch in Colorado. His friends and family knew about these plans, but what he'd told no one except his boss, and his sister Adriana, was that when he got back at the end of those two weeks he was thinking of resigning his job as a police officer. Although he'd always enjoyed his work, lately he'd been feeling unhappy and restless. He didn't really want to give up his job, his career, but he found it a difficult and lonely life. He thought that maybe it wasn't the best thing for him.

That's when he'd decided to go home to see his folks for a while. The change would do him good. The home ranch offered peace and solace, a place to think through one's problems. After spending ten or eleven days out in the open spaces and away from the pressures of the job, he expected he'd be able to decide what it was he wanted to do. And if he wanted any advice, his dad always had some of that to share.

With a concentrated effort Matt brought his attention back to the business at hand, that of windsurfing. *It's your day off,* he told himself. *Relax and enjoy life. Tomorrow will be soon enough to worry about the future.*

That's when he found himself face to face with the oncoming barges.

Precious seconds slipped away while he fought rising panic. Too late, he tried to make a run for it. Adjusting his sail to try to catch some wind, he careened up and over the waves in a hopeless effort to out-distance the oncoming danger.


Matt's best friend, off-duty officer Lt. "Willy" Wilson, stood on the shore watching in disbelief as Matt sailed out into the path of the barges. Matt knew better than to do such a reckless thing as that. *What was that idiot thinking?* Willy asked himself. His heart began to hammer as he watched helplessly. There had to be something he could do, he thought, besides stand there and stare. His hands clenched tightly as he frantically glanced around. A hundred yards up the beach was a boat dock. He could see a fishing boat tied to it.

Willy sprinted across the beach. A tall, redheaded man stood on the deck of the small fishing boat, scrubbing down the deck of the boat. Willy recognized the man as Rusty McGreggor. Rusty worked at one of the local banks, and was also an avid windsurfer and personal friend of Willy's. Willy jumped onto the wooden dock, and ran out to the boat.

"Rusty, I need your boat," he demanded, pointing out into the river. "Matt's in trouble out there. Can you take me out?"

"Sure, Willy. Jump aboard; we're as good as gone."

Willy jumped into the boat before Rusty finished speaking. With a flourish McGreggor started the engine and backed away from the dock, turned a tight reverse semi-circle and thrust the lever ahead to full throttle. "Did you say Matt? Matt Goodell? What's going on?" He'd gotten to know Matt quickly when Matt had come to the region a year ago. They got along well and sailed together often.

While Willy quickly explained the situation, he watched Matt's flight for safety. The barge was quickly over-taking his friend as Willy looked on in hopeless frustration. Willy yelled at the top of his lungs for Matt to sail upriver. *It's your only chance,* he thought. He stood and watched as the distance between man and barge closed.

Matt's sail caught an extra gust of wind that literally hurled him across the waves at speeds in excess of thirty miles an hour.

Unfortunately, it wasn't fast enough. Within seconds the barges would be on top of him.

Matt suddenly felt the wind die from his sail. He was in the dead air zone, that short wind-free area right in front of the barges. He watched his sail slowly sink and felt his sailboard lose its momentum and come to a fatal stop. The barges were just 30 yards from him and he was still 25 yards short of being in the clear. There was no time to stop and rest. He quickly debated his options.

They were damned few. *Live or die. Give up now, or fight for your life,* he thought.

Matt quickly gauged the approaching barges. He'd seen many barges in the Puget Sound, both empty and full. The barges advancing on him now were floating considerably high in the water. He was sure they were empty. He made a quick decision. He'd have to dive under the barges. It was his only chance of coming out of this alive.

Taking a couple of deep breaths, he dove into the water and plunged straight down as the lead barge thundered over him. He felt a severe blow on his left shoulder---it knocked the air from his lungs---sent him rolling and twisting through the murky water.

The river raged dark and turbulent under the barges as Matt fought hopelessly against the current.


Adriana Goodell, Matt's sister, stood at her kitchen sink looking out the window at the river as she washed dishes. Sweat trickled down her face and neck, a combined result of the hot mid-June sun and the steaming, soapy water in the sink. She reached up and opened the window in front of her. The strong west wind blew in and cooled off her face, bringing welcomed comfort. She gazed out at the scene in front of her.

The Columbia River snaked serpent-like through the mountains, effectively dividing the states of Washington and Oregon. It was an incredible view that never failed to move her. Evergreen fir trees intermixed with pine, cottonwood, and oak to make a beautiful combination, topped by an incredibly blue sky that was accented by a clear view of Mt. Hood in Oregon. All this should have given Adriana sufficient reason to be at peace with her life and her world.

On the contrary, she had been plagued all day with an unexplained heaviness and anxiety. Trying to shake off the mood, she blamed the feelings of apprehension on Michael Sans, the principal of the primary school where she worked as a third-grade teacher. Michael had been harassing her for months to go out with him. The more adamantly she refused, the more tenacious he became. He reminded her of a bulldog who stubbornly refused to relinquish a bone.

Now as she stood at the sink, her hands dangling in the water, she suddenly realized that it wasn't Michael Sans she was worried about. She turned her head and looked at a picture of Matt hanging on the kitchen wall. Quickly drying her hands, she reached up and touched the photo. A cold finger of fear ran down her back, causing goose bumps to spread up and across her shoulders in spite of the heat. A vision of Matthew on his sailboard exploded across her mind as real as if it were happening directly in front of her. He was in imminent danger. She could feel it. It gripped her whole being and chilled her to the marrow.

The dishes were forgotten as she ran to the telephone and dialed the number of Willy Wilson. Seconds dragged into hours as she waited and prayed for someone to answer. After ten rings, it seemed her prayers were being ignored when someone finally answered with a breathless `hello'.

"Rose? This is Adriana Goodell."

"Oh, Adriana dear, how are you?" came the reply. "I'm sorry it took so long to get to the phone. I was outside with the children, playing in the wading pool. It's been so hot, hasn't it?"

"Yes, it has. I'm calling about my brother. Is he there?"

"Why, no, he's not. He and Willy were going windsurfing this afternoon, but I'm expecting them back soon. Do you want me to have him call you, dear?"

"Yes, please. I'd appreciate that, Rose. Thank you. 'Bye."

Adriana slowly replaced the receiver. The fact that Rose hadn't heard from the two men meant little. But, she reminded herself, at least there wasn't any bad news...yet. She knew something had happened, but she didn't know what. And that bothered her. A lot.

Down under the barges, Matt fought for several seconds to regain his senses. He'd rolled over and over and was no longer sure which way was up, but he had to make a fast decision. He started swimming by blind instinct. He kicked as hard as he could, his powerful legs pumping like pistons. In spite of his tremendous efforts, the suction created from the barges was dragging him backwards, working against him, pulling him down deeper and deeper. His lungs ached as an invisible band of agonizing pressure tightened around his torso and spread up into his head. It pushed against his eardrums and his eyeballs until he thought they would burst. *Don't think about the pain*, he told himself. *Just swim.*

Matt saw a shaft of daylight penetrating the murky water. He concentrated on that spot, forcibly blocking from his mind the dull roar that was building inside his head. The bright spot grew closer and closer until at last he swam out from under the barges. He frantically kicked himself toward the surface, his lungs screaming for air. The force of his ascent shot him up and out of the water. Gasping and coughing, he inhaled huge gulps of air and water before gravity once again pulled him beneath the river's surface. He popped right back up, however, and this time he managed to stay on top.

He had no time to rest, since he'd surfaced a mere twenty feet from the barges. For several minutes he fought against the strong drag they created. The strong, suction-like pull grew less and less severe until, finally, he was able to swim clear, but the effort it took left him exhausted and helpless. Then he was hit by the first of several high swells caused by the barges. They were almost Matt's undoing. First rising up beneath him and tossing him high on their peaks, then plunging him down farther and farther until all he could see around him were high walls of rolling, churning water. The waves crashing over the top of him threatening to drown him. Finally, they pushed him further away from the path of danger as the barges continued on past him.

Matt heard two long, angry blasts of the tugboat's horn. He turned to look up toward the wheelhouse. The tugboat captain was leaning out the window, shaking his fist at Matt. Every line of the captain's face was etched with vile anger as he shouted obscenities that went unheard above the roar of the boat engines. It was a face Matt would never forget.

In the small fishing boat eighty yards away, Willy Wilson watched anxiously for Matt to surface. After several long minutes, during which time seemed not to exist, Willy saw Matt surface and fight his way through the surging waves.

"There he is, over there!" he pointed. McGreggor nodded and turned the steering wheel toward the spot where Lt. Wilson pointed. Their boat converged on Matt as he struggled in the water. Willy called out to him, "Matt, hang on!"

At the sound of Willy's voice, relief swept through Matt, and he turned and raised a tired arm in response.

Within a few seconds, they reached Matt and helped him into the small boat. Willy's relief and joy battled for dominance against the strong desire to grab Matt and shake some sense into him for being so careless.

"My God, Matt, you scared the crap out of me! You know you could have been killed! What the hell were you thinking of out there, you damn fool?"

Matt couldn't speak. Leaning over the side of the small boat, he vomited up water until he felt like his insides would collapse. After a couple of minutes the convulsions subsided and he was able to sink down onto the seat.

"I don't know, Willy. Oh, Lord, I feel awful. I guess I just wasn't paying attention out there--" another coughing fit interrupted him. When it ended he continued, "Ya' know, ... I didn't even hear him ...blow any warning signal... until it was too late."

Exhausted and weak, Matt sat hunched over on the seat, his elbows resting on his knees, his head in his hands. He tried hard to catch his breath. But to him, it didn't seem like there was enough air available. The harder he breathed, the less air he got. The world started turning dark and closing in around him. He was very cold and started shaking violently.

Rusty threw Willy a blanket out of the storage to wrap around Matt's shoulders. Willy could see that Matt was now hyperventilating.

"Have you got any paper bags in here, Rusty?"

Rusty rummaged around until he found one and handed it to Willy. "Here. It's kind of small, but I think that's all I've got."

"That'll do. Thanks." Willy took the small bag and sitting down next to Matt, he held it over Matt's mouth and nose. "Here. Breathe into this. You'll be O.K. in a minute." Turning around, he said, "O.K. Rusty, take us back."

Rusty turned the boat around and headed back to the dock.

After a minute Matt began to breathe easier. The darkness lightened, then disappeared. The blanket warmed him, and soon the shaking became less violent.

Willy sat beside him quietly, respecting his wearied silence, an arm around his shoulders.

By the time they reached the boat dock, Matt's breathing had almost returned to normal. And he'd regained his composure enough to acknowledge Rusty's presence and to thank him for his help.

Once back on shore, Willy helped Matt out of his wetsuit, then hustled him into Willy's pickup and took him back to his own house.

It had become a habit for Matt to join Willy, Rose and their three children for dinner just about every Monday since Matt had come to Pine Crest. When they arrived, Matt sank into the first comfortable chair he found and remained there, sipping the cold beer Willy brought him. He planned to stay right there until dinner time. He couldn't stop thinking of the close call he'd had. Although he'd never admit it, the fact that he'd almost drowned shook him up badly.

Willy's wife, Rose, told Matt that his sister had called twice in the last hour and seemed worried. Matt immediately asked to use the phone, and called Adriana at home. He wasn't surprised that she knew he'd been in danger. She always seemed to know.

When he got through to her, he admitted he'd had some trouble on the water, but played down the danger and told her he'd give her more details when he got home. He reminded her that he was staying at Willy's for dinner. She seemed relieved that he was all right, but he knew she didn't believe his story. She had enough respect for his privacy not to pressure him, though. He appreciated that. He was too tired to get into it over the phone.

Willy told Rose about Matt's brush with death. She decided what Matt needed most was a quiet dinner, so she kept their normally robust and noisy offspring under a tight rein.

Matt's quiet, reserved manner, so different from his normal behavior, worried Willy at first. Before long, however, Matt perked up and entered into the conversation. With three of his most loyal fans almost busting at the seams to talk to him, it was hard to remain self-absorbed.

The meal revived him a bit, but Matt still felt exhausted. He thanked Rose for the dinner, said good-bye to the children and walked out to his car. Willy walked with him.

"How's Adriana? I haven't seen much of her lately," Willy asked. He'd once thought he was in love with Matt's sister, but it hadn't worked out. Then he'd met Rose and realized what true love really meant. But Adriana still held a special place in his heart, partly because she was Matt's younger sister. In a way, Willy regarded her the same way, as a younger sister.

"Fine, thanks. She invited Connie White over for dinner tonight, so they're probably still swapping gossip."

"Your sister's a beautiful woman. I'm surprised she's not married yet. And that Connie White isn't bad looking either." Willy slapped Matt on the back. "Why don't you ask her out sometime, Romeo?"

"Why don't you mind your own business? I'm not looking for any romantic ties right now. Anyway, she's not my type."

Matt slowly drove back to the apartment he shared with Adriana. His close escape today made him stop and think about the unpredictability of life and death. If he had died today, he would have left this world without an heir to remember him and carry on his name. It was an empty feeling that he didn't like.

There was only one woman he'd ever really been serious about...Lisa McGuire. He'd loved and trusted her with all his youthful, vulnerable innocence. And she'd used him, then left him, crushed and broken. He hadn't been able to trust another woman since.

## Chapter 2

At that moment, Adriana and Connie were enjoying an after dinner glass of wine. Adriana had only partially recovered from her earlier premonition that Matthew was in some kind of danger, and was now making a huge effort not to let her concern show. Lifting her glass up in front of her, she swirled the clear liquid around and watched the light sparkle through it. Bringing the glass closer, she closed her eyes and inhaled deeply, filling her lungs with the light, fruity aroma.

"Umm. There's nothing like a glass of good wine to end the day with." Adriana opened her eyes and turned to look at Connie.

"Well, I can think of one or two things that would compete." Connie's gray eyes twinkled brightly, belying the sober expression on her face.

"Oh? And what would that be, humm?" Adriana asked innocently, joining in on the impromptu game. She knew full well how Connie would like to end her days, and with whom. They had been good friends for almost five years and there was little that one didn't know about the other.

"Well-l-l," Connie drew the word out reluctantly, "it just might have something to do with that handsome brother of yours." Connie could not keep a straight face any longer, as the laughter bubbled up inside her. She blushed and shook her head, sending long platinum-blonde curls dancing about her head. "I think I could easily fall in love with him."

Adriana sobered quickly at that revelation, looked at her friend seriously, and quietly said, "Connie, I hope you're kidding. That's not a good idea. Matt is a tough nut to crack, and I don't want to see either one of you get hurt."

"A tough one, huh? Humm, I always did like a good challenge."

"You don't understand. There's something you don't realize. It's not common knowledge, and you have to promise not to say anything to anybody, especially not to Matt. He'd kill me if he found out I told you this. You know we're both going back to Colorado to visit the folks in a week or so."

"Yeah, sure. So what? You'll be gone, what, a couple of weeks, right?"

"Right---sort of. I'll be back after a couple of weeks. Matt might not be back."

"What do you mean he might not be back? What about his job?"

"Well, he said he's not sure he wants to keep this job. He's asked Chief Baxter for a leave of absence."

"Wow. I don't know what to say. What do you think about it?"

"I don't want him to go, but it's his life after all, and I can't tell him how to live it. I just thought you should know, since you seem to be developing a crush on him. Promise me you won't say anything to him. And be careful, okay?"

"Don't worry, I won't say a word and I'll be very careful."

Adriana seriously considered her friend for a moment longer, than nodded her head. Yes, Connie would be careful. Adriana loved both Connie and Matt more that anyone else in the world, outside of her parents, and she would be delighted to see the two of them get together, but she decided to move on to a safer subject.

"Not to change the subject, but are you planning to go to the Women's Club meeting Wednesday night?"

"Yes, of course."

The Forth of July dinner-dance, a yearly benefit for Pine Crest Memorial Hospital, was one of the biggest events of the year. Since both Connie and Adriana were school teachers, they had their summers free and both worked as summer volunteers at the hospital, as well as being members of the Women's Club which helped sponsor the event. They were heavily involved in the preparations.

They spent the next few minutes discussing food, decorations, and music.

By nine o'clock, they had exhausted the subject of the dinner-dance and the talk had become personal once more, only this time it was directed at Adriana and her problem with Michael Sans.

"I've even considered looking for another teaching job in another town, but I don't want to do that and it makes me mad as hell that he could drive me to even consider that option!"

"I know he was pursuing you this spring, but I didn't think his interest would last this long. What are you going to do, Adri?" Connie addressed her friend by the familiar nick-name. "You can't let this guy continue to harass you just because he's your boss. And don't you even think about quitting your job, girl. I'd miss you too much. And besides we've got several school projects planed together for next year."

"I know, but what can I do?"

"Have you said anything to Matt?"

"No, and I don't want to. I'm going to talk to Michael again myself. I need to convince him that there is no future for him with me."

"You'll have to be more assertive."

"I know."

"Well, I think you ought to tell Matt and let him have a word with Michael. Then he'll leave you alone."

"Not yet. I think I can take care of Michael Sans myself."

They heard a car drive up and looked out the window to see Matt walking up the driveway. Adriana greeted him at the door. Relief flooded over her when she saw he appeared to be all right.

Matt said hello to Adriana, then turned and looked over at Connie. In spite of his earlier declaration that Connie White wasn't his type, she held a strong attraction for him that he tried unsuccessfully to deny. His heart skipped a beat, then accelerated to an unnaturally fast thumping in his chest as he was struck afresh by her unusual beauty. A sparkling halo of light seemed to dance around her hair as she moved across the room. The modest blouse she wore only accentuated her firm, full breasts. When she smiled and said hello, Matt noticed a slight blush in her cheeks and wondered if he was the cause of it. In a swift but sweeping glance, he took in her long legs, her slender hips and waist and her voluptuous torso. He felt the stirrings of sexual desire, something he hadn't allowed himself to feel for a long time. With a shake of his head he thought he must still be experiencing a little reaction to his long day.

While telling Adriana and Connie about his escapade, Matt noticed both the girls had turned a little pale so he poured them each another glass of wine. He hadn't meant to upset them, but he knew if he didn't tell them about the incident they would probably hear it from someone else. He reassured them he was all right, then excused himself and went to take a shower.

When he came out of the bathroom Adriana was alone. He asked her where Connie was and she informed him that Connie had gone home.

"I hope I didn't scare her off," he said.

"Actually, you did," Adriana responded with her usual honesty.

"She was pretty upset about what happened to you today. She's fond you."

"I like her, too; she's a nice girl."

"I mean she really likes you, more than just casually."

"Don't be playing match-maker, Sis. I don't need it." But Matt couldn't keep his thoughts from dwelling on Connie. She really was beautiful and alluring, and a lot of fun to be around. She didn't seem shallow or self-centered like so many of the girls Matt had gone out with before.

"She's pretty smart, isn't she?" he asked.

Turning away to hide the smile tugging at her lips, Adriana innocently shrugged her shoulders. "She was in the top ten percent of our graduating class at college. Why do you ask?"

"I don't know. Just curious. She doesn't seem like the other women I've dated, that's all."

"She's not. There's a side of her that is very serious about life. As a matter of fact, she's thinking of going back to university and working toward a doctorate in psychiatry." Adriana looked at her brother and smiled. She walked over to where he stood and spoke sincerely.

"Matt, I know it's none of my business, but I just want to say one thing. You're my brother and I love you dearly, and Connie is my best friend as you well know. Nothing would make me happier than to see the two of you get together, but I wouldn't let that happen if I thought she would hurt you in any way, or visa-versa." She paused for a moment before continuing. "I know her well enough to promise you that she would never intentionally cause you any pain. She's not like Lisa McGuire, Matt. Don't be afraid to ask her out sometime, if you think you'd like to." Adriana leaned over and kissed Matt's cheek. He wrapped his arms around her in a bear hug that left her gasping for breath.

"Thanks, Sis. That means a lot to me." Embarrassed by the show of emotion, Matt excused himself and hurried off to bed.

Exhaustion began to take its toll. He crawled into bed and fell into a restless sleep. His last thoughts before falling asleep were of Connie White.

But his dreams were about Lisa.

*Thick fog rolled across the moonlit beach, giving a lonely eeriness to the night. Visibility was only about thirty feet. He could hear the roar of the ocean and feel the mist on his face. He could hear, but could not see, the ocean waves breaking against the rocks. The salty, fishy air stung his nostrils as he jogged down the shoreline. He heard seagulls calling his name, over and over and over. Suddenly the fog closed in on him, swirling around him like a cocoon. It caressed his cheek and sent a cold chill down his back.*

*Lisa appeared in front of him, calling to him. He rushed into her arms with the happy thought of asking her to be his wife. The bulk of a jeweler's box rested in his pocket. He could feel it against his thigh. Inside was the diamond ring he had bought that morning. As he kissed Lisa, he reached into his pocket and drew out the ring.*

*Suddenly Lisa was backing away from him, saying "No, no. We can't do this. I can't see you anymore. I just came to say 'goodbye'. I'm sorry, but I've found someone else." Then she turned and disappeared into the fog. Her words echoed strangely, gargled and hallow, mingling with the returning cries of a hundred seagulls. The cries repeated themselves again and again, like echoes in a canyon, "Fool, fool, fool!" they said. And he knew it was true. Then he took the ring and threw it as hard as he could out into the beckoning sea.*

Matt awoke with a start, calling a name that hadn't passed his lips in three years. "Lisa". He shook his head to clear the sleepiness from his brain, got out of bed and walked to the window. The sun was beginning to peek over the horizon. A large blue jay sat on a branch outside his opened window, loudly scolding any and all rivals that dared come too close. Matt looked at his bedside clock: 5:05 a.m. Still tired from yesterday's experience with the barge tow, he crawled back into bed and slept the rest of the early morning hours in peace.

Chapter 3

Tuesday morning June 16 at 10 o'clock

Willy called Matt to see how he was feeling after his ordeal. Matt told him he was fine and planned to spend the afternoon back out on the river. Satisfied that Matt was okay, Willy hung up and prepared to spend his day off with his family. They wanted to have an early lunch, then spend the afternoon in the local swimming pool. Willy was teaching the children to swim.

Matt finished a second cup of coffee. He'd spent a few minutes this morning thinking about the dream he'd had and trying to analyze it. It didn't make sense to him. He was sure he'd gotten over Lisa a long time ago. Surprised that the dream didn't upset him very much any more, he put it behind him and let his mind drift on to a more pleasant subject. Connie White. Maybe it would be okay to go out with her just once or twice. After considering it over his third cup of coffee, he got up, walked over the phone and dialed her number.

She answered almost immediately. Would she like to have lunch with him and then maybe do a little windsurfing? She said she would love to, except that she didn't know how to windsurf. He could teach her, he replied.

At twelve o'clock sharp, Matt pulled his blue Jeep to a stop in front of Connie's rented duplex. His surf board and gear were in the back of the Jeep. The hot June sun beat down relentlessly, but a steady west wind was blowing and the short drive had not been uncomfortable. Connie waited for him in the front yard, under a large, shady oak tree. Two lawn chairs and a small white patio table on which stood two tall glasses of lemonade were all placed in the shade of the tree. Connie sat in one of the chairs and called out to Matt to join her.

The scene in front of him gave his lonely heart a strong tug. He stood for a moment, absorbing the sight, listening to the birds sing. He closed his eyes and could smell the freshly cut grass and the scent of roses in full bloom. He hadn't noticed the roses at first. Now he looked around and saw them, a short, curving row of bright yellows., waving gently in the wind. The whole picture – green lawn, tall shade trees, the roses, and a beautiful woman waiting for him – created a very peaceful and welcoming site. How nice it would be to come home to something like this every day, he thought. *You dunce,* an inner voice growled, *this isn't for you! Don't be fooled by this domestic scene. Don't forget what Lisa did to you. Don't forget the lesson she taught.*

Matthew gave himself a mental shake and pushed his earlier thoughts of 'coming home to this every day' aside. He wasn't going to be taken in by this cunning little beauty and her attempts to win his affection, if that is what she had in mind. As far as he was concerned, they were just out to have a good time together and share what could be a very pleasant afternoon. If they got along, maybe they'd keep company through the summer, starting and ending as friends. No strings attached, no promises made, none broken. Assuming he decided to remain here, that is. He'd forgotten for a moment that he was thinking of leaving his job here.

With a cocky smile on his face, he sauntered over to the where Connie sat. The breeze once again brought the scent of the roses to him. She returned his smile. The warmth in her soft, gray eyes made his heart jump into his throat. *A man could drown in those eyes*, he thought. Momentarily weakened, he bent down and placed a kiss on her cheek and whispered a soft "good afternoon" in her ear. The light scent of her perfume caught him off guard, rocking his senses. She did smell good.

As he accepted a glass of lemonade she offered, his hand touched hers, sending a little shock of heat up his arm. His surprised gasp went unnoticed as he took the glass with a trembling hand. The quickening of his heartbeat frustrated and confused him. Suddenly the warmth of the mid-day sun felt uncomfortable. He took a long gulp of lemonade. The cold drink did little to dispel the gathering heat he felt inside.

"You look like you've recovered nicely from your little adventure yesterday," Connie said. "I'm not sure that I want to take up such a dangerous sport."

"It's not usually dangerous, if you know what you're doing," he replied, recovering his composure. "I made a mistake yesterday in not paying more attention to what was going on around me." He shook his head and smiled. "I never make the same mistake twice." Their eyes met briefly. The double meaning behind his words reinforced what Adriana had told Connie yesterday, but she said nothing.

By the time they finished their lemonade, Matt felt cool and confident. They got into his Jeep and drove five miles west down Highway 14 to a local restaurant named Water's Edge. Located adjacent to a large, newly developed windsurfing spot called Briars Beach, the restaurant was especially well liked by the locals as well as visiting windsurfers and tourists because of its location close to the river as well as its good food. Large oak trees and towering cottonwoods provided ample shade and acted as partial windbreaks for the restaurant.

Matt and Connie went inside and were seated at a table next to a window. They could look out and watch the river with its windsurfers and various passing boats. The wind picked up considerably while they ate lunch. The restaurant itself had modern decor and featured framed prints of windsurfers, wildlife, and landscapes by one of the local photographers, an old timer who'd lived in the area most of his life and still took the most incredible scenic pictures.

During lunch Matt asked Connie if she'd like him to teach her to windsurf.

"I don't think I'm ready to take it on just yet, but I would love to come and watch you for awhile," she said.

"Okay, fair enough. I'll show you how much fun it can be, then maybe you'll change your mind."

After a long, leisurely lunch they drove the short distance to Briars Beach. They changed into their swimsuits in the modern new restrooms. Connie walked down the tree-lined path to where Matt was waiting at the edge of the river with his sailboard.

He proceeded to explain the different parts of his windsurfing gear to Connie, but he had a hard time keeping his mind on what he was doing. She looked so good in her black and red one-piece swimsuit that his eyes and his mind kept wondering away from the sport of windsurfing. With renewed, but useless effort to control his straying thoughts, he finished his short lesson and decided an actual, visual demonstration on the water would be better. It would put some much-needed distance between him and Connie, and get his mind back on track.

Unfortunately, he didn't do much better out on the water than he had on shore. After a half dozen spills, he laughingly gave up and came back in to shore.

"Well, I seem to have lost my edge," he said. His face turned a shade red and he had a hard time meeting Connie's eyes.

"Oh, no," she reassured him, "You were great! I loved watching you. It looks like fun." Secretly, she wondered if she was the reason he was distracted to the point of `losing his edge'. Maybe he wasn't such a tough nut to crack after all. She saw his blush deepen as he grinned shyly. This new, sensitive side of his personality increased her attraction to him. If she wasn't careful, she really would fall for him and, knowing his past history and his uncertain future, she knew she was taking a chance on getting hurt.

Connie looked around and asked Matt if he knew any of the other people on the beach. He pointed out two men who were talking together. One was of medium height with long, dark, curly hair. Connie thought he looked like he was in his early twenties. Matt told her that was Peter Bray, windsurfing hot-shot from Australia. The other man was Tom Morgan, half owner of Briars Beach. He was tall with sun-bleached blond hair and looked like a typical beach bum.

"Are they close friends of yours? I know a Sammy Morgan from up at the hospital. Any relation?" she asked him.

"No. I just met them a few weeks ago. We've sailed together a few times, that's all. And yes, Sammy and Tom are brothers. Peter's here for the summer and works part-time at Thompson's Saw Mill, and loves to sail. He's down here or at one of the other beaches every spare minute he has. He's getting to be a real hot-dog. Actually, he's kind of a pain in the a...neck, sometimes. He's hot stuff and he knows it. Trouble is, he wants everyone else to know it, too. Sometimes it gets him into trouble. Fights and such.

"Tom Morgan, on the other hand, is quiet and unobtrusive. Very friendly. Never been in any trouble that I know of. Not too bright, but an okay guy. They make an odd couple, but they hang out a lot together." He asked her if she was getting hungry. They could go up to the restaurant and get something to eat.

"No, I'm fine thanks," she said. "But, I'm getting hot. Let's get into the water and you can show me how to ride that board."

The rest of the afternoon was spent trying to teach Connie the basics of riding a sailboard, mounting and dismounting, adjusting the sail and balancing on the deck. After two hours Connie was tired and begged to quit. Matt immediately apologized for working her too hard.

He left her resting on the beach while he put away his gear. Then he stretched out on the sand beside her. They stayed there until they were dry and hot.

A shadow suddenly crossed over them. They looked up to see a man standing there holding a tray of cool drinks. The sun shadowed his face and caused a halo of light around his blond, almost white, hair.

"Well, if it isn't Officer Goodell and Miss Connie White. I haven't seen you around here before, Connie," he said. "How would you like a nice cold beer?"

"Hello Victor," Connie said. "Matt, you know Victor Prescott don't you? He's an EMT at Pine Crest Hospital, and one of their best ambulance drivers."

"Yes, of course." Matt stood up and offered his hand to Victor. "How are you, Victor?" Then he took Connie's hand and pulled her to her feet and asked her if she wanted a beer.

"What else have you got there, Victor? Is that lemonade? It looks pretty good." She reached out and helped herself to one of the tall glasses on his tray.

"Oh, that's not very cold now." A dismayed look crossed Victor's face briefly. "Have a beer instead. It's much colder." He tried to retrieve the glass of lemonade from Connie, but she backed out of his reach holding the glass high, laughing at him.

"It's just fine, thank you Victor. Besides, I don't like beer." As she finished speaking she lifted the glass to her lips and took a long swallow of the cold, tart liquid. It refreshed her dry throat and quieted the growing feeling of hunger she was just beginning to notice. Matt accepted a beer and consumed half of it in one swallow.

"What are you doing over here Victor?" Connie asked. "I thought you didn't like socializing with these boardheads?" She looked at him and thought he looked a little pale. "Victor lives just next door, Matt, just around the bend and down the road a little bit."

Before Victor could answer, they were joined by Rusty McGreggor. He carried a sailboard in one hand and the sail in the other. The wind did its best to rip the sail away but his strong grip held tight. Matt reached out and relieved the newcomer of his sail. "Rusty, watch out or you'll get blown away. I want you to meet someone. Connie White, this is Rusty McGreggor. And do you know Victor Prescott, Rusty?

"Connie, Rusty is the other half owner of this beach. He's in business with Tom Morgan, and you'll find him down here almost every day when he's not working at the bank. That is, when his wife lets him." Matt laughed and lightly punched Rusty in the stomach. Matt didn't mention that Rusty helped Willy rescue him from the river the day before. He didn't feel like discussing it in front of Victor.

Rusty ignored Matt's remark about his wife not letting him out to sail as he acknowledged Connie and Victor. He admired Connie's natural beauty and silently hoped that this time Matt had found someone special. Victor offered him a cold drink. He accepted a lemonade and drank it down thirstily, thinking that it was rather out of character for Victor to be over here socializing with the boardheads, considering his well-know dislike of all windsurfers. He gladly took a second glass of lemonade when Victor offered it. He'd been thirstier than he realized. The old axiom came to mind, *"Water, water everywhere, but not a drop to drink."*

The wind seemed to be kicking up stronger than ever as they stood there. Matt was standing close to Connie trying to hold on to his beer and Rusty's sail, which the wind was doing its best to take away. Victor reached up to help control the 6-foot sail when a sudden gust of wind whipped it out of Matt's hand. The sail spun around with a snap, knocking the glass out of Connie's hand.

Victor desperately tried to hang on to the sail. The weight of it pulled him off balance and he tripped as he tried to regain his balance without letting go of the sail. It was a losing battle. He ended up in the sand, on top of the sail. His tray of beer and lemonade went flying through the air and landed with a clatter.

"Are you alright, Victor?" Matt asked him. With a surprised look on his face, Victor replied that he was, and climbed to his feet. Rusty checked that Connie was unhurt, then apologized to everyone.

"Don't be silly, Rusty." Connie said. "It wasn't your fault."

"Yes, it was. It was my equipment and I should have been taking care of it instead of drinking lemonade." Rusty felt especially bad because Connie could have been seriously injured. He apologized again and said good-bye. Then he took his board and sail to the edge of the water to check it over. Nothing had been damaged, so he was soon in the water doing what he loved to do best.

Connie and Matt helped Victor pick up his tray and the few cans of beer and the glasses, which luckily had remained in tack thanks to the reasonably forgiving sand. Victor excused himself, leaving them alone. They sat on the beach and watched Rusty and the other windsurfers.

After about thirty minutes, Connie began to feel light-headed, dizzy and slightly nauseated. "Matt, I think I should go home. I don't feel very well. I think I've had too much sun."

Matt was immediately solicitous. "Yeah, sure. Come on. You probably just need something to eat. Fluids, too. You might be a little dehydrated."

As they walked back to Matt's Jeep, they saw Rusty sailing out across the waves. Matt shook his head and thought, *That Rusty is sure a glutton for punishment. He'll be out there until dark.*

He drove Connie home and insisted on taking her inside. "You're not feeling well," he said. "I just want to make sure you get something to eat and drink."

"No, really, I'm not hungry, Matt." Connie sat down and put her hand to her forehead. "I just have a little headache. I'll be fine."

But Matt insisted on making her a bowl of soup and sat by and made sure she ate all of it, then brought her a tall glass of water.

"Here, drink this. Then lay down for awhile. You'll feel better. Promise me you'll do that and I'll leave you alone."

She laughingly promised she would and saw him to the door. He said he would call her in a couple of hours to see how she was, then kissed her, said good-bye and left.

When Matt arrived home Adriana was pacing the floor. Matt barely got in the door when she confronted him.

"Well, finally!" she said. "I thought you'd never get home. Tell me, how'd it go? Did you have fun? How'd you two get along? Come on...tell all!"

Matt raised both hands as if to ward off an attack. "Whoa...just a minute, Little Sister." He turned and closed the door behind him, then turned to face the onslaught.

"Well, come on. Give!" she insisted.

"Okay, okay -- chill out, would you?" He tilted his head and looked at her quizzically. "You know, it's really none of your business how things went. But since you're likely to bust a vessel if I don't tell you, *things* went just fine, thank you. We had fun, and I think Connie is a great girl. I always have. But that's all there is to it, okay? Except that she got a little too much sun today and isn't feeling too well. So I took her home and made her eat something and said I would call her later to see how she was getting along. End of conversation."

Adriana clapped her hands together and squealed in delight. "Oh, I knew you two would hit it off. I just knew it!" She grabbed Matt around the waist and gave him a big hug.

Matt assured her that they had not *hit it off* particularly well, they had just had an O.K. day, nothing special, and she should not make a big deal out of it. But her eyes continued to twinkle just the same.

At about 8:30 p.m. Matt called Rusty to discuss an upcoming windsurfing competition. Rusty's wife said he wasn't home yet and she was angry because he hadn't bothered to call her. Matt reassured her that he was probably still down at the beach and had just lost track of the time.

An hour later, Matt called Rusty's number once again, but he still wasn't home. His wife's anger had turned to concern. Matt tried to calm her fears and said that maybe Rusty had stopped by the bar to have a drink with his buddies. But after he hung up the phone, Matt himself began to worry. He had a nagging hunch that something was very wrong since Rusty seldom stayed out late visiting with his friends, at a bar or anywhere.


Rusty McGreggor sailed back and forth several times, then began to work his way downriver, away from the mass of windsurfers directly out from Briars Beach, hoping to find a little solitude. He had developed a raging headache that momentarily blurred his vision and interfered with his ability to control his sailboard. A wave of sharp pains in his stomach almost doubled him over, but he kept sailing. Stubbornness and dedication to his sport prevented him from quitting and going home. Cold sweat rolled down his torso, sending a shiver down his back.

He sailed down and around an outcropping of rocks, effectively isolating himself from the other windsurfers. The stomach pains and headache eased up, so he stayed on the river a short while longer.

*One more run, then I'll quit for the night,* he told himself. As he began his run another wave of sharp pains racked his stomach. Sweat stung his eyes and ran down into his mouth, but he held on tightly to his rigging. *Just a little farther. Make this last run a good one.*

He rode the unending supply of waves down the river, unaware of how far he'd traveled. When he finally turned back he was all alone on that part of the river. The outcropping of rock was barely visible. He tried to find a spot to shoot for on the Washington shore, but his blurring vision returned and made it hard to see clearly. The wind felt chilly to him, yet the sweat was rolling off his face like water. His head felt like it was full of cotton. He had trouble keeping his eyes open and wished he could lay down somewhere and go to sleep. He swallowed convulsively as wave after wave of nausea returned.

Rusty continued to guide his board uncertainly toward the shore. Before he was halfway there, he was shaken by a severe bout of chills. That was followed immediately by another wave of stomach pain and nausea that brought him to his knees. As his sail went down in the water, he clung desperately to his sailboard while he vomited violently into the river. When the convulsions finally left him, he was weak and trembling. He collapsed across the deck of his board and rested. Several minutes passed before he had the strength to stand up and pull up his sail.

As he slowly made his way toward the shore, the repeating waves of dizziness and pain converged into one constant, agonizing attack. Now his head felt like it was twice its normal size, pounding like a giant drum. When he looked at the shore there was a double outline of every rock, every tree, even the shoreline itself, making it impossible for him to tell exactly where he was going.

By the time he got to within twenty feet of the shore, his breath came in short, painful bursts. Rocks and trees along the shore seemed to spin around him, going faster and faster, totally disorienting him. Suddenly darkness closed in around him until only a narrowing circle of light remained. *I feel so cold*, he thought, *so cold and so tired.* Slowly and gracefully, his body slid down onto the sailboard, with his legs dangling in the river. *Help me, somebody. Help me, please...*

But Rusty's hoarse whispers for help went unheard. Waves surrounded him while the river enticed his sailboard away from him. He was too dizzy and weak to help himself. He swallowed mouthfuls of river water. Ten feet from the shore a rock jutted up out of the river like a thief in ambush, ready to injure and cripple. A large wave carried the nearly unconscious and defenseless Rusty into that waiting rock and smashed his skull against it with a loud, sickening smack. Blood gushed from the wound and spread out over the water, a blanket of red. Rusty collapsed in a dead faint, face down in the shallow water. With his next breath, water gushed into his lungs. Within seconds he drowned.

In the gathering darkness of night, Rusty's body washed up onto the rocky beach. The waves pounded him and pushed at him until he was wedged in between two rocks, and then left him alone. It was as if the river wanted to leave a message to the world -- "Go home, you're not wanted here."

*A man stood hidden among the trees and watched as Rusty made his last fatal run upon the waves. He waited patiently, knowing what was to come. He smiled when Rusty collapsed on his board, for he knew of the pain ripping through the windsurfer's body. He heard Rusty's weak calls for help, and he softly laughed to himself. He stood and watched Rusty's head smash against the rock. He knew the surfer was drowning. He saw Rusty's body wash up among the rocks, and he stood there and watched until he was sure Rusty was dead. And then he melted back into the night.*

## Chapter 4

### 8 a.m. Wednesday morning, June 17

Lt. Wilson walked into police headquarters eager to go to work. He was breaking in a new police dog, an 85 pound two-year-old German Shepherd named Jazz. Jazz was learning fast and promised to be a good dog. He was also a lot of fun to work with, eager and willing to learn.

"Morning Chief," Willy greeted his boss Ted Baxter. Ted was a good police chief and Willy liked working for him.

Chief Baxter glanced up at Willy and nodded to him. "Good morning, Lieutenant.
How's the dog this morning?"

"Oh, he's fine, but full of piss and vinegar."

"Why don't you take him out and run a little of that energy off him?"

"Right, Boss. I'll take him down along the river."

Willy checked his messages. He made a phone call to speak to a man about a complaint the man had about some young kids playing around his truck the night before. He wanted an update. Then Willy worked on some paperwork he had to catch up with. Jazz became impatient and jumped up on Willy.

"NO, Jazz! Off!" In a quick, deft twist, Willy shoved the young dog off and down to the floor. "Bad dog!" he scolded. But the hurt look in the young dog's eyes pulled at his heartstrings. After a minute, he leaned over and pet the dog, then gave him the command to stay down. Undaunted, Jazz reached up and gave Willy a slobbery kiss with his long, wet tongue, while his tail wagged frantically. Willy straightened up and brushed himself off. He glanced ruefully at the Chief, who was trying unsuccessfully to suppress a grin.

"O.K *Trouble,* let's go. I can see it's going to be a long day. See you later Chief. Jazz, *heel,*" Willy commanded the dog and walked out to his patrol car, Jazz prancing at his side.

Out on Highway 14, Willy turned the car westward and drove

out of town. At Briars Beach he pulled the car off the road and down near the beach, to let Jazz out for a run. Barking and cavorting, the dog dashed down the beach to the river's edge.

Willy took a quick look around. There was a 'No-Overnight-Parking' ordinance posted for the beach, but every now and again someone would ignore it and set up camp there. Then Willy or one of the other officers would have to go and talk to the culprit and issue a ticket, or sometimes they'd just ask the person to leave. This morning the beach was clear. Willy was glad. He didn't like having to run off trespassers so early in the morning. He started walking along the beach, calling Jazz to follow.

Jazz sprang to Willy's side, then ran ahead, investigating every rock and bush along the shore. Willy let him run freely.

Jazz ran about 200 yards ahead of Willy, running through rocks and brush. He spotted something among the rocks along the edge of the water, and stopped. The hair on the back of his neck stood on end. He growled lowly, then barked, but the thing didn't move. He lifted his nose to smell the air. Instinctively, he knew that whatever it was down there in the water was dead. Jazz started barking wildly. He ran back to Willy, stopped and barked three times, then turned and ran back to the dead thing.

At the sound of Jazz's frantic barking, Willy began jogging along the beach. He couldn't imagine what had upset his dog, but thought it might just be a windsurfer out for an early morning run on the waves. When the dog had ran out of the brush, barked at Willy, then ran back, Willy knew something was wrong. He followed Jazz quickly along the beach, but the dog soon left him behind and disappeared into the brush and rocks.

While Jazz waited for Willy to catch up, he sniffed at the thing in the rocks. Once again the hair along his neck and spine stood on edge. It was the young dog's first encounter with death. Wining and whimpering, he reached forward and grabbed a piece of the thing and tried to pull it out of the water, but it was wedged too tightly. He barked several times, then lay down on the sand and put his head down on his paws, watching the thing and listening for Willy.

Willy sprinted over rocks and through brush until he suddenly came upon Jazz, fifteen yards ahead, laying close to the water's edge and watching him as he came through the bushes. The dog jumped up and started pulling at something in the water. Willy couldn't tell what it was until he was almost on top of it.

His quick gasp was followed by a sick feeling in his stomach--a body--face down--in the water. He knew without looking that whoever it was dead. A corpse. He'd seen dead men before. Most cops had, except rookies maybe. But he'd never get used to it, not if he lived to be a hundred. A few quick strides brought Willy to the corpse. Now that he was standing over the body, he could see a nasty gash on the side of the head. It was about two inches long, surrounded with dried blood-soaked hair. With shaking hands, Willy reached over and lifted the head of the corpse. "Please, God, don't let it be anyone I know," he muttered.

But it was. Rusty McGreggor.

Willy turned him over. Rusty's body was cold. In frantic denial Willy checked Rusty's neck for a pulse. None. He knew there would be none. Only the cold, dead eyes staring back at him. Willy broke out in a cold sweat, while icy-hot fingers raced up and down his back. The nausea in his stomach intensified. He ran into the bushes, gagging and heaving.

When Willy recovered, he called Jazz and stumbled back through the bushes and rocks and up the beach to his car. He called headquarters on his radio.

"Chief, this is Willy. I'm out at the west end of Briars Beach. You'd better get out here quick," he sobbed. "I've found a body."

"Would you repeat that, Lt.? It sounded like you said you had a body out there!"

"Yes, Sir, I did. I was out on the beach with Jazz, letting him run off some energy like you said, and he found a body in the rocks along the river. It's a local guy, Chief. A guy name of Rusty McGreggor. Oh, God – I knew him well. He was a friend of mine. He works at the Riverfront Bank... well, he used to."

"All right, Lt. Wilson. I'm on my way; and I'm really sorry. Do you have any idea what happened?"

"No, Sir, not really. It looks like he'd been out windsurfing. He was face-down in the water, and he has a bad cut on his skull."

"Okay, Lt. It sounds like it was just an accident, but you never know. Go back and secure the area. The last thing we need is a bunch of sightseers running around and getting in our way."

Willy did as he told, ribboning off a 50-yard semi-circle on the ground around the body. Then he began combing the area for possible clues.

Chief Baxter drove out to Briars Beach, with the county coroner right behind him. Two other officers drove in behind the coroner. They all walked west along the beach until they found Willy, Jazz, and the dead Rusty McGreggor.

Chief Baxter spoke to the two officers who were with him. "Sanchez, get some pictures of the victim, then you and Nichols pull him up onto the sand so we can get a good look at him."

Then he turned to Willy. "Find anything?"

"Yes, Sir." Willy was feeling better and beginning to think more clearly.

"Let's have it," the Chief said impatiently.

"Over here, behind this bush. I found several footprints in the sand. And some cigarette butts," he said. "It looks like someone spent some time there."

The Chief went over and took a look behind the bush and nodded. Willy pulled a bag out of his pocket. In it were five cigarette butts.

"They're all the same brand, Chief. Pacific Crest. I've never heard of that brand, have you?"

"That's a new company in Portland, Lt." Chief Baxter scrutinized the contents of the bag. "There's no sign of lipstick or gloss on those. There's a good chance they belonged to a man. See that the lab gets them." He studied the ground between the bush and the body in the water.

"Look, Willy. It looks like whoever was behind that bush walked down to the edge of the water and back. I wonder...was he just admiring the scenery or did he see what went on here? Let's get plaster castings of these prints."

When Sanchez and Nichols had pulled Rusty's body out onto the sand, Baxter examined the gash on Rusty's head. It looked pretty fresh. He released the body to the coroner, and ordered an autopsy and a drug screening. Then he helped the others scour the area, but they found nothing more. After an hour they all left except Willy. He sat in his patrol car for a while, just thinking about Rusty. Jazz lay uncommonly quiet on the back seat.


Matt Goodell drove down onto Briars Beach and pulled up next to Willy's patrol car. Matt noticed that Willy looked a little pale and shaky. Jazz raised up and stuck his head out the opened window, his tail slowly wagging.

"Morning, Willy. What's up? I just passed the Chief, Sanchez and Nichols, and the coroner on the highway." Matt was dressed in his windsurfing gear, and carried his sailboard on top of his Jeep. He'd hoped to get in a quick hour of sailing before he had to be to work.

Willy told Matt about Rusty. Matt could hardly believe what he was hearing. His senses reeled from the news. Rusty was a good friend. Now he was gone. Drowned. A couple of days ago he'd almost drowned himself. Now Rusty. It was incredible. For a while he and Willy just stood on the beach, staring out over the water, each absorbed in his own thoughts.

After about 15 minutes, they heard the sound of a car engine. Shaking themselves out of their state of disbelief, they both turned toward the newcomer. The man was of medium height. He had dark curly hair that came down to his shoulders. Matt recognized him as Peter Bray, the visiting windsurfer from Australia.

"Morning, Peter," he said.

"Hey, Matt. Gorgeous day, eh? Thought I'd catch some early waves. You going out, mate?"

"No, not today. Aren't you working today?"

"Oh, well, you know how it is. Gotta 'ave a day off now 'n then, eh?"

Matt turned to Willy and asked if he knew Peter. Willy said he didn't. Matt introduced them.

Matt decided not to say anything to Peter about Rusty. He wished Peter good luck and warned him to be careful. "Hey, mate, don't worry about me. Nothin' ever 'appens to me," he said with a grin. "I'm too good!" And with that remark, Peter headed for the water. Young. Healthy. Indestructible. He thought he had found his own piece of heaven in the heart of the Columbia River Gorge.

"You know, Willy, some guys are just so full of themselves, it's unbelievable. Rusty had thought he was good, too. And he was, really. Not as good as Peter, though. The trouble is, Peter knows he's good and he flaunts it in front of everybody."

"Sounds like the kind to make a few enemies. What's he do for a living? Or is he one of those spoiled little rich guys, living off his old man's money?"

"No, he's not rich, just young and foolish. This summer he's working part-time down at the saw mill. He's not married; there's no one to go home to, so he spends all his spare time sailing."

"Maybe we should have told him about Rusty."

"No. He'll find things out soon enough. Come on. I want you to show me where you found Rusty."

And with that Matt followed Willy back down the beach. Even though the area had already been inspected, they spent an hour studying the sand and rocks for any clues that might tell the story of what had happened. They found nothing.

## Chapter 5
### Wednesday morning. June 17 - 10 a.m.

Located at the west end of town, Pine Crest Hospital was built on a ten-acre lot and surrounded by well-groomed, green lawns and meticulous flower gardens interspersed with a variety of trees that provided shade and beauty.

Victor Prescott and Connie White were inside, doing inventory on the drug supply for the ambulance. Victor had been crowding Connie more and more as the morning went on. He couldn't seem to help himself. To him, she was one of the most beautiful women he knew. She reminded him of his lovely wife, who had died two years ago. They were about the same height and build, had the same color and length of hair, and they both had those same soft gray eyes that flashed little sparks of light when they got angry.

"Connie, what color do you call that hair? I think it's very lovely, my Dear." He reached up his hand to smooth it over her head, but she gently brushed it away.

"Victor, really! We're not here to discuss the color of my hair. We've got work to do." Connie was definitely beginning to feel uncomfortable. Victor was getting just a little too friendly to suit her.

"I know. But I can't seem to keep my mind on the job today. It's partly your fault, you know. If you hadn't worn that dress and put on that nice perfume, I wouldn't be so easily distracted. What kind is that, by the way? Your perfume, I mean?"

"The *job*, Victor. Let's get on with the inventory, okay?" Connie quickly sidestepped around Victor and began counting bottles of medicine. As she counted, she marked the quantities onto a notepad she was carrying.

Undaunted by her chilly responses, Victor laughed. He stepped up behind Connie and gently rubbed his hand along her arm.

"How about dinner tonight, hmmm? I know a nice, quiet restaurant just out of town. You'll like it there. What do you say?"

Exasperated, Connie slammed her notebook down on the

counter. With her hands on her hips, she whirled around to face Victor. Her heaving chest and flashing eyes only made him want her more.

"Victor! I do NOT want to go out to dinner with you, either tonight or any other night. I'm sorry." With that she stomped out of the supply room and down the hall to the nurses station.

Victor shrugged his shoulders and wondered what was wrong with *her*! All he wanted was a simple date. She didn't need to be so rude about it. Oh, well, he thought, one of these days she'll come around. He glanced around the room. It was empty. Quickly scanning the rows of drugs, he picked out a small bottle of pills and slipped it into his pocket. Then he locked up the supply cabinet and left the room.

As Victor stepped out into the hallway, he looked up to see Chief Baxter walking toward him. Victor eyed the Chief warily. He noticed, as he had time after time, what a powerful and imposing figure the Chief made. Victor was six feet tall and he had to look up when they made eye contact. It's probably the uniform, he told himself. A man always looks impressive in a uniform.

He and the Chief of Police knew each other from the time Victor's wife was killed by unknown assailants. They had worked closely together trying to solve the murder for almost a year, but no solid evidence was ever found. Victor had blamed the Chief's department for not being able to find the killers, but he hid his criticism. He couldn't help feeling that the Chief could have done more than he had, although Baxter said he had done all he could. Still, Victor was hoping that some day, someone would come forward with a clue or even a confession that would put the bastards behind bars.

As the Chief approached him now, Victor tried to look calm and friendly.

"Morning, Chief," he said, and continued down the hall.

"Hold up a minute, Victor," Baxter instructed. He reached out his hand and offered it to Victor, who shook it briefly.

"It's good to see you again. Hope things are going okay for you. I just came by to talk to the medical examiner. One of my men found a body down along the river this morning. Looks suspicious, so I've ordered an autopsy."

"Anyone I know?" Victor whispered. His stomach was feeling a little queasy now. Unconsciously, he rubbed his damp palms on his white jacket.

"I don't know, Victor, but I can't release the name until the family has been contacted. Sorry. I understand you were down at Briars Beach yesterday afternoon. Did you see anyone acting suspiciously or weird in any way?"

Victor shrugged his shoulders and shook his head. "No, I didn't notice anything, Chief. Sorry."

The Chief thanked him then said goodbye. Victor walked into the nurses' lounge and lit his first cigarette of the day.

The lounge was not empty. He saw Marie Sanchez, a nurse, sitting in one of the chairs reading a magazine. She looked up at him and smiled.

"Hi, Victor."

"Morning, Marie." Victor's glance took in Marie's long slender legs crossed so delicately, and traveled up toward her head. Her dark skin reflected a warm glow from a nearby lamp. Victor had always considered Marie to be a beautiful woman and he couldn't help admiring her. Her snapping black eyes indicated that she was well aware of his scrutiny. But he just smiled and asked her if she was sporting a new hairstyle.

Marie shrugged off her annoyance at him and said yes, it was a new haircut. "Do you like it?" she asked him. She had known Victor for several years and refused to let his narrow-minded attitude toward women bother her.

"I think it's very attractive, dear." Victor liked Marie a lot, but didn't feel compelled to seek out her company like he did with Connie.

"Well, thank-you. I guess I'll be seeing you at the committee meeting tonight."

"I won't be able to make it. I have an EMT meeting." Victor wasn't much on committee meetings, so he didn't mind missing this one.

Marie said goodbye and left the lounge just as Sam Morgan was coming in. Sam held the door open for her and smiled shyly when she thanked him. Walking over and helping himself to a cup of coffee, he waved a salute to Victor. "Hi Victor," he said.

Sam Morgan had been working as a janitor at the hospital for eight years. He was a little slow in the head, but Victor liked him. He was good with the young children at the hospital, and often spent his spare time entertaining them with games and stories. "My car's in the garage for the day. Can you give me a ride home? I'll feed you lunch. I make good sandwiches."

Victor laughed. "Sure, Sam. I'll meet you back here in about an hour," he replied, then he left the lounge and went back to work.

An hour later, Victor was driving Sam home. Sam lived with his brother Tom, who owned a small home on the bluff above the Columbia River. As they drove along the bluff road, Victor commented on the nice homes they saw. Unlike most of the houses in town, these homes were each on a large enough piece of property to provide seclusion and privacy. After about a mile and a half, the size of the homes became smaller again, but the size of the property remained the same, providing the same sense of solitude.

Just before they reached his house, Sam pointed out a small A-frame cedar home. "That's where Marie Sanchez lives. Did you know that? And this next house, the one you can hardly see down behind those shrubs and trees? That house is empty now. The people just moved out. I don't think they've even put it up for sale, yet."

"I knew Marie lives there," Victor replied. "I have been there a couple of times. But I didn't realize there was another house down in here. It's hidden so well, you can't even see it unless you know it's there." He stopped the car in Sam's driveway and looked over toward the vacant house again.

"It would certainly be private. Do you happen to know who would have a key to it, Sam? One of these days I'd like to take a look at it. I've been thinking of selling my place. I like the view from up here better."

As it happened, Sam and Tom had a spare key to the house, for emergencies, Sam said.

After lunch they walked down to the vacant house and took a quick look around. Victor didn't have time to look inside the house, but the outside was charming. He began to fantasize about living there. With someone who would make him happy again, like he used to be. Someone like his wife. Maybe Connie.

## Chapter 6

At five o'clock Wednesday evening the phone rang in Chief Baxter's office. Dr. Benson, the medical examiner at Pine Crest Hospital reported to the Chief that high doses of sodium chloride and knock-out pills, a deadly combination, were found in Rusty McGreggor's bloodstream.

Chief Baxter called Lt. Williams and told him the results.

"Drugs? That doesn't make sense, Chief. I've known Rusty ever since he came here two years ago. My wife and I have spent some time with him and his wife, and he never used any drugs to my knowledge."

"Well, the autopsy reports don't lie, Lieutenant. But, if you don't think he was on anything, then we'd better look into this a little deeper. You and Matt check it out, will you? And Willy, make this a priority," he instructed.

Matt was in his bedroom sorting through his belongings. The ringing of the phone was only a muted sound to be ignored. More important to him was his present dilemma and the confusion it caused him. He really liked living in the Columbia River Gorge. He recalled the many hiking trails and bike rides he had been on with his sister Adriana and with Willy. He enjoyed the smell of the pine trees, the sounds of the birds, and the abundant wildlife.

It was a beautiful place to live, and he'd made some good friends here. The desire to stay and make a permanent home here was strong, yet he couldn't shake the feeling of restlessness that had plagued him these last few months. The more he tried to sort things out, the more confused he became.

Adriana interrupted his mental turmoil with a knock on his bedroom door and the sharp announcement, "Telephone, Matt. It's Willy."

Matt, jolted out of his thoughts, reached for the phone beside his bed.

Willy filled him in on the autopsy report on Rusty McGreggor's death.

"I never knew Rusty to take any drugs, Willy. Did you?"

"No. It's strange, isn't it? Someone must have slipped him a micky. The boss wants us to check it out. Rusty had no enemies, as far as I know, but we'll have to dig into that possibility. We just might be looking at a murder here," Willy said.

After agreeing to meet at the police station after a quick supper, Matt hung up the phone. *This just doesn't add up*, Matt thought. *I know Rusty wouldn't take drugs.* He sat down on the edge of his bed and tried to make sense of this latest development. He'd known Rusty pretty well, although they weren't really close friends, not really tight like he and Willy were. Just the same, Matt felt terrible that Rusty had died. He would miss seeing him out on the river, competing against him at the windsurfing meets, listening to his easy banter. If Rusty was murdered, Matt knew it was of utmost importance that they begin an immediate investigation before the trail got any colder. However, he wasn't sure he was ready to get involved in a murder investigation. He had less than a week left on his job here, and he didn't want to spend it wrapped up in all the various entanglements of a murder case, which he knew would probably take a lot longer than a week to solve.

Changing out of his summer shorts and tank top, Matt had a bite to eat, quickly showered, then put on a clean uniform. He stared at his reflection in the mirror for a moment. The face looking back at him was lean and good-looking. Piercing blue eyes were his most noticeable feature. Normally a medium Baltic blue, they could go cobalt with passion or like blue fire and ice when he became angry. Tonight they were serious and thoughtful, dark with concern. Matt ruefully shook his head, mentally chided himself for daydreaming, and left to meet Willy at the police station. He picked up his portable police radio from the hall table on his way out.

First, they went to see Rusty's widow, Betty. Willy had already been over there once, to offer his condolences. Now they were on official business and wasted little time on sentiment. They asked all the right questions and received the answers they expected. Rusty was not on drugs, legal or illegal. Not now, not ever. Period. He didn't have any enemies that Betty knew of. He didn't gamble. He didn't owe any outstanding debts, other than to the bank where he worked--they had a loan for their home mortgage. Willy thanked Rusty's widow for her time and he and Matt left.

"Damnit, Willy. If Rusty didn't take those drugs voluntarily, that means someone fed them to him without his knowledge and without his permission. And that's murder, plain and simple. Who the hell would do something like that?"

It was a question they couldn't answer by themselves. Matt knew the local tavern was the best place to go to catch up on the latest news. Even though Rusty seldom stopped at the pub, a lot of his friends did, and Matt hoped they might be able to learn something there.

Jake's Tavern, located along highway 14, was the local hot-spot for night life. The building was sixty years old, but still in good shape, and was decorated in the German Rhineland theme to go along with the rest of the town's businesses that had remodeled in honor of Pine Crest's sister city on the Rhine, in Germany.

As he pulled up in front of Jake's Tavern, Matt looked in disdain at the Rhineland decor. He thought the whole idea of decorating a whole town after a city in another country halfway around the world was rather silly. There were plenty of local points of interest around which to build a town theme. There were the two mountains, Adams and Hood, the Columbia River, the Hood River Bridge, tugboats, sailboats, skiing, hiking, not to mention the abundance of wildlife. Ever since he'd first arrived, Matt wondered why the town hadn't picked a more personal and appropriate motif. He shook his head and got out of his car. Making a mental note that there were twenty-three vehicles parked outside, he walked up to the entrance of the tavern and went inside.

Even at 8:30 in the evening it was still plenty light outside at that time of the year and after the brightness outside, the interior of the tavern seemed darker than it actually was. Matt couldn't see anything for several seconds while his eyes adjusted to the change of light. He could, however, smell cigarette smoke, mingled with human sweat and dust, and hear the jukebox playing quietly over the sound of people talking and glasses clinking. Then he spotted Willy waiting for him at the far end of the bar.

Willy sat facing the doors, where he could watch anyone who came inside. He was waiting patiently for Matt to find him.

Matt casually walked over to where Willy was sitting on a barstool, saying hello to a couple of local men he knew as he walked across the room.

"Hey Willy. How's it going?" Matt eased his lanky frame onto a barstool next to his long-time friend. He looked around the room, studying its occupants silently.

"Kinda quiet, Matt. You want anything to drink?"

"Sure, I'll have a diet coke," Matt replied as he patted his stomach. "Gotta watch the weight, ya' know."

Jake Evens was a man about six feet tall, with broad, well-muscled shoulders, bald-headed, forty-eight years old and getting a little paunchy around the middle. A well-kept beard covered most of his face. He came over and placed his big, powerful hands on the bar in front of Matt and Willy, leaned forward and glared at each of them in turn. His voice was deep and raspy when he spoke. The twinkle in his eyes belied his gruff appearance.

"What can I get you boys?" he growled, not even flinching when they smiled at him.

They ordered two diet cokes, and laughed when Jake complained that they weren't drinking something stronger. He brought them their order then went on about his business.

A man and woman sat down next to Matt, making it difficult to discuss business, so the two kept the conversation casual. Willy asked Matt how his sister was doing.

"Fine. She and Connie had a meeting to go to tonight. Planning meeting for the big Fourth of July dance. You going?"

"Oh, yeah, we wouldn't miss it. Let's see, that must be about three weeks away. Right?"

"Yeah, sounds about right."

"I thought so. That Connie White. She's a pretty good-looking woman. You ask her out yet?"

"Maybe. We might have spent the day together yesterday, down on the beach."

"Oh, really? Well, now. That's interesting. What did you two do, down there on the beach?" Willy asked with obvious insinuation. Matt took exception to the innuendo.

"Hey, don't be a jerk. She's a nice girl. We didn't *do* anything. Just had lunch, then went down to the river and I gave her some beginning sailing lessons, that's all. But, you're right. She is beautiful. And we hit it off pretty well, I guess."

"Good. I'm glad you had a good time. You gonna see her again?

You two would make a good couple."

"Come off it, man. You're as bad as my sister. To hear Adriana talk, you'd think I was getting married next week," Matt said. "But, still, the truth is, I think I could get used to Connie's company real easy. Too easy. It's scary. What I don't need right now is to get involved with anyone. I had enough of that with Lisa. I've learned my lesson, thank-you. Besides, I'm leaving in less than week."

"Yeah, but you'll only be gone two weeks. Then you're coming back, right? You two could pick up right where you left off."

"I don't know, Willy. Maybe. Maybe not."

"What the hell you talkin' about, Matt?"

"Well, to tell you the truth, I've been re-thinking my future. Maybe this job's not for me. I can't seem to settle into it, you know?"

"Come on, Matt. Don't talk like that. Police work's the only thing you've ever wanted to do as long as I've known you. You're just going through a rough spot. We all do. Maybe all you need is a good woman to take care of you. Maybe it's time you got married. Give Connie a chance, buddy. She's a great gal.

"And Matt, you're smart enough to know that not every woman is going to be like Lisa. I know Connie. She's a wonderful person. If there could be something there for you two, you'd be a fool to let it go by because of one bad experience. I think it's worth hanging around for a while to find out. You owe yourself that much."

"I don't know. It still hurts when I think of Lisa and what she did to me. I had another dream about her the other night. It seemed so real. I woke up in a cold sweat. But, you're right. I need to let that go, once and for all. Unfortunately, I don't know if I can. Not just yet."

"Maybe you need to go see Lisa again. Just to say good-bye. Who knows, maybe it would be a catharsis."

"Yeah, maybe I do. Maybe when I go on vacation, I'll make a quick trip to Seattle and look her up."

The couple who had sat down next to Matt got up and moved over to a booth.

Getting back to what they were there for, Matt and Willy looked around for someone who might have seen or talked to Rusty in the past couple of days before he died.

They asked questions without appearing too anxious. Jake overheard them and said he'd seen Rusty the night before he died. "He was here, in the tavern. I remember because he doesn't come in here that often, and I thought it was kinda unusual."

Matt asked him if he remembered anything else unusual happening while Rusty was in here. "Did he meet anyone or talk to anyone?"

"Well, now that you mention it, he did get into an argument with someone. Yeah. It was some tugboat captain. I think his name was Roachea--Ed Roachea. Yeah, that's it. He a tugboat pilot. He comes in here now and then. They had a pretty good "discussion", if you know what I mean. No fists or nothin', but a lot of ugly words flying back and forth between the two. It started getting pretty loud, so I told them to put a lid on it or get out. Then this Roachea fella, he slammed outta here like a locomotive. He was real pissed. Yessiree."

"What were they arguing about? Could you tell?" Matt asked.

"Best I could tell, it was somethin' about right-of-way on the river. Roachea started in on Rusty as soon as he came through the door, calling him names and such. He told Rusty in so many words that he and his boardhead buddies had better stay the hell out of his way or get run over. And Rusty, that dumb hothead, he was carryin' on about the tugs hoggin' the river."

Matt and Willy looked at Jake, then at each other. They had their first suspect.

"Thanks Jake," Willy said. "Do us a favor and call us if he shows up again." Jake nodded to him and went on down to the end of the bar to wait on another customer. Willy looked at Matt and quietly said, "Let's go."

In his car, Matt radioed for an address on one Ed, Edward or Eddy Roachea. While they waited for the call-back, Matt checked the time. It was after nine o'clock and the sun had finally gone down. After a minute, the dispatcher called back and gave them the Roachea address. Willy followed Matt to the address. It took only ten minutes to get there.

The Roachea home was dark except for the front porch light, and a light glowing through one of the frontroom windows. There was an old Buick parked in the driveway.

They parked out on the street and walked up the driveway, looking around cautiously. When they got closer to the house, an old black lab raised up off the porch and slowly walked toward them, wagging his tail from side to side.

Willy spoke quietly to the dog and put his hand down for him to smell, then scratched the dog's head and ears. That's all it took to win the dog's affection. It went over and laid back down as Matt knocked on the door.

No one answered, but they could hear the sound of the radio coming from the house. Matt knocked again, this time louder. Still no answer. After trying a third time with the same results, they rattled the doorknob and found it to be locked. Giving up, they returned to their cars.

They would have to either sit and wait for someone to come home, or leave their questions for another time. They decided to wait.

Their plans changed when, after a few minutes, Matt received a call from dispatch saying that Jake Evans had called to let him know Ed Roachea had returned to the tavern. They started their cars and headed back in that direction.

## Chapter 7

Back at the tavern, Peter Bray, hotshot that he was, sat at a table with several other windsurfers, both men and women. They were drinking beer and congratulating themselves on a day well-spent -- on the river doing what they liked to do best. Peter was bragging about himself in his usual, obnoxious manner when Ed Roachea walked in.

Peter was so caught up in the telling of his own accomplishments that he didn't notice Roachea, whose body occupied the whole doorway as he stepped through it. He was six feet-three inches tall, 250 pounds, somewhere in his mid-fifties. He looked like he hadn't shaved in a week.

Roachea looked around and saw that the tavern was full except for two seats at the bar near the table where Peter and his friends sat. Roachea sat down and ordered a double whiskey. When Jake delivered the drink, Roachea downed it in two swallows and ordered another, which he also knocked down in short order. It was while he was enjoying his third double whiskey that he began to get irritated at the constant babbling of the self-important idiot sitting at the table close by. Looking at the man and his friends, he noted their sun-bleached hair and dark suntans, as well as their style of dress. *Looks like another bunch of damned boardheads*, he thought. *Just what I need.*

Roachea had come here to relax and enjoy a couple of drinks, so he turned his back and tried to ignore the conversation going on at the table. But as he sipped his drink he found it harder and harder to block out the chatter.

He thought of the hundreds of boardheads he encountered each day as he made his way up and down the Columbia River. The river that was once almost like a private domain was now polluted beyond recognition with hundreds and hundreds of sails of every color and size. The situation had gotten way out of hand. The question of right-of-way was a major issue all up and down the river. To Roachea, there was no question about it -- he had the right of way. That's all there was to it.

His head began to pound; his shoulders tensed. His big hands slowly clenched until his knuckles on the glass turned white. In spite of the air-conditioned room, sweat formed on his brow and ran down his face, like rivulets down a mountain. His heart pummeled against his chest, screaming to get out. Whipping the sweat off his brow, he thought, *God, it's hot in here! These damned walls feel like they're closing in.* The ordinary chatter of the crowded tavern had turned into a mind-boggling roar, becoming louder and louder with each passing moment. Breathing deeply, he tried to block out the noise. The fruitless effort served only to aggravate him further. Clear, rational thought became impossible.

Roachea's blood pressure had shot up 20 points. With an angry growl he slammed his drink down onto the bar. The glass broke in his hand. Blood flowed freely from a small cut, but went unnoticed as he whirled around and growled at Peter.

"HEY! Put a lid on it, you babbling son-of-a-bitch. You have a hell of an opinion of yourself, don't ya'? Well, I think you're nothin' but a bastard on a board and a damned fool, and I'm getting a little tired of listening to you brag about yourself!"

Mouth agape, Peter Bray stared at Roachea in stunned silence. An embarrassed blush slowly crept up Peter's face. He looked around at his friends, then smiled sheepishly. Turning back to Roachea, he apologized.

"Sorry, mate. I guess I was getting a little carried away. I didn't mean to brag. No hard feelings, right?"

Roachea responded with a snarled oath. He wanted nothing more right then than to get his hands around the scrawny neck of that little jerk. But the noisy crowd had suddenly quieted. Many of the customers had stopped their chatter and were watching him with open hostility. Realizing he was outnumbered, he decided to let the matter drop. He would deal with the loud-mouth foreigner another time. Turning his back on Peter, he ordered another whiskey.

Peter's friends reassured him that they didn't think he'd been bragging and that some people--referring to Ed Roachea--were just plain rude. Soon their conversation resumed its original boisterous level as they forgot about the rude interruption and regained their cheerful reminiscence of the day's windsurfing events.

Roachea finished his drink and sat at the bar, mumbling to himself.

Jake kept a close eye on the tug captain. When Roachea had first come into the bar, Jake had taken a minute to call the police station and leave a message for Willy and Matt that Roachea was there if they still wanted to speak with him. Now, when Roachea started getting worked up again and ordered another double whiskey, Jake told him he'd had enough to drink.

Roachea became angry and abusive, but Jake, being used to angry and abusive customers, handled Ed with a fine expertise that he had honed over the past ten years that he'd owned the bar. Within minutes, he'd convinced Roachea that it would be to his advantage to leave quietly. So, much to Jake's relief, Roachea got up from the bar and started for the door. Jake hoped Matt or Willy showed up before Roachea left the premises, but decided against trying to detain him. He didn't want to end up in a fight with this guy. Best to let him go on his way. He did offer to call a cab to take Roachea home, but Ed refused his offer, called Jake a couple of choice names and stumbled out the door.

Jake was glad to see him go. Ed Roachea would not be served in his bar again.


At nine-thirty-five that evening, Matt and Willy pulled up in front of Jake's Tavern for the second time. Darkness had set in and it was hard to count the number of cars still in the parking lot. They went inside and looked around but no sign remained of Ed Roachea. They walked over to the bar where Jake was polishing glasses.

"You just missed him, boys. He was causin' trouble, so I kicked him out. Sorry." Jake laid his polishing cloth down and spread his big hands out on the bar.

"Never mind, Jake. We'll catch up to him later. Was he talking to anyone in here?"

Jake told them about Roachea's sullen and hostile behavior toward Peter Bray. Willy thanked Jake, then he and Matt walked over to Peter's table and asked him if they could speak to him for a minute. Peter said sure.

They questioned Peter for almost ten minutes, but didn't get any satisfactory answers. They asked him not only about his run in with Roachea, which didn't seem to amount to anything, but also about Rusty McGreggor.

Rusty and Peter were not close friends, but they hung out with the same crowd and Matt thought Peter might know something to help them. As far as Peter knew, Rusty didn't use drugs or have any enemies.

Peter looked at his watch, said he had to get home, and asked if there was anything else they wanted to know. There wasn't. He walked back to his table, said good-bye to his friends and went out the door.

Matt and Willy sat down and ordered coffee. There were several other people in the tavern who knew Rusty. The detectives spent the next half hour talking to these people and asking pointed questions concerning Rusty's habits and lifestyle. They needed some answers. They got some. All the replies were the same. Rusty didn't use drugs. And he had no known enemies. It seemed more and more that Rusty's death was not accidental or self-imposed.


Peter Bray whistled as he walked through the dimly-lit parking lot of the tavern toward his car, his keys jingling in his right hand. Just before he reached his car, a large shadowy image jumped out from behind the bushes.

With a startled gasp, Peter jumped back. "What--?", then recognition registered in his eyes and he relaxed. "Hey, mate. Aren't you the guy who was...?"

Before he finished speaking, the big man grabbed him by the shirt-front and shoved him up against a parked car. Then he slammed his fist into Peter's belly. With a loud *whoosh!* the air exploded from Peter's lungs. The jackhammer punch drove him to his knees. Reaching out his hand, he grabbed the car fender and pulled himself up. He shook his head and looked at his attacker.

"God, what'd you do that for? Are you crazy?" Peter's breath came back in short gasps.

With staggering swiftness, the attacker hit him again. This time on the jaw. The blow spun him around and he slumped to the ground a second time. The world was spinning around him as stars exploded in his head. He put a hand to his jaw. Blood ran from a jagged cut on his lower lip. It was several moments before he was able to raise his head.

The man was standing back, waiting for Peter to get up. He held something long and shiny in his right hand. A hunting knife. Tired of waiting, he reached down and hauled Peter to his feet. Something fell unseen out of the man's shirt pocket; a small pill bottle that rolled quietly along the gravel on the ground before stopping beside the tire of the next car.

Peter swayed against the car. Blood streamed down his chin and onto his shirt. He spat, and more blood poured forth. Angry now, he glared at his attacker. "You son-of-a-bitch!" He leapt at the man and slammed his fist into the man's face, but the attacker was ready for him. He jerked his head to the side so that Peter's fist only grazed his cheek. Then he hit Peter and knocked him down a third time. Fear suddenly replaced Peter's anger. *This lunatic's doing some real damage,* he realized.

He groaned and rolled over onto his back. Looking up at the man, he asked, "What do you want?"

"You, man. I want you." With that, the man knelt down beside Peter. He grabbed the front of Peter's shirt and jerked him up so that their faces were only inches apart. Peter smelled the strong odor of whiskey on the man's breath.

"It's time you paid for what you and your friends did. It's time to die!"

"Shit! What the hell are you talking about?"

"You know damned well what I'm talking about, you little no-good pile of shit. Remember? Two years ago!"

"You're crazy. You got me mixed up with someone else. I didn't do anything. I swear!"

Peter had no idea what the man was talking about. But he suddenly realized that it didn't matter. He was about to die and he didn't know why. He watched in helpless terror as the man lifted his arm high. Peter saw the knife and tried to lunge away, but the man had an iron grip on him. The arm came down with a blur of motion.

Peter felt the hot, searing pain as the knife plunged into his chest, cracking and splintering bones. It ripped through the left ventricle of his heart, tearing flesh and spewing blood in a great, red, sticky puddle as it spread down across his belly. He reached wildly for his assailant's shirt, grabbing the front in a tight death grip.

The man jumped back, jerking his arm free from Peter's grip but letting go of the knife --leaving it in Peter's chest. He turned and ran to a small, red car, jumped in and sped away.

## Chapter 8

Inside Jake's tavern Willy and Matt concluded their informal question-and-answer session with the tavern patrons, said their good-byes to Jake, and prepared to leave. It was 10:15 PM.

Once outside, it took a few seconds for their eyes to adjust once again to the darkness. Adequate outdoor lighting was obviously not high on Jake's list of priorities, but the three-quarter moon had risen above the mountains, providing sufficient light to guide them. The wind whipped through the trees and bushes, causing spooky shadows that danced and dodged back and forth.

Matt stopped and looked around. He felt a shiver run down his back. Listening to the night, he realized the only sounds he heard were coming from the tavern. Nothing else. No crickets. No frogs. No little night animals scurrying through the bushes. Nothing. It was eerie. He continued toward his car, still searching the dark shadows.

Willy, who was walking ahead of Matt, stopped suddenly in his tracks. Matt bumped into him.

"Oops, sorry. What's up? Something's wrong, isn't it? I can feel it." Then he looked over Willy's shoulder. Thirty-five feet ahead, the moonlight vaguely illuminated the shape of a body crumpled on the ground. The moonlight also reflected off the blade of a knife sticking out of the victim's chest.

"Oh, Lord," Willy murmured, "somebody's been killed." He started toward the body, but Matt grabbed his arm and held him back.

"Be careful," he whispered, "The assailant might still be around." He pulled his .38 out of its holster, as did Willy, and together they proceeded cautiously toward the body. Willy knelt down beside the corpse.

"Sweet Jesus. It's Peter Bray!" He checked for a pulse, and finding none, he leaned close to see if Peter was breathing. He wasn't. Willy laid his ear on Peter's chest and listened for a heartbeat. After several seconds, he slowly stood up, a look of disbelief on his face.

"He's dead, Matt," Willy whispered. Willy looked at Matt, who motioned for Willy to check around the nearby cars. Matt unclipped his police radio from his belt and called in the report, asking for backup forces, then worked his way around one side of the parking lot. Willy did the same on the opposite side.

They each kept flashlights in their cars, and when they'd worked their way around to their cars, they took these out and continued to search the parking lot once again while they waited for backup to arrive. They looked into and under every car on the lot. Nothing.

The piercing wail of sirens could be heard in the distance, growing louder and louder; their backup and an ambulance.

After a few minutes they had eliminated the probability of the perpetrator being there. Returning to their cars, they got evidence bags and returned to Bray's body. First they checked through all his pockets. His wallet was still in his back pocket, and contained $54 in cash. While kneeling beside Bray's body, Matt noticed something in the palm of Bray's right hand. He carefully picked it up and examined it.

"Look at this, Willy. What do you make of it?"

"A button. Off who's shirt, though? It's white, and Peter's shirt and buttons are blue. It's gotta belong to someone else."

"Yup. His attacker most likely." Matt pulled a small plastic bag out of his pocket, put the button in it, and labeled it. They pulled small notepads out of their breast pockets and busied themselves making quick notes of all the relevant facts like date, time, location, their exact location when they noticed the body, what officers were at the scene (themselves). They also wrote down the number of vehicles in the parking lot at the time and the license numbers of every vehicle, what the victim was wearing, the color of his clothes, whether he was laying face up or face down, etc.

The tavern was surrounded with shrubs and trees, which could hide any number of people who didn't want to be seen. After coming up empty in the parking lot, Matt and Willy began searching the surrounding greenery. They had just started when three patrol cars came screaming into the driveway. The flashing lights lit up the sky like it was the Fourth of July. Gravel and dirt sprayed in every direction.

Chief Baxter climbed out of his car and hurried over to Matt and Willy, who'd returned to the body. He took a quick look at the corpse, checked for vital signs, and nodded. Not that he didn't trust his men, but sometimes he liked to double check things for himself.

He ordered his six officers present to secure the perimeter and make a thorough and complete examination of the property for the purpose of collecting evidence.

An ambulance arrived and two emergency medical technicians were examining Peter's body. When they had concurred that there was no hope of reviving the victim, they reported their findings to the Chief, who thanked and dismissed them. Chief Baxter then called the county coroner and told him his services were needed.

He sought out Willy and Matt for a short conference. He wanted to know exactly what happened. Every detail.

For the next fifteen minutes, Matt and Willy read over their notes until they exhausted every single detail they could think of. They even read off the approximate outside temperature and weather conditions that they had written down. Seemingly irrelevant details could become invaluable later, perhaps helping to solve a case or prosecute a suspect, so they always wrote down *everything*. And the Chief would be angry if they weren't completely thorough. "Be thorough," he always said, "Be completely thorough." They were especially precise when relating the run-in Jake Evans said Peter had in the bar with Ed Roachea.


The past year had been a quiet one, with no major crimes committed. But now Chief Baxter was uneasy. Two deaths in his town in as many days; one of those, at least, was murder. He didn't like it--not at all. Still, he had seen more unusual things happen in his thirty years' experience in law enforcement. He vowed he'd get to the bottom of these two deaths in record time and soon have Pine Crest back to business as usual.

After dispatching two officers to go and pick up Ed Roachea for questioning, Chief Baxter himself supervised the investigation of the crime scene. *It's going to be a long night,* he thought.

He ordered flood lights to be brought in and set up. Everyone still left in the tavern was questioned unmercifully for two hours before being allowed to go home. Every square inch of land around the tavern and parking lot was searched over and over again.

One of the officers found a small bottle under one of the cars close to the body. There was no name on the bottle label--no doctor's name, no patient's name, no drugstore name. It had to have come from a supply store somewhere. He carefully scooped it into a small plastic bag, labeled it and handed it to the officer in charge of collecting evidence. They also collected dirt and gravel samples.

After three long hours without finding any other clues, the Chief sent his exhausted men home.

He gathered his thoughts together and mentally went through the short list of evidence. All he had to go on was an argument in a tavern full of people--nothing unusual there; a bottle of pills that could belong to anybody; and of course the knife that was found lodged in Peter's chest. Hopefully the lab would find some usable prints.

When Chief Baxter got back to the police station, he read the reports made out by the officers who had picked up Ed Roachea. He saw that Roachea had come in with minimal resistance, in spite of the fact that he'd been drinking. According to the report, Roachea claimed he'd gone straight home from Jake's Tavern and that is where he'd spent the rest of the night. The officers had talked to his wife and she confirmed her husband's alibi, saying that he'd gotten home at 9:35 p.m. She noticed the time because she'd just gotten home from the planning meeting, and she looked at the clock when she came through the door. She was just taking off her coat when she heard Ed's car pull into the driveway. When asked if anyone else had seen him, he said no but he'd talked to his boss on the phone about ten minutes after he got home. They called his boss, who confirmed the phone conversation and the time, 9:45 p.m. The Chief knew that Willy and Matt were talking to Peter Bray at the tavern from 9:40 to 9:50, after which Peter left the tavern. Unless Ed could be in two places at the same time, he couldn't have done the murder.

Chief Baxter finished reading the report and tossed it onto his desk. *Damn!* he said. It was 4:30 a.m. Thursday, June 18th. Baxter went home and went to bed.


Matt and Willy spent Thursday afternoon again talking to family, friends and acquaintances of Peter Bray, but to no avail. Although Bray was a show-off and a braggart, he hadn't made any real enemies in his short lifetime. The money found still in Bray's wallet ruled out robbery as a motive for killing him, unless the attack was interrupted by the arrival on the scene of Wilson and Goodell.

There were very few clues to work with. The knife and the bottle of pills might not even be related. They were able to lift one good fingerprint off the pill bottle. Matt ran it through the computer, but no match was found. There were no prints on the knife, leading him to believe that the attacker either wore gloves or wiped the knife clean after killing Peter.

Matt thought it was unlikely that the killer would wipe the knife off when it was still in Peter's chest, so he assumed the man must have worn gloves. And if he was wearing gloves, that most likely meant he'd planned the attack enough in advance to bring the gloves and to put them on before committing the crime. And that meant this was not a spur-of-the-moment killing. It was premeditated. They were dealing with a dangerous and cold-blooded killer.

Other than the report on the prints, which turned out to be no information at all, Matt and Willy seemed to be playing a waiting game, which neither one of them liked. After working all day yesterday and spending half of night at the crime scene, they were both exhausted and more than a little out of sorts. After a fruitless afternoon, the two detectives called it quits and prepared to go home.

Just before Matt left, Chief Baxter called him into his office and asked him to postpone his vacation until these two murders were solved. Baxter wanted Matt to work the case with Willy. The deaths of McGreggor and Bray had really shaken up the town. There were few people, if any, who weren't watching to see how the Chief handled the situation. He knew that a quick solution was needed to reassure the townspeople that their police force could protect them.

When Matt got home, he told Adrianna about having to postpone his vacation.

"That's okay," she replied, "The Forth of July committee really needs my help. They don't have as many volunteers as they'd hoped this year. And I'd like to be here for the party, too. We can go home another time."

## Chapter 9

Friday - June 19 - 9 a.m.

Connie White sat in the nurses' lounge at Pine Crest Hospital drinking a cup of coffee and watching Adriana pace briskly back and forth. Adriana's hands became animated as she told Connie about the latest exploits of her boss, Michael Sans, and his never ending attempts to get a date with her.

"I don't know what to do. The man is absolutely obsessed." Adriana's blue eyes flashed in anger. "He just doesn't want to take NO for an answer. I thought now that school's out for the summer I wouldn't have to deal with him again until next fall, but he keeps calling me! The damn phone hasn't stopped ringing all week."

"Adriana, if it goes on much longer you'd better let Matt handle it. He'd soon straighten Michael out."

"I know. You're right. But not just yet. I still want to deal with Michael myself. After all, I'm a full-grown woman. I should be able to handle it."

"O.K. You know what's best." Connie secretly doubted that Adriana did indeed know what was best in this case, but she would respect her friend's wishes--for now.

The door to the lounge opened and the janitor, Sam Morgan, walked in.

"Hi, Connie. Hi, Adriana."

"Hi, Sam," they answered in unison.

"You girls went to the planning meeting last night, didn't you? Is everything set for the dance? I can't wait to go. You're gonna go, aren't you?"

"Yeah, sure. We wouldn't miss it," Adriana responded. "But, you know Sam, the Fourth of July's not for a couple of weeks yet. You'll have to be patient."

"Oh, I know. But I enjoy it so much every year, that's all I think about all summer!"

The change of subject helped Adriana to forget about Michael Sans. And Connie was glad for the interruption, since she didn't have any answers for Adriana's problem with Sans; at least not any that Adriana would listen to.

For the next ten minutes, the three of them discussed the dinner-dance and all the preparations that were being made.

Finally, Adriana looked at her watch and said she had work to do at home, and since they were through with their work at the hospital for the day, she thought she'd better be going. That reminded Sam that he'd better get back to work, too.

Victor came into the lounge at that moment and asked Connie if she would stay a minute. He wanted to talk to her. Adriana and Sam said good-bye and left.

Connie eyed Victor suspiciously, not trusting him after their last encounter in the supply room. She didn't know what had gotten into him that he had become so overly friendly with her, but she hoped it was just a passing thing.

"Connie, I wanted to apologize for the way I behaved the other morning." Victor handed her a small bunch of pink carnations he had hidden behind his back and gave her his most brilliant smile. "I don't know what I was thinking. Forgive me?"

"That depends." Connie wasn't going to forgive him so easily. "What was that all about anyway, Victor? I've known you for, what? about three years or so, right? I've never known you to act that way before, and I've never given you any reason to think I was romantically interested in you."

"I know. And you're right." He turned away, toward the window, to hide the pain her words caused. "I guess I've just been feeling real lonely lately. And you kind of remind me of my wife, God rest her soul. You know, she died two years ago this summer, and I really miss her."

The suspicion and anxiety Connie was feeling melted away. She felt pity and compassion as she watched Victor. Here was a sad and lonely man who only wanted a little love and companionship in his life, and there was no one to give it to him. She knew she was not the woman to provide these things for him, but she couldn't help feeling sorry for him.

She walked over to where he still stood by the window and placed a warm hand on his arm. If she had known that her touch and the smile she gave him sent his blood rushing, she would have been more reserved.

"I'm sorry, Victor. Maybe I over-reacted. Let's forget the whole thing, O.K.?"

Victor felt his heart skip a beat, and suddenly life didn't seem so gloomy. He smiled at Connie and offered her the flowers he still held in his hand.

"Friends?" he asked.

"Friends," she replied, taking the flowers.

"I'd like to make it up to you," he offered tentatively. "Will you let me buy you lunch tomorrow? No big deal. No strings attached. Just two friends having lunch. I promise." He gave her an innocent and beguiling smile that he hoped she would perceive as harmless.

Connie hesitated only a moment. It appeared that Victor was being open and friendly and only wanted to make up for treating her badly. She could see no harm in a simple lunch with him, and she told him so.

He smiled and promised her she wouldn't be sorry.

"I'll see you tomorrow then," Connie said. "I've gotta run. I have some shopping to do. 'Bye." Matt was picking her up at seven for dinner and she wanted to find a new dress to wear.

Victor said he'd pick her up about noon on Saturday and they'd have lunch at the Harbor Inn. After she left, he walked over to the window and stood staring out at the trees. He wished he could reveal his intimate desires to Connie, tell her how he dreamed of her. But he didn't dare. She would surely refuse to go out with him if she knew how much he wanted her. Some day soon, he'd find a way to win her love.

Earlier that same morning, Matt and Willy were working on the two murder cases. The fruitless morning turned into a long, frustrating and unproductive day. The autopsy report came back on Peter Bray. A small percentage of alcohol showed up in his blood, but nothing else.

Willy had a short list of possible suspects in Rusty McGreggor's case. Only three names were on the list.

Ed Roachea was the first suspect. It was widely known that he had it in for windsurfers, and he'd been seen in Jake's arguing with Rusty on Monday night -- the night before Rusty died. When Roachea was brought in for questioning by two other officers the morning after Peter Bray was murdered, Matt and Willy interrogated him for two hours, but finally had to let him go. There was no solid evidence to link Roachea to either death. Now they decided to question him again. Maybe he'd make a mistake, let something slip that would give the police something on which to build a case against him.

They drove out to Roachea's house and asked him to come down to the station with them. At first he refused, but when Willy insisted, he reluctantly complied. They sat down with him in a quiet room and questioned him for 45 minutes. He repeated the same story he'd told them on Thursday morning: he was working the day Rusty died, and had no contact with the victim. When Matt asked him if he ever used drugs, he became angry and abusive. Pushing his chair back, he rose to his full six-foot height and glared at Matt, tight-fisted and ready to fight.

"I ain't never touched drugs in my life. Hell, I wouldn't even know where to get any. And if you was any kind of detectives at all, you'd already know that."

"Take it easy, Ed. These are just routine questions," Matt said. "Sit down and relax."

"I don't want to sit down," he bellowed, "and I'm as relaxed as I'm gonna get, so don't treat me like some stupid kid who don't know his way around.

"You don't have the right to harass me like this. First you drag me in here and accuse me of Peter Bray's death. And now you're trying to somehow pin the death of Rusty McGreggor on me? I didn't do anything, and you're treating me like a mass murderer!" He paced across the room to the far wall, turned sharply and faced his accusers. "Am I under arrest?" he growled.

The two detectives exchanged glances, then looked at Roachea. Willy shrugged his shoulders and gave his reply.

"No, Ed. You're not under arrest. But you are a suspect, so stick around. Don't leave town, except to go to work, and we'd appreciate it if you made yourself available to us, in case we have any more questions."

As Ed stormed past Matt toward the door, Matt reached out and placed his hand on Ed's arm to detain him for a second.

"Thanks for coming in, Ed," he said.

Eddy threw Matt's hand off with an easy flip of his powerful arm, sending Matt backwards a step. "Go to hell," he spat, and continued out the door. Willy started to go after Roachea, but Matt called him back.

"Let him go."

Matt made a phone call to check out Roachea's alibi. It turned out Roachea was telling the truth. He had been working. There was no way he could have been involved with Rusty's death.

The next suspect was Tom Morgan. As half-owner of Briars Beach, he had an interest in Rusty McGreggor, who owned the other half of that section of beach, which was becoming a lucrative enterprise. Every windsurfer who used the beach had to pay a fee, plus there were two small snack stands set up on the beach that McGreggor and Morgan got a percentage of. Morgan was also present at the scene of the crime, and therefore had access to the victim. Matt knew that if he could prove that Tom would inherit Rusty's half of the property, they would have their motive.

Tom Morgan was called in to police headquarters.

While questioning Morgan, it was discovered that Rusty's wife, and not Morgan, would inherit his half of Briars Beach. So much for motive. Without a motive Matt knew Morgan's presence on the beach that afternoon meant nothing. There were at least fifty other surfers on that particular beach that same day.

Tom Morgan was released, with appropriate apologies.

It was one o'clock, time for lunch. Willy invited Matt to have lunch with him at his house. Willy's family provided a short but pleasant distraction from the day's work. After lunch they went back to the station and spent the next few hours working on the case.

The last name on Willy's list of possible suspects was Nick Truman. Truman was a dock worker who lived twenty-five miles upriver, in a small town in Oregon. His only connection with Rusty McGreggor was that he had recently been involved in a legal battle over a piece of river-front property he had leased for ten years. The state refused to renew the lease. The land went up for sale.

In all fairness, the state gave Truman the first opportunity to buy the land, but Truman did not have the money to buy it. He applied at the bank for a loan, and McGreggor, as a loan officer, had turned him down. Truman made quite a scene, and the police were called to usher him out of the bank. He was consequently asked to take his business elsewhere. Willy remembered the incident.

It was a weak connection, Willy knew. But he was getting desperate.

He should have listened to his instincts. Upon further checking, it turned out that Truman had a very solid alibi for the day of McGreggor's death. He was out of town, visiting relatives in southern Oregon.

"Well, that's that, I guess." Willy threw his notes down onto the table with such force they flew in every direction. "I feel like we're just beating our heads against the wall."

"Well, it's got to be here somewhere. We're just not looking in the right place." Matt pushed his chair back, and raked one hand raggedly through his tousled hair. His shoulders and neck muscles felt incredibly tense. His head ached. And his eyes burned. He took a deep breath, held it for a few seconds, then exhaled slowly. He looked at his watch, then stood up and spoke to Willy.

"It's almost five-thirty. Let's get out of here." He had a date with Connie at seven that he was looking forward to.

## Chapter 10

At home Matt changed into shorts and a tee-shirt. His Jeep Cherokee was badly in need of a wash job. While washing the car, he had time to think about his budding relationship with Connie, although he didn't like to think of it as a *relationship*. He knew he didn't have any business starting a real relationship right now. Not when there was the possibility he'd be going away for good. He and Connie got along well and enjoyed each other's company, so there was no harm in dating her. Or was there?

Suddenly he wasn't so anxious to go on this date tonight. He didn't want her to get the idea that they were becoming a *couple*. After tonight, he realized, he probably shouldn't see her again. Adriana had told him that Connie liked him. A lot. It wouldn't be right to lead her on. And Adriana would never forgive him if he hurt Connie by letting her think they had a thing going on, and then dumping her in a couple of weeks.

*So, it's settled then*, he thought. *Tonight, I'll tell her that I'm going to be leaving and that there's no future for us.* That thought gave birth to a feeling of loneliness that swept over him. He couldn't understand it, or even clearly discern it. But it was there, all the same.

He finished washing his Jeep, then returned to the house to take a shower. The hot, steamy water rushed down over his tense shoulders, pleasant and strangely sensual. He stayed in longer than normal, letting the pulsating stream massage his fatigued muscles. When he finally stepped out of the shower, he was thinking of things from a new, relaxed point of view. His life wasn't so bad, really. Getting a little complicated, maybe, but he felt he could control that easily enough.

Matt pulled into Connie's driveway at 6:55. He sat there a moment thinking over his earlier decision not to get involved with her, and the feeling of loneliness returned, an emptiness that he couldn't explain to himself. He put it down to the overall restlessness and dissatisfaction with his life that he'd been struggling with over the last few months.

Giving himself a mental shake, he got out of the Jeep and went up to the apartment door. Before he could ring the doorbell, the door opened. Connie stood in the doorway in a cool, light-blue, sleeveless cotton dress. Her hair was washed and dried to a brilliant glow. *A halo in the evening light*, Matt thought.

She smiled at him and stood aside to welcome him into her home. He looked into her eyes and thought he could easily drown in the depths of those soft, gray eyes. As he stepped past her into the house, he caught the smell of her shampoo, mingled with bath soap, and a light, erotic perfume. The combined fragrance had a heady effect on his senses. He leaned down and kissed her on her eagerly awaiting lips.

Closing his eyes, he deeply inhaled the scent of her. The world seemed to fall away, leaving just the two of them together, no problems, nothing to worry about, no complicated romantic situations to figure out. In spite of his earlier resolutions, Matt couldn't help the excitement he felt at seeing Connie. The feelings of sadness he'd had lately evaporated in her presence, replaced by a physical longing that he couldn't control.

He felt a little foolish and awkward, like a kid in high school. *This is ridiculous. What's the matter with me?* He had a sudden sensation of losing control of his life, of his world, and he didn't like it. Somehow, he had to regain command of his senses. The best way to do that, he decided, was to put a little distance between himself and this beautiful creature before him.

"You ready to go?" he asked brusquely. *The sooner I get through this evening, the better*, he told himself.

"Yeah, sure," Connie replied. "Is something wrong?" She wondered at his mood change. When she'd first opened the door to him, she detected a warm welcome in his eyes and that kiss held an unmistakably hunger. Then for some reason, he seemed to change, to turn almost angry.

"No. Nothing's wrong. I've just got something on my mind. I'm sorry. I guess I'm a little preoccupied with work. *O.K., you idiot,* he condemned himself, *Chill out. There's no sense in spoiling the whole evening. Just relax. Be pleasant. Have a good time. Damn!*

They drove out to the trendy Aeolus Restaurant and Hotel, located three miles east of town on a stretch of land that overlooked the Columbia River and Gorge, with Oregon's Mt. Hood in the background. It had been developed into a beautiful establishment, aptly named after the mythical Greek god of the winds, *Aeolus*. In spite of the almost constantly blowing wind, or perhaps because of it, it had quickly become the in vogue place to go. Its popularity was due in part to the fact that it was a new restaurant with a spacious and airy atmosphere and partly because it was built on a hill that commanded a magnificent, panoramic view, with lush gardens and lawns that sloped down to the river below. A gravel path wandered through the property to the riverfront.

Giant fir and pine trees surrounded the hotel, providing much welcomed shade in the hot summer, shelter for squirrels and birds, and wind-breaks in the icy winter months. The trees filled the air with the essence of the mountains. One could stand among the them, eyes closed, and breathing deeply, imagine oneself to be high on a mountain top, isolated from the rest of the world.

Inside the restaurant, immaculate tables awaited. The squeaky-clean windows gave the impression of nonexistence, as if only open space existed where windows belonged. Soft lights created an intimate glow in the room. As the Maitre d' steered Matt and Connie to a window table, they were serenaded by soft piano music being feathered on a black, baby grand piano in the center of the restaurant.

An attentive waiter brought them ice water, then left them alone for a few minutes to study the menu. Flowers and candles adorned every table. The master chef had been brought in from France and enjoyed a growing reputation as one of the best chefs in the Northwest.

From their table, they could see for miles in both directions up and down the river. Tall fir and pine trees in various shades of green, interspersed with multi-colored wildflowers and mountain grasses that had turned golden in the summer heat, covered the distant hills.

They could see dozens of windsurfers on the river, sailing back and forth with seeming lack of effort, their bright sails in a multitude of colors creating a confetti-like effect. Matt watched as they sliced through the waves, or flew off the tip of a whitecap and remained suspended in air for a second before dropping back onto the surface of the water. He grimaced whenever a surfer lost his balance and tumbled from his sailboard. It made Matt wish he was out there with them.

Connie was admiring the furnishings of the restaurant. This was the first time she had eaten here, and she looked around in appreciation. The modern decor was refreshing after the older and somewhat dismal interiors of most of the other local establishments. This was much more to her liking. The off-white walls, eggshell tile floors, and open design made for a light and spacious feeling. For contrast, the tables boasted black slate, a color repeated in the ceiling lights. The walls displayed many paintings and photographs by local artists. Numerous large planters of living flowers and plants added to the feeling of life and light.

    After perusing the menu, Connie decided she wanted a crab salad. Matt chose the baked Columbia River salmon, the house specialty. He also ordered a bottle of white house wine recommended by the waiter, who took their orders, then left them alone.

    Matt relaxed and let his worries slide away, to be dealt with another day. He looked at Connie and couldn't help but admire her beauty. The shining golden mane of hair tempted him to want to run his hands through it, to feel it between his fingers. He was sure it must feel like silk, all shiny and soft. But he resisted the temptation.

    During dinner, Matt kept their conversation light and impersonal. His thoughts, on the other hand, were very personal. In fact, he couldn't stop thinking about what it would be like to get really close to Connie, to hold her in his arms, to make love to her. The harder he tried not to think of her that way, the more he found himself doing just that.

    After dinner, Matt suggested a walk through the quiet restaurant gardens and down to the riverfront. The restaurant excluded windsurfing from its beach so that its patrons could have somewhere to walk, or just sit and enjoy the scenery. There were a few tables and chairs scattered under the trees along the river for those who were adventurous enough to take advantage of them.

    There were several other people on the pathway when Matt and Connie left the restaurant. Matt hoped they would have some time alone, as he renewed his determination to end their short-lived relationship and tell Connie goodbye. He felt nervous and at a loss for words. He had think. *How do you end something that never really got started?* he wondered. *Carefully. Very carefully.*

    The sun was sinking low over the western sky, giving a golden glow to the landscape. The earlier wind had died down to a gentle breeze that brought the coolness of the river with it as it feathered across their skin.

    As they walked along the beach, Matt reached down and picked up a small stone, and with a deft twist of his wrist sent it skipping out across the water. Connie grabbed his hand in hers, laughing lightly at his surprised look, and pulled him along the beach.

At the touch of her hand, an electric jolt shot up Matt's arm, quickening his heart. He tried to remember all the reasons why he was going to tell her goodbye, but they became like wisps of smoke in the wind. He was overcome for a moment with a strong desire to take her in his arms and kiss her.

The mood was broken when another couple walked by with their three noisy young children. Brought back rudely to the present time and purpose of their walk, Matt decided the beach wasn't a private enough place after all to say goodbye to someone he knew he could come to care about if time and circumstances were different. He abruptly suggested they go home.

Disappointment showed on Connie's face, but Matt was determined to carry through with his plans. *Another time, another place, and maybe it could have worked out for us, but not here and not now.* Right now his life was complicated enough without introducing another person into it. So he led Connie back to the car without further explanation.

The drive back to Connie's apartment was accomplished in awkward silence. Matt formulated what he would say to her, and how he would control his emotions while he did it. Fortunately, the Jeep was roomy enough to allow some separation during the short trip. He used the respite to gather his thoughts and to reason with the part of himself that was telling him not to throw away a good thing.

Once inside Connie's small apartment, something became apparent that Matt hadn't thought about. They were indeed isolated from the outside world. But that suddenly became a disadvantage as Matt became even more aware of, and more vulnerable to, Connie's charms and sensuality.

This wasn't the way he'd planned the evening to go, he reminded himself. Trying to distract himself, he looked around her apartment.

From where he stood by the front door, Matt could see the living room and the kitchen. Both were simply furnished in modern decor and light, pastel colors, which made the whole apartment look bigger and more open than it actually was. He admired the results.

"This is really nice," he said, suddenly nervous. "You've done a great job of decorating."

"Thank you. You should have seen it when I first moved in.

What a mess." Connie walked over to a small side bar and asked, "Would you like a drink? I have some good brandy."

Accepting her offer, Matt followed her across the room.

A gas fireplace occupied one corner of the room, and Connie asked Matt if he would light the fire for them. "We'll keep it low, so it won't get too hot in here," she said. "I love to sit and watch the fire. It's so relaxing." She, in turn, pulled out a large, fluffy fake fur rug and laid it down in front of the fireplace. Then she threw down two big, overstuffed pillows.

They sat down on the rug, leaned against the pillows and sipped their brandies. It was warm and cozy, and very, very relaxing. And before long, Matt forgot all about telling Connie that he couldn't see her again.

The brandy was having its effect on them both. By the time they'd finished two glasses of the fiery liquid, the talk had progressed from the weather, work, and the Fourth of July dance, to more personal matters. Connie talked about her work at the hospital, and the strange way Victor Prescott had acted lately. When she mentioned that she'd promised to have lunch with Victor the next day, Matt objected firmly. He felt strongly that it was a bad idea.

"Victor might misconstrue your agreeing to have lunch with him as something more personal. You don't want to be leading him on, Connie." *Look who's talking*, he reminded himself. He was not really that concerned that Victor might read more into the lunch date. What he was feeling, much to his own surprise and regret, was jealousy. It angered him that Connie was going to have lunch with another man. What made him even madder was the inner knowledge that he had no business feeling that way. He had no claims on Connie. He reminded himself that he was there to tell her he was leaving.

But he couldn't. Not yet. That acknowledgment confused him even further. He was beginning to think he was losing his common sense.

"Matt, I've already promised Victor I would have lunch with him, and I have no intention of breaking that promise. I've known him for a long time, and I know I can handle him. Don't worry." Connie suspected Matt was jealous, and that thought sent a shiver of hope through her. *Maybe Matt's beginning to take an interest in me at last!*

She didn't know how much of an interest Matt was taking in her until a moment later when he reached across the short space that separated them and pulled her into his arms. She went willingly and eagerly.

A short time later she was pushing him away from her. Her breathing was fast and ragged. A thin layer of perspiration glistened on her face. She smoothed down her dress and gave him a shaky smile.

"I think we'd better take a breather here. I could use another drink. How about you?"

Not only was Matt in the same state of disarray, he also seemed to be in a mild state of shock. His hair hung down into his face in damp tendrils. Longing had turned his blue eyes to cobalt. After several seconds in which he seemed to struggle with himself, he stood up and pulled Connie up off the rug.

"I'm sorry. I guess I got carried away." His deep voice was raw with barely controlled passion. Looking into her eyes, he felt himself lost, and fought desperately to save himself. "I think I should be going."

"Oh, no, I didn't mean that. You don't have to leave just yet, do you?" Connie spoke softly. It was like a caress to his ears. Her eyes were liquid pools and he felt himself going down into them again. Taking a deep breath, he looked away and nodded.

"Yeah, I do."

She wrapped her arms around his neck and gave him a deep and promising kiss. The result left him shaky and weak in the knees. He found himself returning her embrace, and the kiss.

"But I'd like to see you again," she purred. "Will you have dinner with me tomorrow night?"

It was more than he could resist. "Yeah, I'd like that."

"Umm, okay. Pick me up about seven."

"Okay, I'll be here," he promised.

Chapter 11
Saturday, June 20th.

Adriana spent Saturday morning shopping in the new Columbia Mall at the east end of town. By 11:00 a.m. she was already hot and tired. The sun beat down in full force, promising to be another scorching day, with the wind just beginning to pick up. A tall glass of iced coffee sounded wonderful, just the ticket to pick up her fading energy. Her arms full of packages, she stopped in at a small coffee shop.

The shop was almost full of customers, most of them tourists on their way through town or visiting for a few days. Adriana didn't recognize a single person, but being the friendly, outgoing person that she was, she smiled at several people as she walked through the shop, and said hello to a couple of elderly women who looked as tired as she. She found an empty table near the rear and dropped into the seat gratefully.

The shop was small, but unique in that its motif reflected the local attractions of river and mountains. Adriana appreciated the owner's display of independence in daring to deviate from the accepted German theme decor. Adriana liked its originality and spirit. She thought the scenes of wildlife in the meadows, skiers on the mountains slopes, and tugboats on the river were much more indicative of the area than the Rhineland theme.

After she ordered her cold drink, her mind returned to her present problem with Michael Sans. He didn't seem to take the hints she'd given him that she didn't want to date him. When school started up in September and she'd have to work with him every day, it could turn into an impossible situation. She knew she had to talk to him before then, and make him understand, in no uncertain terms, that she would not go out with him. She dreaded the inevitable confrontation, but felt they would both be better off once they came to an understanding.

The devil must have been listening to her thoughts, because just at that moment she saw Sans walk in through the front door of the coffee shop. *Great,* she thought, *just what I don't need.* She turned her head away, hoping that he would not see her, but it was too late. Fate mocked her today. His look of recognition told her that he had indeed seen her, and he proved it by heading over to her table. *Well,* she decided, *I guess now's as good a time as any.*

"Adriana," he said, "how nice to see you. You don't mind if I join you, do you?" Without waiting for her to answer, he took the seat across the table.

"Actually, yes, I do mind," she said. He laughed and smiled that conceited smile of his that made Adriana want to cringe. "But, as long as you're here, there's something I want to say to you," she added.

"Well, of course there is. I must say, you look especially beautiful today."

Adriana knew *that* statement wasn't true. She could still feel the perspiration running down her face, ruining her makeup, and the wind had blown all the style out of her hair. She knew how she looked when she was tired, as she certainly was this morning, and it wasn't beautiful. But she decided to ignore his condescending remark and get right to the point.

"Michael, you've been after me for months now to go out with you and I keep turning you down."

"I know, my sweet, but today is your lucky day. I've got the rest of the day off, and I want you to go home and change and we'll go spend what's left of it in Portland. We can go sightseeing, then have a nice, quiet, romantic dinner and then catch a movie." The lecherous grin he gave her spoke volumes. "Finish your drink and we'll get out of here."

Adriana fumed at the presumptuous way he expected her to eagerly fall in with his plans. He must have sensed a little of her hostility, because the smile slowly faded from his face.

She counted to ten in an effort to control her anger.

"Michael, I have tried to tell you politely that I don't want to go out with you. I never have and I never will. I want you to get that straight!"

"What are you talking about? You never said you didn't want to go out with me. We just haven't been able to work it out to when we're both free, that's all."

"No, Michael. That's not true, and you know it. I've turned you down at least a dozen times. You're not my type, Michael. I'm sorry".

"What do you mean, I'm not your type? What's that supposed to mean? And how do you know I'm not your type, if you won't even try to get to know me better?"

"I've known you for two years, Michael. We've worked together at school. We know each other pretty well, really. Look, we don't have anything in common. We don't like the same foods, or the same movies, or the same hobbies; we don't have the same friends; we don't have the same beliefs. We just aren't right for each other."

"You're wrong, Adriana! We do have some things in common. We both like kids. We both like to teach. Hey, look, we both ended up in the same coffee shop. And those other things don't matter. We could make new friends. We can find new hobbies to do together."

"Are you saying you're prepared to give up your friends for me, Michael? To stop doing the things you enjoy? To change completely to please me? Because that's what you'd have to do! And you know what? You wouldn't be happy, and you'd end up hating me for making you change. And I wouldn't be happy either, because I know that you couldn't do it. I couldn't either. No one can change that much and still be happy. We have to be true to ourselves, Michael. You know I'm right!"

"No. I don't believe that. You don't know what you're saying. You're wrong! *You* are what I want, Adriana. Come with me tonight. I'll prove it to you!"

"I can't do that. More importantly, I don't want to. I don't know how else to put this, except to just say it outright. I'm not attracted to you, Michael, and nothing you do will change that. You have to accept that and stop pursuing me like this. Because if you can't, we can't continue working together." Adriana noticed that some of the other customers were beginning to look at them curiously, but she was beyond caring. She had to make Michael see that she was not going to let him continue to harass her.

Michael's face started turning a dark red as his anger and frustration grew. He wasn't used to being turned down, and now he felt like he was being threatened.

"What do you mean, we can't work together? What do you plan to do, file some kind of stupid complaint against me? What good will that do? There's no law against asking a girl out on a date, for Pete's sake!"

"No, Michael, that's not what I mean. I only mean that I might have to quit my job at the school and apply somewhere else. I'm prepared to turn in my resignation, even if that means having to find work in another town."

"My God. You're serious." Reaching across the table, he tried to take her hand in his, but she pulled back. Her chin raised just that little bit, and she looked him in the eye. She had strength and courage, and she wasn't going to back down from him.

"Dear, sweet Adriana, surely things aren't that bad? We can work this out, if you'll just give us a chance." He was beginning to beg, now. His voice had taken on the wining quality that Adriana hated. It made her skin crawl. Trying to keep her voice under control, she withered him with a glance. Fire sparked from her eyes. Her voice trembled in anger.

"I am not your dear sweet anything, and don't you ever call me that again. Do you hear me? There is nothing to work out! I don't like you. I don't want to get to know you any better. And I will not go out with you. So get that straight! And if you ever bother me again, I *will* file a complaint against you. And don't make the mistake of thinking it will do no good. That would be a mistake you can't afford to live with. Goodbye, Michael!" And with that, Adriana grabbed her shopping bags and her purse and stormed out of the coffee shop.

Michael Sans sat in stunned silence. The message that dear sweet Adriana Goodell simple didn't like him had finally sunk in. It hit him hard, and it would take his over-inflated ego a while to get over the shock.


Adriana drove from the shopping mall back to her apartment, still seething. She stopped there just long enough to drop off her packages and quickly freshen up and change into a clean outfit. Then she headed for Pine Crest Memorial Hospital where she was due for an afternoon of volunteer work.

By the time she arrived at the hospital, the big clock on the wall chimed the noon hour. Adriana had calmed down enough to see a little humor in her chance meeting with Michael. Surely he had finally gotten the message that she wanted nothing to do with him. And she hoped that by the end of summer he would have forgotten all about her and set his sights on some other *dear, sweet thing*.

As soon as she entered the hospital, she ran into Victor Prescott who was just leaving. They exchanged pleasant conversation for about five minutes, then Victor told her something that surprised her.

"I have to run," he said. "I have a lunch date with Connie White."

"Really? When did this come about?" she asked him. She never would have thought Connie would go out with Victor, and this new development puzzled her.

"Oh, just yesterday. I think she likes me. And I find I'm very attracted to her. Do you think we'd make a nice couple?"

"Victor, it's only lunch. I wouldn't read anything into it. I happen to know that Connie's already seeing someone else."

"Who? Who's she seeing? You know what? I don't care! Even if that's true, I'm still going to give it my best shot. I won't know if I have a chance with her if I don't try, will I?" And with that, Victor waved goodbye and hurried out the door.

Adriana stood as if in a trance and watched him walk across to the parking lot. Then she shook her head and decided to leave that puzzle until later. She would find out what was going on the next time she talked to Connie.

Since it was lunch time, Adriana walked down to the hospital cafeteria to grab a bite to eat. She saw Marie Sanchez and Sam Morgan sitting together at a side table. Adriana took her tray of food over to their table.

"Hi, you two. Mind if I join you?" She knew they wouldn't, since they had all been friends for a long time, so she didn't wait for an answer. She set her tray on the table and sat down.

The other two smiled hello and Marie asked her what she was doing there. Sam just said hello and grinned at her and helped her unload her tray. Adriana told them she was going to help out for a few hours.

Lunch was pleasant and relaxing. It helped Adriana to put the Michael Sans incident completely put out of her mind, and restored her to her normal good humor. When Sam excused himself to leave, she asked him where he was going.

"I have to go," he said. "I promised the children I would read them stories before nap-time. If I'm not there, they will be mad at me." He was serious, and obviously didn't want to incur the wrath of any of the hospital's young patients. Adriana smiled at him and assured him that his young friends would never get mad at him. They loved him too much.

As they watched him leave, Adriana and Marie decided they too should be getting to work. They walked out into the hall to the elevators, where Marie invited Adriana over to her place for lunch the next day. After gladly accepting the invitation, Adriana went on her way.

She spent the afternoon working with the nurses on various duties. Nursing had been her second choice as a career and she sometimes wished it had been her first. But this way, she got to do both jobs --teaching and nursing. During the summers she had more time to devote to working at the hospital than during the school year, and she thoroughly enjoyed the hours she spent there helping the nurses and patients. It was a fulfilling and personally rewarding experience.

The numerous and varied duties that she performed kept Adriana's mind off the fact that Victor and Connie were having lunch together. On her way home, however, she once again pondered that strange event, and wondered how it had gone.

## Chapter 12

In fact, Connie's lunch date with Victor went quite well. The Harbor Inn where they ate had a good reputation as one of the most popular restaurants in town. Located at the parkway near the Pine Crest Marina, it offered both the convenience of being close to the water, and entertainment for children and adults alike. The park had swings and slides, as well as benches and shade trees under which to sit and rest or visit. Squirrels, blue jays and wild Canadian Geese were among the frequent visitors to the parkway. Sailboats, fishing boats and windsurfers all used the marina.

Connie was surprised at how pleasant Victor could be when he wasn't being a jerk. It seemed like his whole attitude had changed once he got his way and she agreed to go to lunch with him. During lunch, he was relaxed and happy, catering to her every wish. He applied no pressure, no subtle innuendoes. They discussed impersonal topics, from the weather to world problems.

After lunch however, Victor began once again to focus on his hopes for a personal relationship between the two of them. He complimented her several times on her looks, and hinted strongly that he thought they made a nice looking couple. Then he hinted at an evening date, and Connie frantically searched her mind for a way to change the subject.

When Victor mentioned how much she looked like his deceased wife, Connie took that opportunity to turn his point of interest. She soon realized that Victor still carried a grudge for his wife's murderers, and that he believed that some day they would come back this way again. When that happened, he planned to be ready for them. He would make them pay for what they did to his beloved Amy.

Lunch ended and Victor drove her back to her apartment. She began to think things had gone very well when he abruptly asked, "Will you have dinner with me tonight, Connie?"

"I'm sorry, Victor, but no, I don't think that's such a good idea.

I'd like us to just stay friends, okay? I'll see you next week at the hospital." For a moment she didn't know how he was going to react, but then he shrugged and smiled.

"Well, then, until next week."

She was relieved when he left.

Later in the afternoon, Matt called Connie to confirm their date for that evening. She almost told him she'd changed her mind. Although Matt had told her that he had a vacation coming up and he was going home to visit his parents, he hadn't revealed the fact that he might not be coming back, but Adriana had. That possibility weighed heavily on Connie's mind and on her heart and it bothered her that he was keeping it from her.

She knew if she became involved with Matt, especially if she really fell in love with him, which she thought might easily happen, she would be badly hurt when he left. On the other hand, she told herself, she had only a short time to get to know him better. Maybe she would decide he wasn't for her after all. And if she discovered that he was the one she wanted to spend the rest of her life with, she owed it to herself to take that chance. If they did hit it off, she knew she would be willing to follow Matt wherever he wanted to go. So she decided to give it her best shot. She was reminded of the old saying, *It's better to have loved and lost, than never to have loved at all!*

The evening couldn't have gone better if she'd planned it. Matt had suggested they go to dinner and a movie, and she agreed, but after dinner, she suggested they skip the movie, and retreat back to her apartment. In order to build on their relationship, Connie wanted to spend as much undisturbed time with Matt as she could. No distractions. Nothing to interfere with the process of laying the foundation on which to form a permanent bond between them. The attraction she felt toward him held a strength that surprised her. She found herself willing to do almost anything to capture his love.

Once back in her apartment, she poured them each a glass of wine and invited Matt to join her on her couch. He felt a little awkward, but sat down beside her and tried to think of something pleasant to say. He needn't have worried. Connie picked up the conversation and spent the next half-hour entertaining him with stories of her and Adriana's years together at college. She made him laugh as he hadn't laughed in a long time, and before long, he felt completely at home.

She gave him every opportunity to tell her about his plans to leave, and when she began to think he never would, he did just that. Although it wasn't news to her, hearing him speak the words hit her unexpectedly hard. Her breathing became rapid and shallow; her eyes misted over. She turned her head and pretended to look out the window so he wouldn't see her tears. The clear realization struck her that she was already falling in love with Matt.

Blinking away her tears, she was determined to remain cheerful and optimistic. Then Matt surprised her when he told her that Chief Baxter had asked him to postpone his vacation/leave-of-absence until these recent murders were solved. Delighted that his leaving had been delayed, she arose gracefully and retrieved the wine bottle from the kitchen. While she poured the golden liquid into their goblets, she quickly analyzed the situation. She would now have more time to strengthen their acquaintance and cement their relationship before he left.

On his part, Matt felt a deep sense of relief now that Connie knew he might be leaving for good and that there was little hope of a future for the two of them. He should have been happy, but there was a heaviness in his heart. He tried to shake it off and enjoy the evening.

After his second glass of wine, Matt felt like he was in a trance. If he could admit the truth, he'd been feeling that way most of the evening.

As soon as he'd picked up Connie, wave after wave of sensuous sensations had swept over him--feelings that he could do little to repress. He felt an unbridled urge to make love to Connie right there on the couch. He knew such thoughts had no business in his life right now, but he couldn't stop them from coming. His need was great and he put his drink down onto the coffee table with trembling hands.

Connie also set her drink down and, with a boldness that surprised him, she leaned over and tenderly kissed him. Caught off guard, Matt responded ardently. As his passion flared, he tightened his arms about her and lowered her down onto the couch. He searched her face for any signs of rejection. Finding none, he kissed her softly on the corner of her mouth, on the tip of her nose, and on her closed eyes, trailing kisses down her face and neck. Breathing heavily, he forced himself to stop after he had thoroughly explored the deep crevice between her breasts.

"You're so beautiful. I want to make love to you. I can't make you any promises. But right now I want you more than I've ever wanted anything in my life."

"I want you too, Matt. I don't expect any promises tonight."

Matt rose off the couch, took Connie by the hand and led her into the bedroom.

---

The next morning, Matt awoke to find himself alone in Connie's bed. He looked at the clock on the bedside table. It read 9:30 a.m. He felt lazy and relaxed. And happy. He decided he'd better get up and get a move on or the whole day would be shot, although he didn't have to report to work until the next day.

He opened the bedroom door and heard sounds coming from the kitchen. The smell of coffee awakened his appetite.

"Connie, do you mind if I take a quick shower?"

"No," she called, "go ahead. Towels are in the cupboard. Are you hungry?"

"Starved."

"Good. I'm making breakfast. You have ten minutes."

As he showered he spent the time analyzing his feelings for Connie. He tried to convince himself that last night didn't mean anything. They were both lonely and had needed to be together. It wasn't anything permanent. But the more he lectured himself, the more he knew he was only kidding himself. He realized that if he didn't watch it he would find himself emotionally entangled with Connie White and unable to easily extract himself.

He came out of the shower and picked his clothes up off the floor where he'd thrown them the night before. Picking them up brought back the events of last night vividly. What a night.

The need to replenish his spent energy made itself known. His stomach growled for the third time since he'd come out of the shower. The wonderful aroma of fried ham permeated the room, increasing his hunger. He followed his nose to the kitchen.

She stood in front of the kitchen stove, making them a big breakfast of hash brown potatoes, toast, ham and eggs, and juice. She looked up at him and smiled.

"Good morning, sleepy-head. I hope you're hungry. I was starving, so I made us a feast."

Matt almost forgot his hunger as he drank in the scene in front of him. He was beginning to feel kind of strange. It was a good kind of strange, though. Peaceful and secure. Homey. *I guess this is what it would feel like to be married*, he thought. He liked the feeling. It made him happy inside.

For the next several days, Matt and Willy were kept busy with work. The town was full of tourists and windsurfers, but nothing unusual happened. A couple of accidents, a lost child, and two young boys picked up for shoplifting. There were no further leads on the murders of McGreggor and Bray. Matt took Connie out three times, and ended up spending the night with her each time. She always said their lovemaking came with no strings attached, and he began to feel free and happy for the first time in years.

The temperature climbed into the nineties and stayed there. The wind had switched around and was coming from the East, and dying down in the evening, making the nights unbearably hot. Pressure increased from the town council members to solve the murders. Tempers grew short. Chief Baxter called for more overtime. He wanted the murder cases solved, and soon.

## Chapter 13
Friday, June 26th. -- 2:30 PM

Victor Prescott walked down the hospital corridor carrying a box of supplies for the ambulance. His long stride ate up the distance in double-quick time. Private and very sensual thoughts of Connie White occupied his mind. He remained totally unaware of how much the nurse beside him struggled to keep up with his fast pace.

Nurse Marie Sanchez hadn't walked so fast nor felt so insignificant since her days in Army boot camp. Her dark skin glistened with perspiration from the effort to keep up. She especially didn't like being ignored.

"Victor, slow down, for crying out loud! This ain't no race we're runnin' here. What's your hurry?" She glanced up at Victor and could tell by the blank look on his face that he hadn't heard a word she said. *What is the matter with that man?* she wondered as she hurried down the hall and out the door.

As they put the supplies into the ambulance, Marie finally got Victor's attention by snapping her fingers in front of his face. "Hey! Victor. Wake up. You've been a million miles away. What's on your mind that has you so preoccupied?"

"Sorry, Marie. Did you say something?"

"Yes, damnit. And you didn't hear a word I said. You raced down that hallway like the devil himself was after you. You got somethin' on your mind?"

"Oh, I was just daydreaming. Actually I was thinking about someone. Connie White. You two are friends, aren't you?"

"Yeah, sure I know her. She's pretty cool. Why you thinking about her?"

"Well, I like her a lot and I was thinking about her, that's all." Victor suddenly felt self-conscious and wished he hadn't mentioned Connie's name. He quickly put the last of the supplies into the ambulance and stood beside the vehicle waiting for Marie's reply.

Surprise and mild shock played across Marie's face. That was the very last thing she would have expected Victor to say. This sounded like something she would rather not get involved in, but she knew who held the key to Connie's heart and it wasn't Victor Prescott. Still, she didn't want to see Victor get hurt. She decided it would be kindest to let him know right now how things stood with Connie.

"Hey, man. You're chasing after the wrong fox there. I happen to know for a fact that Connie has very strong feeling's for another man. You might as well save yourself the trouble of running that race and set your sites on someone else, 'cause you don't have a chance with her. Sorry, Vic, but that's the truth."

"I know she fancies herself in love with someone else, but she's wrong! I would be better for her than anyone else could be, and I'm going to prove that to her. If she'll give me a chance I'll show her how good we can be together."

"That's a bad idea. You should forget about that girl. I'm tellin' you, let it go."

"I can't, Marie. I think I'm falling in love with her. I'm not going to let her just walk out of my life."

Marie didn't know what to say or think, but she was worried about Victor. They'd been friends for a long time, since before his wife died. She had watched him go through that awful ordeal and she didn't want to see him go through the loss of another woman.

"I have an idea," she said, wanting to distract him, "Why don't you come over to my place tonight. I'm cooking some of my famous spaghetti with venison meat sauce. Yes?"

Victor reluctantly agreed, but didn't see how that was going to help him convince Connie that he was the man for her.

"I have to work until five o'clock. Dinner will be ready about six-thirty. What time do ya get off work today Vic?" Marie asked.

"Two-thirty, today and tomorrow." Victor looked at his watch. It was 2:29 p.m. "Which means I'm now off duty. Okay, I'll see you tonight then."

# Chapter 14

Saturday, June 27th, dawned warm and still. As the day wore on, the heat increased and a strong east wind blew up, leaving everyone feeling wilted and cranky. Matt and Willy were sitting at the big double desk they shared and tried to ignore the 95-degree heat as they worked on their cases. A large oscillating fan in the corner of the room provided small relief and intermittently blew loose papers off the desks and onto adjacent desks and/or the floor. An odd assortment of coffee cups, books, pencil holders, car keys and even an occasional rock lay scattered atop the desks as paperweights. The dispatcher, Gloria, sat at her chair in the corner monitoring the radio and answering the phones.

A repeated banging and hammering came from the janitor, Benny, who was diligently working on the broken-down air conditioner. Every few minutes a string of curses blasted the air, adding fuel to the already growing fire of tension in the room.

Matt looked at his watch. Four o'clock. *Another two hours to go in this hell-hole, and we're getting nowhere with this investigation.* He threw down his pencil and abruptly stood up, causing his chair to crash over backwards.

"Nothing. We have absolutely nothing to go on. How in the hell are we supposed to solve a crime when we have no clues, no leads, no witnesses, no nothing?" He walked over to the water cooler and reached for a paper cup. The ancient water cooler gave up its contents reluctantly. Matt waited impatiently. "God, it's hot. Too damned hot to even think."

Over in the corner the janitor yanked and banged on the air conditioner, then emitted another angry spate of swearing. That only resulted in getting Matt's attention, which was a mistake, since it provided Matt with a target on which to vent his frustration.

"Benny, when the hell are you going to have that old, warn-out piece of junk fixed? We're dying in here for crying out loud!"

Benny pointed out that he was working as fast as he could and that it didn't help for Matt to be yelling at him. Matt muttered something under his breath, then went back to his desk where Willy sat looking at him like he was a child who'd just thrown a temper tantrum.

"What are you lookin' at?" Matt growled.

"Don't let it get to you, Partner. Something's bound to break soon. There's got to be somewhere we haven't looked, yet. Someone who knows something, or saw something. We'll break this case soon, so be patient. And in the meantime, don't be taking out your frustration on poor Benny, or he may never fix that damned air conditioner."

"Yeah, I know, I know. I've got some things on my mind, that's all. And this heat makes it hard to concentrate."

Before Willy could ask him what kind of things he had on his mind, the telephone rang. The dispatcher answered it, then signaled to Willy to pick up his phone. Willy reached over and lifted the receiver.

He sat up straight, grabbed a pencil and pad of paper. "This is Detective Wilson. Just calm down. Where? Are you there now? Good, O.K. We'll be there in five minutes. Keep everybody away from the body, O.K.? Can you do that for me? O.K., good. We're on our way." He looked at Matt, "We have a hit-and-run."

While listening to Willy's end of the conversation, Matt strapped on his Smith and Wesson .38 Police Special and grabbed his hat. His heart pounded wildly as adrenaline raced through his blood. The investigation and everything else was forgotten in the face of this new emergency. Willy told the dispatcher to send out another unit and an ambulance.

Matt fired questions as Willy snatched up his own firearm and headed for the door, answering Matt's questions as they ran to the patrol car.

The double-crossing fan slowly swung around toward their desk once again, scattering forgotten papers across the room before they floated gracefully down to the floor in slow motion.

Siren screaming and lights flashing, Matt and Willy raced out of town, heading west on Highway 14. Unusually light traffic made for a speedy drive.

Eight miles west of town stretched an expanse of land, 30 yards wide by a half-mile long, between the highway and the Columbia River. The wind blew stronger at this spot on the river than anywhere within 20 miles. A new name had been given to this particular stretch of land in recent years. It had been dubbed the High Wind Strip, or "the Strip," for short.

Tall oak and pine trees provided ample shade for weary travelers who wanted to stop for a few minutes of rest. Access to the river itself was rocky and dangerous, but people always found a way across the rocks. Just west of this wide spot, the highway narrowed dangerously. Two miles of new guard rails had just been installed there the week before.

The influx of windsurfers had taken over the place in recent years, taking every spot along the Strip that was wide enough to park in. Now the ordinary traveler found it all but impossible to get a parking spot.

Matt knew that many of the local people held a deep resentment towards the intruding windsurfers. Tempers were flaring, and there was a rumor of a secret organization, the purpose of which was to undermine, and even try to eliminate, the sport of windsurfing on the Columbia River. Looking at the crowded parking at the Strip, Matt could well understand their resentment.

When he and Willy arrived at the Strip, a crowd had already gathered. Someone was diverting traffic around a spot about a hundred yards down the Strip. Matt was relieved that someone at the scene was helping to control the situation until they arrived. The crowd parted reluctantly to allow the police car through.

Matt tried to park off the road, but there was no space left. He parked the car in the road with the lights flashing. He and Matt grabbed their hats and jumped out of the car. A man approached them and introduced himself as the one who had called, then led them to where a body was lying face-down on the side of the road.

Matt knelt down and pressed his fingers against the side of the man's neck, searching for the carotid artery. He felt no pulse. He turned the man over and put his ear close to the man's mouth and nose to listen for breathing. He heard none.

"Oh my God," Willy quickly knelt down next to the body. "That's Michael Sans, the grade school principal."

"Are you sure?" Matt asked. Matt had never met the principal, but had heard his sister speak of him occasionally.

"I'm sure." Willy rose and quickly walked back to the patrol car to get flares and flags from the trunk. A second police unit had arrived and Willy directed them to handle traffic control around the scene.

The ambulance arrived and the paramedics rushed to the victim's side. *It's too late for him, boys*, Willy thought. After a quick examination, they pronounced Michael Sans dead, packed up their equipment and left.

Willy took some pictures of the body and the scene, then called the coroner. He had noticed a large tear in Sans' yellow life jacket, with a small piece of the material missing. He spent several fruitless minutes looking around on the ground for the missing piece of material. He told Matt about it.

"If we can find a car with that patch of yellow material hanging off the grill, we'd have our perp," Willy said.

"Sure, but what are the chances of a small piece of material staying on the front of a moving vehicle for very long? I don't think we can count on that. Come on, let's take a look around."

Two more patrol cars arrived and Willy asked those two officers to take names, addresses and statements from the bystanders.

He and Matt walked west along the highway, looking for signs or clues as to where Sans had first been hit. They could see where his body had been dragged through the gravel. Following this trail they soon discovered the point of impact about 25 yards from where the body ended up. The trail through the gravel ended next to the guard rail. A fresh dent marred the new guard rail and in the middle of the dent, a narrow smear of red paint. Matt collected a sample of the paint for evidence. Matt marked the location, then they continued following the road.

Two parallel streaks of rubber angled from the point of impact out into the center of the road, beginning as almost transparent tire tracks and becoming darker and more vivid until they ended 20 yards further down the highway. Matt and Willy looked at one another.

"This was no accident, Willy."

"No. Whoever ran down Michael Sans knew exactly what he was doing. He gunned his vehicle hard enough to lay rubber from here clear up to where he impacted the body. That's cold-blooded murder."

They measured the tire tracks, took samples of the rubber, and pictures of the tracks, then walked back to where a crowd of people was still milling around. The next hour they spent questioning everyone who was on the scene. There was only one witness; a young man of about 18 heard the squeal of tires and had turned and caught a glimpse of a small red sports car racing by. No one else saw anything. They were all either out on the water or busy inspecting their equipment or otherwise preoccupied. Willy finally dismissed everyone and he and Matt drove back to the office to fill out all the paperwork.

At eight o'clock that evening Matt finally finished going over all the reports and details of the hit and run and went home.

Adriana had saved him a plate of food and warmed it up in the microwave oven for him. Matt poured them each a glass of wine and told Adriana to sit down. He broke the news of Sans death to her as gently as he could, but she was obviously shocked and upset by the information. She told Matt all about how Sans had been after her to date him and about the confrontation she had had with him a week earlier.

"I didn't want to go out with him, Matt. But I wouldn't have wished this on him for anything. I feel really bad."

"Listen, Sis. What happened to Michael Sans today had nothing to do with what was going on between you and him. That's history. You did what you had to do. There's no reason for you to feel bad about that now."

"Do you know who...?"

"No. It was a hit and run. But we do have a lead, although a small one."

"What is it?" she asked.

"I can't discuss that, Adri. You know that."

"But Matt, this is me. Surely you can tell me. Michael was my boss. I need to know!"

"I'm sorry, but I can't say. It's only a small lead. Nothing substantial. Don't go getting all worked up about it, O.K.?"

Adriana was already worked up, but she knew better that to pursue the matter. She said good-night and went to her room for the rest of the evening.

Matt poured himself another glass of wine, sat down and ate his supper, and tried to unwind.

Chapter 15

Over the following week Matt spent most of his time working on the murder cases with Willy. Bad luck plagued them on the long road to discovery. Every small lead they dug up turned out to be false. The people in the county were screaming for results. Tempers were short, the atmosphere charged with tension. The Mayor approved more funds for extra work hours.

The Chief asked them to work ten-hour days, six days a week, with no exceptions. The temperature stayed in the mid-nineties.

Matt saw Connie twice during the early part of the week, for short periods of time. Too busy and too tired to do more than take her out to dinner, he made no excuses to her for neglecting her the rest of the time.

Glad of the reprieve, he told himself he needed a little time to let his passions cool off. He thought they both could use some time alone. So he kept as busy as he could, much too busy to closely examine his relationship with Connie, working longer hours than the Chief asked for. However, he still couldn't stop thinking about her, and he dreamt about her every night.

Connie was busy dealing with Victor Prescott. Having set his sights on her, he was becoming a regular nuisance. She managed to keep him at bay most of the time, but in one moment of weakness, she'd given in to the pressure and had lunch with him again, and the next day she agreed to have dinner with him, Marie Sanchez and Sam Morgan.

As the week wore on, he grew more demanding and possessive. Realizing she'd made a mistake in spending any time at all with Victor, she vowed not to see him again. So, over the next few days, she'd refused several invitations from him, and he was becoming impatient with her. But she had no intention of leading him on, and she certainly didn't want to give Matt any reason to think she was interested in Victor. It appeared that Matt was looking for any excuse not to get involved with her, and she didn't want to help him find one.

On the afternoon of Friday July 3rd, Connie was once again working at the hospital. It had been a long day. She'd never seen so many cranky patients wanting fresh water or something cold to eat or a backrub. Everyone had a complaint about something, and nothing seemed to go right.

Her own back ached almost as badly as her poor feet. The heat had not let up in days. Perspiration ran down her face and back, making her clothes sticky and limp, and she wanted a shower more than anything. It didn't help her mood that she hadn't seen Matt in several days.

At four o'clock, she was in the nurses' lounge enjoying a cold Coke. She sat in one of the chairs with her feet up, looking out the picture window at the hot sun beating down on the parking lot. She didn't know why the nurses couldn't have a nice view out their window like in the doctors' lounge, but she guessed that was just one of the advantages the doctors had. *Maybe I should have been a doctor,* she mused. But she knew she wasn't cut out for that line of work. She had let Adriana talk her into doing volunteer work at the hospital, and she did enjoy it, but it wasn't something she would have done on her own and she wasn't sure how much longer she would continue with it.

She finished her Coke and was preparing to leave for home since she was done for the day, when Victor walked into the lounge.

"Just the person I was looking for," he said. "Are you free for dinner tonight?"

*Oh no,* Connie thought to herself, *here we go again!* She took a deep breath then blew it out slowly, and tried to remain cool and detached. Thankfully she had a legitimate reason to turn him down, and didn't have to tax her tired brain for an excuse not to see him.

"Sorry, but I have plans. Adriana invited me to dinner this evening." She reached for her purse and headed for the door.

Victor caught her by the arm and detained her. His grip was tight. Too tight. Connie stiffened and tried unsuccessfully to pull away.

"What about tomorrow night, then?"

"No, I don't think so, Victor. Thanks anyway."

"When, then, Connie. When *will* you go out with me again? Lately, every time I ask you out, you make up some excuse not to go. You're trying to avoid me, aren't you?" Victor's face was flushed and beads of perspiration stood out on his forehead. His grip on her arm tightened.

"Victor! Let go of my arm. You're hurting me!" She wretched her arm away in anger. "What the hell do you think you're doing?"

"I'm sorry, Connie, but you won't talk to me, you won't go out with me, you won't even give me a chance! If you would just give me a chance, get to know me better, I know you'd like me."

It was about the sixth time Victor had asked her to go out with him and Connie was tired of the same old argument. She was beginning to appreciate what Adriana had gone through with Michael Sans. And she realized she had to be perfectly blunt with Victor. *Subtleties be damned. The only thing this big ox is going to understand is the candid truth.* She looked directly at him and spoke as firmly as she could.

"Look, Victor. I like you all right. You're a nice guy. But I already have a boyfriend, whom I'm very serious about. And that's not the only reason why I don't want to go out with you. You're not my type, Victor. I'm just not interested in you that way. I'm sorry, but there's just no chance of you and me ever getting together. We can only be friends. Do you understand?"

"No, I don't understand. Answer me this; is this boyfriend of yours Matt Goodell? I mean, I think I have a right to know."

Connie didn't really want to tell Victor that Matt was her boyfriend, but she had a feeling he wasn't going to let the subject drop until he found out. Maybe once there was another man's name connected to hers, he would leave her alone.

"Okay. Yes. It is Matt. Now that you know, I hope you will stop asking me out. And please, don't tell anyone else about Matt and me. It's not common knowledge, and we're not ready for it to be."

"I won't tell anyone, because it doesn't matter. Matt doesn't love you. Hell, he's not the right person for you. You two will never be happy together."

Anger boiled up inside Connie. Anger and cold, dark fear. She withered Victor with a glance. Her voice shook uncontrollably.

"That's not true! You have no idea what you're talking about. From now on you had better mind your own damn business and stay the hell away from me!" She whirled away from him and reached for the door, but he caught her by the shoulders and turned her around to face him. His hands squeezed her shoulders and he shook her roughly. Tears came to her eyes, but she refused to acknowledge her pain. His next words frightened her more than she wanted to admit.

"I'm making *you* my business! Get that into your head and stop this nonsense about Matt Goodell!" With that said, he pulled her roughly against his chest and swiftly lowered his mouth to hers in an angry, savage kiss.

Connie struggled against him, trying to break free from his vice-like grip. With her hands flat against his chest she pushed in vain. She couldn't breath and felt like she was being crushed. Balling her hands into fists, she pounded fiercely on his arms. When he finally released her, she stepped back, swung her arm back and slapped him soundly.

"You son-of-a-bitch! Who the hell do you think you are? You've just destroyed any chance you ever had of being friends with me. Understand? My friends don't treat me like this, and neither will you!" Fire blazed in her eyes and she stood there like a mad goddess, commanding and getting respect from her disobedient servant. She quickly stepped to the door, then stopped and turned toward Victor and delivered a parting remark.

"If you ever try anything like this again, I'll report you to the hospital administrator! Is that perfectly clear?"

Standing as she was like a regal queen, Victor loved her all the more and wanted her more than anything in his life. He realized he'd made a bad mistake and offered his humble apology, but Connie was too angry to listen. Victor watched in despair as she whirled around and marched out the door, slamming it behind her.

The last echoes of her enraged voice died in the silent, empty room. Victor slumped down into a nearby chair and dropped his head into his hands. *Fool! You big, stupid fool. She'll probably never speak to you again. And who would blame her? No one... not even me.*

He sat there for a long time. He thought about his life and how empty it was. Loneliness was an unforgiving companion. He thought about the vacant house out on the bluff next to Sam Morgan's place. It was a beautiful house. With a little work, and the right woman in it, it would make a perfect home. That woman should be Connie, he thought. She'd love it up there where she could overlook the river and see for miles around. *I wish I could make her understand that she and I could be happy together if she'd just give us a chance! If I could get her alone for just a few days, I'd make her see things my way. I know I could!*

Empty wishes. Empty thoughts.

## Chapter 16

At six o'clock Friday evening, Adriana's doorbell rang. Dressed in a cool cotton sundress and airy sandals, she placed the salad she had just finished making into the fridge, before dashing to the door. Opening it, she smiled at her visitor.

"Connie, hi. Come in quick, and get out of the heat."

"I hope I'm not too early."

"No. Don't be silly. You're just on time." Adriana ushered Connie into the living room as she spoke. "Dinner's all ready except for the steaks, and Matt will put those on the grill in a few minutes. Let's sit down and relax awhile first."

Down the hall a door opened and closed, drawing the women's attention. Matt walked into the living room, freshly showered and dressed in casual pants and a new cotton dress shirt.

Adriana thought he looked a little over dressed for the simple dinner they had planned, but she didn't say anything.

When Matt saw Connie, he suddenly realized how much he'd missed her over the past few days. Forgetting everything else, he walked over to her with a big smile on his face and, engulfing her in his arms, kissed her with more than just a friendly little kiss. Adriana couldn't leave that alone. She raised her eyebrows in question.

"Well, well, well. What's this? Since when do you greet our dinner guests so ardently, Brother?" But Matt and Connie just smiled at her and remained non-committal, so Adriana asked Matt to get them something cold to drink. She invited Connie to sit down on the couch, while she chose to sit in her favorite rocking chair. When Matt brought their drinks, he joined Connie on the couch.

After a short while she sent Matt outside to grill the steaks on the barbecue, and she and Connie spent a few minutes discussing the annual Fourth of July dinner-dance to be held the following night. They expected to have a big crowd turn out for it, as usual.

When the steaks were done, they went into the kitchen table and enjoyed a meal of salad, French bread with garlic, and the grilled steaks. Matt noticed that Connie seemed tired and tense, but decided to wait until later, when they were alone, to ask her about it.

In fact Connie's earlier run-in with Victor had left its mark on her, but she didn't want to spoil their dinner by raging about him. Instead she summoned up the energy to pretend nothing was wrong.

After dinner they decided to have coffee outside in the shade of the trees. The sun, lowering toward the horizon, cast long, cool shadows across the yard. Combined with the breeze that was beginning to pick up, it helped make the evening pleasant and restful. Adriana couldn't help but notice that Connie and Matt were having a hard time keeping their eyes off each other. She wondered how soon it would be before they made up some excuse to leave together.

She didn't have long to wait. Declining a second cup of coffee, Connie said she was tired and really should be getting home. Matt jumped up and offered to take her home, but she reminded him that she'd driven her own car over.

"That's O.K. I'll just follow you and make sure you get home safe." A lame excuse, but Matt didn't care. He just wanted to get Connie alone for a couple of hours.

Connie rose from her lawn chair and thanked Adriana for the dinner. Confirming their plans to help decorate the Community Center for the dinner-dance the next day, she hugged Adriana goodnight and walked to her car.

"I'll see you in the morning, then," Adriana said as Connie got into her car and closed the door. Stepping back out of the way, she waved at Connie as the latter drove away, then turned to her brother. Matt kissed her on the cheek.

"Thanks for the dinner, Sis," he said. "Don't wait up for me, I might be late." With a wink and a wicked grin he sauntered to his Jeep.

"So what's new," she called after him. "It's been a long time since I waited up for you to get home." She laughed and turned toward the house, then sobered as a strange feeling came over her. She called out to him.

"And Matt..."

"Yeah?" He had one hand on the door. There was something in her voice that made him turn around.

"Be careful," she said. Something passed between them. A thought or a feeling. Subtle. Indefinable. But there, nonetheless. He looked at her critically.

They'd always been close, and ever so often something like this would pass between them. She'd get a sudden foreboding that something was going to happen to him, and inevitably it did. He had long ago come to respect and fear those premonitions, and he knew they would come true, just as sure as he knew the sun would rise tomorrow.

He walked back to where she stood, the laughter gone from his face. "What is it?" he asked.

"I don't know," she said. "A feeling. Nothing more. Probably nothing. Maybe it's the heat. I don't know. It's nothing I can put a finger on. Just be careful. O.K.?"

But Matt knew it wasn't just the heat. It had happened too many times in the past. He gave her a big, brotherly bear-hug.

"O.K. I will. I promise. Hey, try not to worry. I'll be extra careful." He looked into her sober eyes, trying to see what she had seen, but they looked only dark and troubled. He leaned down and kissed her again, this time on the other cheek. "Goodnight, Adriana. I love you, kid."

She watched him get into his Jeep and drive away. The strange feeling became stronger, making her pulse quicken and her heart hammer. She walked to the house and went inside and sat down in her rocking chair. Next to the rocker stood a small end table upon which lay a thick, leather-bound book. She picked up the book and folded it to her chest with both arms crossed. She began to slowly rock back and forth, staring out the window at the spot where Matt had parked his Jeep, unaware of the two tears that slowly rolled down her cheeks.

The book she held was an heirloom, her old family Bible.


Although nothing like the harrowing traffic congestion one found in big cities like Portland and Seattle, Matt found there were still plenty of vehicles on the road to slow down someone in a hurry.

Driving to Connie's apartment, he pushed aside the strange, ominous feeling that arose from Adriana's sudden premonition, and devoted his attention to his driving and the late evening traffic. He was following a blue van carrying two windsurfing boards on top. He noticed that about three-fourths of the cars and vans had windsurfing boards on them. He'd be glad when the summer tourist season ended.

As Matt approached an intersection, the van directly in front of him merely slowed down before rolling through the stop sign and making a right turn. Matt shook his head, quickly noted the out-of-state license number of the offending vehicle, then drove on toward Connie's place, giving the other driver the benefit of the doubt.

However, a stop sign is a stop sign no matter what state you're from, so Matt wanted the license number for future reference. One never knew when that kind of information might come in handy. *Or maybe*, Matt told himself, *I'm just a little jumpy.*

He reminded himself he was off duty and promised himself not think about work for the rest of the evening. Connie was waiting for him and he was really looking forward to spending some time alone with her.

Once at her apartment, Matt forgot all about anything else. She made it easy for him. By now the evening breeze had cooled them both down, but once they were together they found themselves warming up all over again. She greeted him with long, slow kisses that started at the corner of his mouth, whispered across his lips and down his neck and torso, and ended at his naval. Hot sensations jolted through his body, intensifying the shock of her sudden onslaught. With trembling arms, he swept Connie up and carried her to the bedroom where he proceeded to explore and adore every inch of her lovely body.

He would later wonder how he had let himself get into that situation. Lately he seemed to have lost control of his life and his destiny. It was like he was just going along for the ride and at times hanging on for dear life.

Two hours later, showered and dressed, Connie made coffee while Matt sat at the kitchen table and watched. While they drank the hot liquid, Connie found herself feeling very comfortable and safe with Matt. Wrapped in this blanket of warm feelings, she began telling Matt about Victor and his ardent, though fruitless, pursuit of her attention. Before long, though, she wished she had never mentioned it.

"Victor has always been friendly, but has never imposed himself on me like he's been doing lately," she confessed to Matt. "I don't know what more I can do to discourage him. Do you have any advice, Matt?"

Matt had tensed at the first mention of Victor. Anger and sudden dislike toward Victor flamed up within him. He never thought of himself as a jealous man, but all of a sudden he had a strong urge to beat Victor into a pulp.

"Don't worry about him anymore. I'll have a little heart-to-heart talk with him next time I see him."

"No, Matt. I don't want you to get involved in this," she said. "I probably shouldn't have said anything about it. I'm sure I've made my position clear to him and I really don't think he'll bother me again."

Watching Connie talk, he thought she looked as helpless as a wild animal caught in a trap. His natural instinct to protect her ran hand in hand with a new feeling, a feeling that he didn't like to admit to himself. The thought of another man wanting Connie's attention, wanting to make love to her, created a hard, cold knot in his stomach. When he spoke his voice was ragged.

"It doesn't sound to me like he's going to leave you alone! I'm going to have a chat with him and make it perfectly clear that he's not to harass you." Matt stood up and began pacing the floor. He ran a shaky hand through his hair. The house suddenly felt hot and stuffy. Beads of sweat erupted across his face.

"No, Matt. Please. Victor's attentions are harmless and temporary," she insisted. "Promise me you won't go see him!"

"I can't make that promise, Connie. I'd be lying to you if I did." Then he said he should go home.

"Stay here with me tonight, Matt. Please." As tempting as that sounded, Matt had something that he wanted to take care of. He was determined to find Victor and give him a piece of his mind.

Connie walked over and wrapped her arms around his neck. Her body was hot and supple. She clung to him tightly, pulling herself up and wrapping her legs around his hips.

At first Matt tried to resist her, still thinking of what he'd like to do to Victor. But few men could have resisted such a fervent show of passion, and Matt was no different. With hungry arms he carried her back to the bedroom and laid her gently on the bed. Any thoughts of Victor and what he'd like to do to him vanished like a puff of smoke in a high wind. Their hearts beating wildly, their breath hot and moist, they soared together as one on a blanket of raw emotion.

## Chapter 17

### Saturday, July Fourth

The Fourth of July was starting out to be another hot summer day. The Gorge winds were blowing strong, making it seem a little cooler than it was, but by 10 AM the temperature was already hovering around the 80-degree mark.

The police station was buzzing with activity. All vacations had been canceled until further notice. Matt and Willy sat hunched over their desk, going through their notes once again. Matt pushed back his chair and took a deep breath and stretched out his arms and back, running the fingers of both hands up through his hair and then down across his face.

"I've been over these notes so many times I've got them memorized. There's not much here to go on. We still don't know if we're dealing with only one perpetrator or several."

"I don't think it's just one guy," Willy replied. "We have three different murders, and three different MOs."

"If it is just one guy," Matt said, "then he's one damn clever bastard. We may never find him."

"Oh, we'll find him alright. Sooner or later he, or they, will make a mistake, Matt, and when that happens, we'll get 'em."

Chief Baxter entered the room amid a swirl of hot air and dust. Wiping the sweat from his face, he addressed the room in general, "I just returned from a meeting with the mayor. His office has received just about as many calls and letters as I have from concerned citizens, not only of Pine Crest, but of the whole damned county, who want to know what we're doing to solve these murders. I hope to God that one of you gentleman has something new for me today!"

He looked around the room at each man in turn, hoping that someone had found the lead that would break at least one, if not all, of these cases.

"Sorry, Chief. There hasn't been anything new."

"We're at a dead-end, boss."

"Nobody knows nothin' out there."

"You know how it is, Jess. These things take time."

One by one the officers had to admit that they were up against the proverbial wall. Things were at a stand-still.

"Well, somebody's got to have seen something, or heard something, or knows somebody else that has. And, quite frankly, we're starting to look bad. People are getting restless, and restless people are spooky people. Spooky and irritable. They're demanding action. Action and results--something I'd like to see myself."

Matt looked across the desk at Willy. The chief was right. The people around town had been acting strange the past week--whispering in small groups, glancing around furtively while walking down the street, stopping him on the street, asking all kinds of questions. It was only natural, given the present circumstances.

Chief Baxter instructed them all to be especially careful in their investigations, not to assume anything, and to go over every little detail from every possible angle.

That's exactly what they were doing, and Baxter knew it, but there was nothing else he could do except remind them again. Matt thought it must be frustrating to be the head of the team that was supposed to keep the town safe, and to come up against a situation like this where you were up against that wall, and there was nothing you could do except stand there and beat your head against it.

After two more mind-numbing, nerve-wracking hours of going over details, Willy and Matt stopped for lunch. They drove across town to their favorite hamburger joint. Willy parked in the shade of a large oak and left the windows down so that Jazz would stay cool. He commanded the dog to "stay," then met Matt at the front door of the small restaurant. They found a booth back by a corner window where they had a good view of everyone who came and went in the restaurant as well as passing traffic. Willy looked at his car and saw that Jazz had his head out the window watching the passersby with interest.

Willy ordered his usual hamburger and fries and a chocolate milkshake, while Matt decided on a taco salad and iced tea. There was the usual rush of lunch-time teenagers, working people and young mothers with their children out for a treat. Amid the noise and confusion Matt tried to relax and enjoy his meal.

When they were finished eating, he and Willy made their way through the crowd to the exit door. The West wind had increased in intensity. Matt grabbed his hat just as it started to blow off his head. "Oh, God, what a day! Perfect for hittin' the waves, and here I am. Stuck in a hot, sticky office all day. Life ain't fair, Willy."

Willy just shook his head and grinned.

"Forget about playing in the water. We're not going to see any time off for quite a while. Let's take a drive down to Briars Beach again. Maybe we can scare something up."

"Fine. I'd sure like to find someone who knows about the car that ran over Sans. Maybe we'll get lucky."

Once down at the beach, Matt and Willy asked Tom Morgan if he had seen anyone acting suspicious, or heard any hint of foul play since they had last talked to him. Tom was little or no help to them. While he had seen several strange-acting people come through that area, it was nothing unusual. He pointed out there were a lot of weird people in the world and he saw more than his fair share of them.

After a frustrating hour Matt and Willy climbed back into their patrol cars and headed back to town. The traffic had picked up considerably, mostly of them windsurfers heading for Briars Beach and other access areas along the river.

They had gone only a mile when they became trapped in heavy eastbound traffic on a 300-yard-stretch of narrow highway. Built between the rocky hillside and the river, the road was bordered on the river side with safety rails to prevent motorists from careening down the twenty-foot embankment into the water.

Traffic in their eastbound lane slowed to a crawl as cars up ahead waited for someone in a blue van to park. The driver of the van was having trouble getting into a small parking space just beyond the long bottlenecked stretch of road. Westbound traffic was just as heavy, but moving along at a good clip.

Horns up ahead started honking at the van. The driver seemed not to notice the congestion he was causing or else he just didn't care. Matt wasn't sure which, but he radioed to Willy and growled, "I think we'll stop and have a little chat with that driver. Maybe give him a lesson in parking."

When they finally made their way up to the van, Matt turned on his flashing lights and pulled his car off to the right shoulder of the road, behind the van. Traffic now had to pull out and around him, too, adding to the confusion. Matt swore as he got out of the car and slammed the door. Willy pulled his car around to the other side of the van and off the narrow road as far as he could. Jazz was excited by all the traffic and wanted out of the car, but Willy was concerned for his safety and made him stay. He strode over to Matt who stood looking at the license plates on the back end of the van.

"I remember this van. Someone driving this van ran a stop sign in town last night," Matt said. Willy stood back and directed traffic, while Matt walked around and talked to the driver of the van. Matt remembered the driver, too.

A young man with long, straggly dark brown hair sat behind the wheel looking rather embarrassed. He had on a pair of wildly colored cotton pants, leather sandals and dark sunglasses, but no shirt. When Matt approached his window and showed his badge, the man removed the sunglasses and smiled.

"Hi, mate. Say, I'm real sorry about this foul-up. I thought I could get parked in here, but I can't. And now, with all these bloody cars on my ass, I can't get out, either."

"Yeah, well, you had no business trying to park here anyway. Anyone can see there's not enough room."

"You're right. I know. It was a stupid thing to try. I guess I was just in too big a hurry."

"You seem to be in a big hurry a lot. Last night I saw you run a stop sign up in town. What's the matter? Don't they have stop signs where you come from?"

"Well, now, mate. I can explain that. I didn't mean to run that sign. I was lost and trying to find my way back to my motel, and quite honestly, I didn't see it until it was too late. I was already out in the middle of the intersection, so I figured I might just as well go on across, right?"

"What's your name and where you from?" Matt took a notepad from his shirt pocket and jotted notes.

"Name's Dewy, Jonathan Dewy. I came up from Down Under, as they say. Australia. Came for the gnarly surfin'. You do any sailin' yourself, mate?"

"I'll need to see your driver's license and registration, Mr. Dewy." Matt didn't care for Mr. Dewy's overly friendly attitude, but put it down to nervousness. When Dewy handed over his papers, Matt ran a check on them. They both checked out. Matt ordered Dewy to be more careful in the future, and halted traffic in both lanes long enough to let the Aussie back his van out onto the road and take off. Carefully avoiding the long line of impatient drivers as the traffic quickly picked up again Matt turned and started to walk back toward the patrol car. Engines roared as the line of vehicles in the Westbound lane turned into a long, flowing echelon of grinding gears and spinning wheels, picking up speed with each passing second.

From the corner of his right eye, he saw a brief flash of red streak by in the Westbound lane. Jerking his head toward the flash, he searched for the car, but got just a glimpse of it before the following traffic obscured his vision. *"I heard the screech of tires and saw a red sports car race by"*, Matt remembered that's what the young man had told him when he was interviewing people at the scene of the hit and run incident that killed Michael Sans.

"Willy! Let's go!" he yelled and jumped around the side of his car, mindless of oncoming traffic. Tires squealed and horns honked as cars came to a halt. Cursing his own foolishness, Matt just managed to get inside the car without getting hit.

Hearing the urgency in Matt's voice, Willy ran around from the back of the car where he'd continued directing traffic, jerked open the door, and leaned into the car.

"What's going on?"

"I just saw a little red sports car go by! Let's go!" Matt yelled as he threw the car into gear.

Willy ran up to his own car, jumped in and quickly buckled up his seatbelt and flipped on the siren, which shrilled into a crescendo. Gravel spit out behind his tires like a shower of hail as he quickly made a U-turn on the highway.

Matt, too, maneuvered his patrol car around in the middle of the narrow road. More breaks squealed and horns honked from the oncoming vehicles, but Matt ignored them. Precious seconds were slipping by.

Although he kept the siren howling, their pursuit was hampered by the dense traffic. Motorists were moving as quickly as they could, but it wasn't fast enough. By the time they got out of the narrow strip of road, where the other cars could get out of their way, several minutes had passed. They continued West for fifteen miles before Matt could admit to himself that they'd lost the car.

In the meanwhile, Willy had radioed ahead to Skamania County for assistance from that county's sheriff department, and had them set up a roadblock on Highway 14 just outside the small town of Stevenson.

Frustrated and disappointed, Matt pulled his car off the road and sat in stunned silence. He couldn't believe he'd come so close and lost.

"Damnit!" he swore, slamming his fist against the steering wheel. He got out of the car and leaned his folded arms across the top, resting his head on his arms. Rivulets of sweat ran down his face. "Damnit, damnit, DAMNIT!" he bellowed. He kicked the tire as hard as he could, and felt a little better.

Willy pulled over as well. He was on the radio with Skamania County once again. When he finished, he stepped out of the car, walked around to the trunk and opened it. Reaching in, he pulled out a jug of ice water and took a long drink, then offered it to Matt.

"Skamania County boys still haven't seen anything. They said they'd station a couple of men where they could watch the road for another hour or so in case our car turns up. They'll keep their eyes open."

"Yeah, well, I guess that's about all they can do for now." He took a long drink of the cold water, then poured some into his hand and splashed it on his face. "There are dozens of little side roads that car could have gone up between Briars Beach and Stevenson. There's no tellin' where he's at by now."

"I'm afraid you're right, Matt. Look, it might not have been our man. You didn't get that good a look at it, and we don't even have a positive ID to go by."

"I know. You're right. But, I sure would have liked to find out who that was." Matt looked at his watch.

It was almost 6 p.m. Quitting time.

## Chapter 18

Earlier that same day, Victor Prescott made himself a simple lunch consisting of a bowl of vegetable beef soup, a cheese sandwich and a cup of black coffee. He took it out onto his deck, which faced the river, and sat at a small table he'd placed near the edge of the deck, under the shade of an old cottonwood tree. The wind blew his napkin away before he could anchor it down. Quickly retrieving it, he put it on the table beside his bowl and set his cup of coffee on it.

As he sat eating, he watched the river, the windsurfers, and the birds. A gull screeched at him as it flew overhead, and a black crow flew in and landed on a fence post, watching him. He threw a crust of bread to the bird and watched it swoop down to gather its bounty.

Three long, deep blasts sounded from a passing tug. Victor stared out at the river. The windsurfers dispersed, leaving a wide path for the tug. Victor watched absent-mindedly.

His psychiatrist had warned him to avoid any undue stress, but he couldn't stop this demon from taking over his mind. All he could think about was Connie. *I know she likes flowers. Maybe I'll go into town and buy her some.*

With that he stood up and took his lunch dishes into the house, rinsed them off and put them into the dishwasher. He sat down and made out a list of things he needed from the grocery store.

When he was finished, he put away the writing pad and pencil, and made sure everything was straightened up before leaving the house. There was a small scrap of paper on the floor which he picked up and threw in the trash. The house was spic and span.

Out in the garage, Victor backed his little MG out into the sunlight. A blue Buick La Sabre occupied the other space in the double car garage, and that was the car he usually drove. But today he'd chosen to drive the small car. He saw it was covered with dust, and remembered that he'd planned to wash it today. For a minute he thought about waiting until tomorrow for the wash job, but looking at it critically, he decided he'd better go ahead and do it now, before driving into town.

Pulling it up under the shade of an oak tree, he proceeded to hose it down. He didn't mind the task, in fact it gave him a satisfying sense of accomplishment and pride.

The little car was one he'd bought ten years ago in a small town in Alabama. While he and his wife were there on vacation, he'd spotted it parked in front of a modest home that had a real estate company's "For Sale" sign planted in the lawn. The car also had a "For Sale" sign on it, so Victor had stopped and asked about it.

It turned out the car belonged to a recent widow; actually had belonged to her husband, who had passed away two months earlier. She was moving in with her sister in the city and had no use for the car.

The price was right and Victor was thrilled to find such a treasure. Against his wife's wishes, he bought the MG and drove it home to Washington. That meant, of course, that his wife had to drive their family car all the way home, and she wasn't very happy about that. But Victor couldn't resist the MG, and his wife knew who the boss in their family was, so she kept quiet and did as she was told.

Looking at it now, dirty and neglected, it was hard to believe that he cherished it as much as he did. He was ashamed of himself for letting it get so dirty, but he remembered that the last time he drove it home, he was in a tremendous hurry to get into the house. He'd been shaky and light-headed. He'd quickly parked the MG in the garage and closed the door, then had gone into the house and poured himself two fingers of bourbon. Taking the bottle with him, his trembling steps took him into the living room where he collapsed into a chair. After a few minutes the trembling had decreased and his breathing returned to normal.

Remembering that day made Victor nervous. As he washed the dirt off he chided himself for being foolish. *It's just all that's been happening around here lately*, he told himself. *Everything's going crazy. Half the time I don't even know what I'm thinking. Sometimes I feel like I'm loosing my mind. Maybe I should go and see Dr. Westgate again.* Having decided that, he felt better and concentrated on the task of washing the car.

That activity diverted his mind, for a few minutes at least, from thoughts of Connie.

As he was finishing up the front end, he noticed a small piece of ragged yellow material hanging from the front grill and pulled it loose.

Looking at it, he wondered how it got there, but his mind was on other things and he simply shrugged his shoulders and threw the rag into the garbage can next to the garage.

Deciding he'd better change his clothes, he hurried back into the house. When he came out five minutes later he was pleased with the way his car shone. *Like a bright, red apple,* he thought as he climbed into the driver's seat and revved up the engine.

Driving into town he passed by Briars Beach, which was overflowing with windsurfers. He also noticed two police cars parked among the other vehicles in the parking lot; and Matt Goodell and Willy Wilson were down on the beach talking to Tom Morgan.

Traffic was beginning to pick up, though, and Victor didn't have time to wonder about what was happening down at Briars Beach. He had groceries to pick up and flowers to buy.

Once in the grocery store, he spent as little time as possible getting what he needed. Shopping wasn't his favorite pastime. He used to leave all that to his wife. He resented the inevitability of having to do it himself and considered it a necessary evil. Therefore, he accomplished the task as quickly as possible, spoke to no one unless he had to, and paid no attention to ads, specials or bargains. The only pleasurable thing about the task was that, with his wife gone, there was no one to nag him about how much ice cream, cookies or beer he bought.

Today he stocked up on all three. As soon as he could get out of the grocer's, he headed for the florist. He was more comfortable there, having patronized the place often over the years. The clerk smiled at him when he stepped into the shop.

"Well, Mr. Prescott, how nice to see you again. It's been a long time since you've visited us," she said. "What can we help you with today?"

Victor ordered a dozen red roses accented with white Baby's Breath to be delivered immediately to Connie. He thought it would be better to have them delivered than to take them to her himself, since she was probably still mad at him for kissing her yesterday.

The florist smiled and asked him if he had a new girlfriend, ending the question with a wink.

"Not just a new girlfriend," he replied. "I've found the woman I want to be my new wife." And with that comment he walked out the door, leaving the florist with raised eyebrows and a half-smile on her lips.

Having completed his self-assigned tasks, Victor climbed into his car and headed home. The afternoon traffic was still just as heavy as it was when he came into town an hour earlier. About a mile East of Briars Beach the movement of vehicles heading West slowed to a stop. Victor peered up the line and saw two patrol cars with lights flashing and a blue van turned crosswise in the road, blocking the lane. The delay was aggravating. He was in a hurry to get home with his groceries and relax in front of the television with a couple of bottles of his favorite beer.

The wait was short-lived. Within a minute the van had maneuvered around and was heading East, toward town. The traffic in Victor's lane began to move and quickly picked up speed. It seemed everyone was in a hurry to get going, and that suited Victor just fine. He revved up his engine and sped down the highway, past the patrol cars, which were still parked in the same place, and disappeared around the next bend in the road.

Within two minutes he was pulling his car into the garage. He pushed the button on his remote control that closed the garage door and got out of the car. Gathering up his two bags of groceries, he quickly walked into the house and placed the softening ice cream into the freezer and the other perishables into the fridge. After putting away the rest of his groceries, he opened the refrigerator and pulled out a cold bottle of beer. He walked into the living room and sat down, staring out the big picture window at the river and the mountains of Oregon. He forgot about watching TV.

Time passed by unnoticed as Victor's thoughts wandered. He thought about how much he still missed his wife and realized that it wasn't so much that he missed his wife as it was that he was so lonely. Connie could alleviate that loneliness for him. He couldn't get her out of his mind. He wanted her. He needed her. He swore he would have her, one way or another.

Chapter 19

At 7:30 p.m. Matt knocked on Connie's door. When she opened the door, he stepped inside and embraced her warmly. After a long, hungry kiss, she leaned back and studied the haggard expression on his face.

"Hard day, huh?" she asked as she walked into the kitchen to mix some pre-dinner drinks.

"Oh, just very frustrating. And hot. And I'm starving." He sniffed the air with obvious appreciation. The smell of home baked bread and fried chicken assailed his nostrils. "What have you got to eat?" He lifted the corner of a casserole dish and smelled the contents. "Umm, that smells great. Can I have some?" he asked as he reached a finger in to sample the chicken.

Connie swatted his hand. "Get out of that! That's for the party tonight. Here, if you're starving you can have a hot bun." At the look on his face she re-phrased her words,

"A hot roll, I mean. *Dinner* roll."

He grinned wickedly and grabbed her around the waist, swinging her around and around the kitchen. She laughed, and the sound echoed in the small apartment. "You're a depraved man, Officer Goodell. I don't think I should trust you in my house without an escort. Maybe I should call that watchful sister of yours."

"Oh no you don't. She's the one you should worry about. Why, she's probably sitting at home right now conjuring up all kinds of things about us."

Connie had never felt so happy as she did right now, slowly dancing around the room in Matt's arms, joking and carrying on as if they'd been together for a long time. And more importantly, as if they would be together for a long time to come. She wrapped her arms around Matt's neck and laid her head down on his shoulder, closing her eyes. She wanted them to stay like this forever.

Matt was thinking along the same lines as Connie, and when he realized this, it gave him a little shock. Somehow he didn't seem to mind anymore. In fact, it gave him a tremendous sense of peace, a feeling of belonging. The restlessness that had plagued him all summer was gone. And with it, the loneliness. He felt as if he had been gone a long time and had at last come home. Now he knew what people meant when they said something gave them a warm, fuzzy feeling inside. They finished their drinks and gathered up the food Connie had made. The trip to the Community Center was a short one and took only a few minutes. On the way they chatted about insignificant subjects of no importance to either of them. Connie repeatedly smoothed the skirt of her dress and chattered more than normal. Matt fiddled with the buttons on his shirt and avoided eye contact with her.

Something important had passed between them. Something momentous and yet fragile. Connie had known all along that she was falling in love with Matt. It was what she wanted. She knew that he was falling in love with her, but she also knew that he was unaware of it.

Matt, on the other hand, was living for the moment, enjoying this close and wonderful feeling he got whenever he was with Connie. But he was a little embarrassed by it, too. A little afraid of it. He didn't want her to read anything into it. He wasn't ready to accept any deeper meaning in their brief relationship. He told himself his motto was going to be--*One date at a time.*

When they arrived at the Community Center, Matt helped Connie carry her food inside. The band was in place up on the stage, warming up. Most of the guests were already eating, so Matt and Connie found the plates and proceeded to dish up. The long tables were laden with all kinds of main dishes, casseroles, side dishes and salads, as well as every kind of dessert imaginable, and they had no trouble finding enough of their favorite dishes to fill their plates.

Laughing at each other for being gluttons, they wandered through the crowded dining hall until they found Adriana. There were two empty chairs next to her. Matt seated Connie before sitting in the other chair. As they ate, he took time to look around at the festive decorations the girls had worked so hard on.

Sticking with the traditional color scheme of red, white and blue for the Fourth of July, the decorating committee had filled the hall with streamers and balloons. On the walls they had mounted posters of the War of Independence, depicting American soldiers marching along the streets of New England and fighting in battle against the English. One whole wall was devoted to reproductions of the Boston Tea Party, with authentic costumes of that era on loan from the local museum. All in all, the committee had done an outstanding job and everyone was talking about it.

Not wanting to be outdone, Matt generously added his verbal approval and sincere appreciation. Judging by the bright rosy glow on Connie's cheeks, she was flattered by his show of interest. Adriana, on the other hand, acted as it something was troubling her. Throughout the meal she was quiet and withdrawn. She answered in monosyllables when spoken to until Matt proclaimed another stream of compliments pertaining to the decorations. Then she snapped at him, "Matt, shut up. Stop babbling. Unlike the typical male, we don't need constant affirmation from the opposite sex to know we've done a good job."

"Don't be rude, Sis. I was trying to express my admiration for the work you did. If you can't appreciate that, then forget it!"

Connie looked at Matt and then back at Adriana, raising her eyebrows at the unusual display of tension.

"Hey, you two. What gives? Did you two have a fight this morning?"

"No, we didn't have a fight. How could we have a fight when I haven't seen him since last evening?"

Suddenly Matt knew what was bothering Adriana. Last night, he and Connie had been so caught up in their passionate lovemaking that he'd forgotten all about Adriana's premonition that he was in danger. She would naturally be worried about him when he didn't come home all night. She was worse than a mother hen after having one of her premonitions.

He realized he should have called her sometime during the day, but he'd been so busy that he'd not thought about it. An expression of contrition crossed his face when he thought about how her day must have gone, worried about him yet not wanting to be a nuisance and call him at work. A quick phone call could have relieved her mind, at least for the time being.

He reached across the table and took her hand in his. Giving it a gentle squeeze he said, "Oh man, Sis. I'm sorry. I should have called you. I've been so busy, I just didn't think. Forgive me?"

Adriana appeared to struggle with her emotions, but she could never remain mad at Matt for long. She gave him a cross look, then reluctantly returned the hand squeeze and gave him a little smile. That made him feel a lot better. He turned to Connie, who was looking at them like they'd both lost their minds, and explained about Adriana's premonition.

Connie was aware of Adriana's gift of insight where her brother was concerned, and knew of the accuracy of her premonitions. She asked Adriana about what she'd seen and Adriana assured her that there was nothing concrete to go on, just a feeling of unease.

"Well, come on," Matt said. "Let's not let it spoil this evening. We're here to dance and have fun, so let's get on with it."

"Matt's right, Connie. Get him out on that floor and dance off that huge meal before it all turns to fat. He gets kind of ugly when he gets fat, so keep an eye on him," she kidded.

So the other two got up and headed for the dance floor. The band was playing a slow song, which Matt preferred since his talents on the dance floor were not exactly up to date.

The dance hall was beginning to fill up with other couples who'd finished eating. Matt saw Willy and his wife dancing across the room, as well as several other people he knew. After a couple of times around the floor he noticed Victor Prescott standing against the wall, talking to Marie Sanchez. Matt deftly steered Connie away from that part of the room. He pulled her tighter against himself. Her soft and supple body boldly molded itself against the outline of his own. He felt the stirring of passion and lost himself in the motion of their dance.

The soft music lulled him into a dreamscape where only he and Connie existed. The rest of the world was muted and lost in his subconscious; forgotten for the present. He buried his face into the soft pillow of golden hair and inhaled the essence of her perfume, heady and sensual.

They danced and talked for the next hour, totally absorbed in each other, unaware of the stares and whispers of their friends. All in all the evening was going very well, Matt thought. He had never seen Connie so happy and full of life. For that matter, he couldn't remember ever feeling so happy himself.

After a while he came to the shocking realization that he might be falling in love with her, and he wasn't at all sure what to think about that. Somehow that idea didn't scare him as much as he thought it would.

He drifted along in a daze for a while, lulled by a feeling of happiness and security. He wouldn't think about what "falling in love" meant, he told himself. He was happier than he had ever been and he wanted to just relax and enjoy that feeling before he had to stop and analyze what it would mean to him and his life.

About 9:45 they were sitting at a table talking to Adriana, resting between dances. The room was becoming quite warm, so Matt offered to go and get them all something cold to drink. The offer was quickly accepted. While he was gone, the music started up again. Connie looked around and saw Victor staggering across the floor toward them. Just as he reached their table he tripped on a chair and almost fell into Connie's lap. The smell of alcohol was so strong she grimaced and turned her head away.

"Victor, you're drunk!" she berated him.

"No, I'm not, Honey. Come on, lez danze." He pulled her up by the arm and began dragging her onto the dance floor. She tried to pull free but his grip was too strong.

"No, Victor. I don't want to dance. Let go of my arm!"

"Oh, com'on, now. Don't be a shpoil shport," he slurred as he continued to haul her through the crowd. She stumbled over the leg of a chair that was in her way and painfully whacked her shin.

Anger boiled up inside her. How dare he come along and grab me as if I belonged to him, she thought. Drawing back her free arm, she punched him as hard as she could in the mid-section and jerked her other arm free.

"I said NO, Victor! What the hell do you think you're doing? You can't just come in here and drag people around. What's the matter with you?"

"Hey, all'z I wanted was jus' a lil' danz. You don' `av ta be-zo-mean 'bout it."

Adriana had watched as Victor drug Connie onto the dance floor and immediately got up and followed them through the crowd to Connie's side. She reached out and put her hand flat against Victor's chest and pushed him back hard. People were starting to stare at them.

"That's enough, Victor," she said. "Connie doesn't want to dance with you. You either behave yourself or leave. Don't bother Connie again or I'll have my brother throw you out of here. Understand?"

"Oh, yeah. The brother. The cop. I know all 'about 'im," he said. "Okay, I'll go. But I'll be back later. Gotta 'ave a dance with my girl." Victor mumbled something to himself and staggered around the room until he found someone else to talk to. The curious onlookers lost interest and returned to what they were doing, and the party returned to normal.

Back at their table, Connie calmed down. She and Adriana spoke about other things. Willy Wilson and his wife, Rose, joined them just as Matt returned with their drinks, so he asked them if they would like something to drink. Willy and Matt started back for more cold drinks.

At the same time, Marie Sanchez dropped by their table to say hello and Connie asked her to join them. Marie cheerfully accepted and Connie called after Matt to bring an extra glass of punch for Marie. Adriana introduced Rose to both Connie and Marie, who had never met her. Then the women settled down into a discussion about the new bicycle store in town. They were all talking about getting new bikes and doing some serious biking this summer, but Adriana was hesitant. It had been a long time since she was on a bicycle. But the way Rose and Connie talked about the handsome young owner of the bike store caught Adriana's interest. She'd always loved bicycling when she was younger. *Maybe it is time I took up that sport again,* she thought.

After a few minutes Sam Morgan walked over to their table and greeted them, then he asked Marie to dance. She smiled and said she'd be pleased, and followed him onto the dance floor. Connie said to the other two, "Look at Sam. He's so shy, he's blushing!"

"I know. Isn't it sweet?" Adriana replied.

"I've known Sam for about seven or eight years," Rose said. "And he's always been like that. It's too bad more of these men aren't that sweet."

Willy and Matt came back with the punch and sat down. Adriana told Matt what Victor had done, and Connie made light of it by saying that he was just a little drunk. Matt wanted to go over and confront Victor. But Connie made him promise not to pick a fight, and only after eliciting this promise from him, changed the subject and managed to draw Matt's attention away from Victor.

At the end of the dance, Sam brought Marie back to their table and asked Connie for the next dance. He grinned like a little boy, his cheeks once again tinted pink, and Connie couldn't resist. She let him lead her out onto the dance floor as the band played the opening strands of "Louie, Louie."

As he watched Connie and Sam dance, Matt felt a little jealous. He turned to Willy and asked if he knew much about Sam. Willy laughed gleefully and slapped Matt on the back.

"You'd better watch out, Partner. He'll sweep your gal right off her feet if you're not careful."

"Very funny. Anyway, what makes you think she's my girl?"

"Are you kiddin' me? Anybody looking at you two together can see the chemistry between you. It's written all over your faces."

"You're crazy. You don't know what you're talking about, Willy."

"Yeah, well--whatever. But don't worry. Sam's perfectly harmless. He's just a big, ol' friendly kid. He's no competition for you."

When the dance ended, Sam brought Connie back to their table and asked Adriana to dance. The dance was a waltz, Adriana's favorite, and she was happy for the chance to enjoy it to the fullest.

"Sam is really quite a good dancer," Connie commented to Matt. "He's got a lot of natural rhythm and grace for such a big man."

Matt jumped up, pulling Connie with him. "Come here, you. I may not be much of a dancer, but I guarantee you'll enjoy it more." Then he led her out onto the dance floor and danced better than he'd ever danced in his life. The music lent itself to romance and love, and he took advantage of every step and twirl. Their bodies molded together perfectly as he swung her around and around the room. When the song ended, they were both breathless and hot.

Walking back to their table they passed by Victor arguing with Madge Smith, a local woman who had helped organize the dance. The smell of alcohol permeated the immediate area around Victor, who's speech was even more garbled than it had been earlier in the evening. Mrs. Smith was obviously uncomfortable with the situation. Victor had hold of her arm and was trying to pull her out onto the dance floor, while she was doing her best to disengage herself without creating a scene.

Matt stopped. It was time to put an end to Victor's abusive behavior. Matt pulled Connie off to the side, then excused himself. He turned and crossed the space between him and Victor in three long strides. Grabbing Victor by the arm, he pulled him around and pushed him back against the wall--hard.

In his surprise Victor released his hold on Madge. His eyes held a blank, unfocused expression. After a brief moment, recognition showed on his face, and with it, anger, resentment, and even hatred.

Matt had a firm grip on Victor's left arm with one powerful hand, and with the other held solidly against Victor's chest, pinned him to the wall. They stood face to face, only inches apart, both breathing heavily.

"I believe the lady said no, Victor," Matt hissed. "I think you'd better leave her alone."

"Mine' yer own dam' binniz, *copper*. Me an' the lady's jes gonna `av a lit' danz." Puffy, bloodshot eyes met icy-blue ones narrowed in anger.

With a sudden thrust, Victor propelled Matt backwards into a nearby chair, sending it clattering across the floor. Clenching his massive hand, he closed in on Matt as Matt tried to avoid tangling with the chair.

Matt's youth and agility served him well. He instantly regained his balance and twisted sideways as Victor swung at him. Victor, thrown off balance, tripped over Matt's foot and landed face-down in a drunken heap on the floor. Reaching down, Matt grabbed him by the left wrist and twisted upwards across Victor's back in an effective arm hold.

Willy had noticed the scuffle and came to Matt's assistance. Together they hauled Victor to his feet. "That's enough for one night, Victor. You're going home," Willy said as he helped Matt escort Victor to the door. As Willy passed his wife, he asked her to call for a cab.

Victor didn't seem very appreciative of the efforts to get him home safely. He tried several times to jerk free, cussing and ranting. Once outside, the cooler air and quiet helped to calm him down. That, and the fact that Matt threatened to take him to jail. He chose to sit peaceably on the park bench until the cab arrived. When it came, Willy gave the driver directions to Victor's home and ten dollars for his trouble.

As the cab drove away, Willy turned to Matt. "I wonder what the hell's gotten into him. I don't recall ever seeing him drunk and nasty like that." Shaking his head, he slapped Matt on the shoulder and said, "Come on. Let's not let this spoil our evening."

Back inside, the band had struck up a lively tune and the dance floor was crowded with couples cavorting around the room. Grabbing their Partners, Matt and Willy laughingly joined the fun, the incident with Victor all but forgotten.

Looking around the room as they danced, Matt spotted Adriana dancing with a tall, dark haired young man and asked Connie if she knew who he was.

"Oh, that's Bret Stone. He's new in town. He owns that new little bicycle store on 2nd Street. You've noticed it, haven't you?"

"Yes; I was wondering who owned that. Bret Stone, huh? Well, he looks nice enough, but you never know these days. I think I'd better go meet him."

"Oh, no you don't. Adriana's old enough to take care of herself, and besides, tonight you're mine, Lover Boy," she laughed and pulled him tighter as they swung around and around the room. Matt soon forgot all about Adriana and Bret Stone.

Later, Matt and Sam stood in a quiet corner talking. Soon they were joined by Willy. The women were taking a powder-room break, leaving the men to entertain themselves for a few minutes. Sam was enjoying the attention, proud as he could be that the two police officers were interested in him. Ordinarily modest and shy, Sam showed no such inclination now.

"Sometimes I help take inventory and things like that," Sam revealed. "I'm not really supposed to, but Victor says it's OK. He lets me help him, but just once in a while. Not very often. He's real smart. Do you know, he knows all kinds of names of all those medicines, and bandages, and everything. It's real interesting."

It seemed like the perfect opportunity for Matt to find out a little more about the man who was interested in Connie.

"You seem to know Victor pretty good, Sam," he said. "Do you two ever spend any time together outside of work?"

"Not much. He asked me to go hunting with him last year, but I don't like to hunt, so I didn't go. But he showed me his guns once. They're real pretty. Big, too. Boy, he's got one that I bet is big enough to kill an elephant!"

"You know anything about his wife?"

"His wife? No. Oh, well, if you mean the one he used to have. Yeah. She was real pretty. But she died, you know."

"Yes, I know," Matt replied. "But does he see anyone now. I mean, does he ever talk about going out on dates. You know, stuff like that?"

"Naw, he doesn't talk to me about private things. We really don't spend that much time together. Anyway, he doesn't need to talk to anyone about stuff like that. If he needs to talk to someone, he goes to see Dr. Westgate."

"Dr. Westgate? Who's that?"

"Oh, that's Victor's psychiatrist. Over in The Dalles. He sees Dr. Westgate twice a month. Anyway, he used to. I don't know if he still does."

"What else can you tell us, Sam?"

"What'd you mean?"

"I mean," Matt explained, "what other kinds of things does Victor like to do? Does he like to fish, or play golf, or watch movies? Stuff like that."

"Oh, yeah. Well, let's see. I don't know. I've never heard him talk about fishing or golf. But he has had me over to watch movies a couple of times. I didn't like them much."

"No? Why not, Sam? What kind of movies were they?"

Sam hung his head and shrugged his shoulders, reluctant to answer. His cheeks turned red. But he didn't want to lose his new-found friends, so he answered their questions.

"Well, they were girlie movies. You know, the ones for adults only. Victor really liked them. But I didn't. I didn't think they were very nice, and I told Victor that, but he just laughed at me and told me to grow up and stop being a baby. But I'm not a baby, Matthew. I just don't like those kinds of movies. Do you think that makes me a baby?"

"No, Sam. That doesn't make you a baby. You're a good man. Don't ever let anyone tell you any different. O.K.?"

The smile returned to Sam's face and he sat up taller in his chair. "Yeah, O.K. Matthew. Thanks." Sam felt really good about himself and vowed that he would do anything he could to help out his new friends. "Oh, yeah, and one other thing," he said.

"What's that, Sam?" Willy asked.

"Well, I think Victor likes houses."

Willy looked inquiringly at Matt, who only shrugged his shoulders and shook his head in wonder.

"Houses? What do you mean?" Willy thought he'd lost Sam's train of thought.

"Houses. Homes. You know, houses where people live!" Sam shook his head and laughed, "Houses!"

Willy frowned at him and cocked his head to one side. "What makes you think he likes houses, Sam?"

"He told me so. A couple of weeks ago. We were at my place and he asked me who lived next door. I told him the house was empty, but that I had a key. The owners gave it to me. Well, to my brother, really. You know, for emergencies. Victor said he'd like to take a look at it, so we walked over there. He really seemed to like the place. Said he was thinking of moving away from the river. Too many windsurfers.

"He hates them, you know. Windsurfers. Always has, ever since his wife was killed. Hates them with a passion. `Damned boardheads,' that's what he calls them." He nodded his head importantly, looking back and forth between Matt and Willy.

Matt gripped Sam's shoulder in a friendly gesture and smiled. "Thanks, Sam. You've been a big help. But the girls are coming back now, and I don't think we should talk any more about this, O.K.?"

"Yeah, sure Matthew. Hey, I'm gonna go get something to eat. I'll see you later."

As they watched Sam walk away, Willy could almost see the wheels turning in Matt's head.

"I know what you're thinking, but it's no good. Even if all of what Sam told us is true, it's not enough to really mean anything. A lot of men like sex films. A lot of them hunt and, therefore, own at least one rifle. A lot people don't like windsurfers. And as far as having an interest in houses, well...I don't know what that meant. Nothing as far as I can figure."

Matt slowly turned his head around to look at Willy. His eyes were clouded, the lids half-closed. "I don't like it, Willy. And I think you're wrong. I think it does mean something. A lot. Victor could be our guy. He has access to some pretty potent drugs, right? He sounds real wacky. And he's messing with Connie. I don't like that one damned bit!"

Willy could tell there was no use arguing with Matt. "Well, then. What do you propose we do about it?"

"For starters, we need to get a subpoena to look at Prescott's psychiatric records and see just how unbalanced this guy really is."

"That's not going to work. We have nothing to go on, and the judge isn't going to give us a subpoena without cause, but if it'll make you feel better, we'll talk to him first thing Monday morning."

"We need it sooner than that, Willy. This is a murder case, for God's sake!"

"Look. This is a long shot at best. And Victor lives and works here. He's not going anywhere. We can wait another day."

Matt didn't like that answer, but before he could say anymore, Connie and Rose returned and began coaxing their Partners into another dance. Not wanting to spoil their fun, Matt and Willy allowed themselves to be pulled back onto the dance floor and spoke no more of Victor Prescott.

## Chapter 20

Sunday morning at approximately 8:30, Sam Morgan woke up sneezing and coughing. His head throbbed. His throat felt sore and raw. His eyes hurt from the bright light coming through his bedroom window. Shivering, he walked to the bathroom and looked in the mirror. Bright rosy spots appeared on his cheeks, contrasting strongly against his unusually pale face.

He rummaged through a box of first-aid supplies until he found a thermometer, then stuck it in his mouth and stumbled back to bed. He pulled the blankets up to his neck. It felt like it was still winter to him. Two minutes later he pulled the thermometer from his mouth and read it. 101 degrees. He sneezed hard and fumbled in his drawer for a clean hanky, and blew his nose. Then he wrapped himself in a warm robe and went in search of the cold medicine.

After looking through every drawer and cupboard that might possibly conceal some pills, he finally gave up and sank into a chair at the kitchen table and lay his aching head down on the cool table top, trying to think what to do. His brother Tom had already left and Sam didn't know where he was, but he thought he was probably down at Briars Beach with some of his windsurfing buddies. He tried to think of someone else he could call, but his thoughts were all jumbled and fuzzy, and it only made his head hurt more.

After a few minutes he thought of Victor Prescott. Victor had always been nice to him. Maybe he would help. So he called Victor at home and explained how sick he felt. He asked Victor if he could go to the drugstore and get some cold pills for him. Victor sounded grumpy and irritable, but agreed to bring Sam some medicine. He said he would have to wait until his lunch break since he was just on his way to work and was already late. He told Sam to make himself a cup of hot tea and go back to bed until he got there. Sam thanked him and hung up the phone, rubbing his sore throat. Then he fixed himself a cup of hot lemon tea and took it back to the bedroom, inhaling the steam from the tea as he walked.

What he needed, he told himself, was a vaporizer to clear up his sinuses. Then maybe his head would stop pounding. He had one somewhere. At one time, before his mother had passed away, she had brought him a vaporizer, saying it was an essential piece of equipment that no home should be without. That had been several years ago, and he'd used it only a couple of times since then. If he could just remember where he'd stashed it. Coughing and sneezing, he went in search of the essential piece of equipment.

In the bathroom cupboard he found the old vaporizer, added some water to it, and carried it into the bedroom. He plugged it in and watched to see if it worked. The motor purred and soon began sending out moist vapor into the room. With a sigh of relief, Sam shuffled over to the bed and crawled under the covers. With shaky hands, he sipped his tea and watched the vapor stream rise to the ceiling. The tea flowed warm and soothing down his raw throat. He drank it all and within minutes was sound asleep.

He was still sleeping at 1:15 p.m. when Victor knocked on his front door. At first Sam didn't hear the increasingly severe pounding, but after a while it began to penetrate his feverish sleep and he stumbled through the house in his pajamas.

Victor stood at the door looking angry and formidable, but when he saw Sam's condition he mellowed considerably. He stepped inside and closed the door, then took Sam by the arm and helped him back to bed. "My God, man. You look terrible! What have you done to yourself?"

"Oh, I don't feel so good, Victor. I guess I caught a cold somewhere. Did you get me some medicine?" By now his eyes had a bleary, sunken look. He was shaking from the effort of answering the door and crawled into bed without protesting.

"Where's your thermometer? I want to take your temperature while I get you a glass of water to wash down these pills, OK?"

"It's right here by the bed, but I already took my temperature this morning. It was a hundred and one."

"Let's take it again. You look pretty bad. Here, stick it under your tongue, and keep your mouth closed for a couple of minutes. I'll be right back." Having given this directive, Victor went to the kitchen and found a clean glass, filled it with water and returned to the bedroom, where he opened the bottle of cold pills and aspirin and took out the right dose for Sam. "Here," he said, taking the thermometer out of Sam's mouth, "take these, and drink as much of this water as you can. You need the fluids."

He read the thermometer while Sam did as he was instructed. It read 102.9 degrees. "Well, it looks like you're going to be in bed for a few days, Sam. Have you had anything to eat or drink today?"

Sam rolled his head slowly back and forth.

"No? O.K. Stay in bed. I'll make you a bowl of soup. You'd better stay home and get some rest. You should be O.K. until your brother gets home."

Sam felt too weak to argue, so he accepted Victor's help as gracefully as he could. After he was through eating and settled into bed for the afternoon, he thanked Victor and asked him to tell his boss at the hospital that he wouldn't be in to work for a few days. Victor promised to do that for his friend and prepared to depart.

Just as he was leaving, he asked Sam if he could take a look at the empty house for sale next door, to which Sam had the key. That reminded Sam of the things he had told Willy and Matt the night before about Victor, and he felt a little bit ashamed of himself. But he hadn't really betrayed Victor's friendship, he told himself; only answered a few questions the police had asked. Still, he wished he hadn't said anything. Victor was his friend.

"Yeah, sure, Vic. The keys are in the dresser next to the front door. Top drawer. Right-hand side. You can get them back to me later."

"Thanks. I will. Bye."

After he heard the front door close, Sam reached for the remote control for the small TV he had in his bedroom, and tuned in to one of his old favorite reruns. After a short while, the effects of the medicine and hot soup took over and he fell asleep. Even the blare of the TV could not wake him.

The empty house was small, only about 1200 square feet, but it held a coziness and charm that immediately appealed to Victor. Large picture windows looked out across the Columbia River at Mt. Hood and the Hood River Valley. The morning clouds had receded, leaving the clear blue sky sparkling in the summer sunshine, dotted with white puffy clouds dancing along the horizon. Looking down, he had a clear view of the river. A tugboat bulldozed its way through the water on its way upriver.

Victor walked quickly through the rooms and liked what he saw. In his mind he pictured the house furnished with Early American furniture, cherished antiques and valuable paintings hand-picked by himself. He also imagined classical music playing and the sound of a woman's laughter drifting across the room. A face seemed to appear before him, smiling, inviting him to kiss her. It was the face of Connie White. He ached for her, and knew that one day soon he would have her.

The spell was broken at the sound of a dog barking nearby. The music and laughter vanished along with the furniture and artwork. He force himself back to reality by taking a deep breath and expelling it slowly, then gave himself a good all-over shake.

As he turned to leave, a sudden depression overcame him. His life was so lonely and unhappy. He really had nothing to live for, no one to live for, and he wondered if life was worth living any more. Nothing seemed to matter lately, and he sometimes found himself feeling like he just wanted to stop the world and get off. It would be easy to do, for a man like himself.

He glanced out the window and down at the river. As usual, the river was dotted with tiny-looking windsurfing sails. It looked like a sea of brightly-colored sharks swimming back and forth, back and forth, back and forth. Never ending. In endless supply. There was no getting away from them. They would never go away.

In reality, there were only a few windsurfers out. The wind had died down earlier and most of the windsurfers had headed downriver to Stevenson, in search of more wind. But in Victor's mind, the few windsurfers looked like a hundred. His overactive imagination was playing games with his head.

Victor thought of his dead wife and what those windsurfers had done to her. His heart began to pound at the memory of her torn and bleeding body. He could still hear her screams of terror, and see the empty way her eyes looked when he'd found her laying on the bedroom floor. They had no right to do that to her. She didn't deserve the beating or the rape. They had no right.

## Chapter 21

Having decided his men needed an occasional break, Chief Baxter had relented on his earlier decision to revoke all days off. Accordingly, on Sunday, Matt enjoyed the first day off he'd had in two weeks. He slept in until 8:30 and lazed around the living room for an hour drinking coffee and watching Adriana clean house. He knew he should be helping, doing his share, but he was too tired to care. He apologized to his sister, who only laughed at him and told him to relax and enjoy himself for a little while.

It felt pretty good to have nothing to do for a change. Connie would be busy all morning at the hospital, so Matt had no plans until later in the day, when he and Connie planned to go for a swim in one of the nearby lakes and share a picnic supper.

After a while he ate a bowl of cereal, then spent a couple of hours helping Adriana with some much neglected yard work. They enjoyed an easy comraderie and the morning went quickly. When they were done, the yard once again looked well groomed and cared for. Adriana made sandwiches, and they relaxed in a pair of lawn chaises in the shade of a large oak tree, surveying their work and sipping iced-tea. The day, which had started out cool and cloudy, had cleared off and was promising to be warm.

Matt got up and went into the house. In a few minutes he came back out with two plates, each holding a large slice of cold watermelon.

After a few minutes, Adriana ventured to ask her brother, "So, did you enjoy the dance last night?"

"Very much, thank you. And you?"

"Oh, I had a great time," she replied.

Their mock formality was a way they had of teasing each other and had been going on since childhood. Now Matt smiled at the old, familiar game. It took him back a long way and made him feel young and carefree. He lay back on his chaise lounge and closed his eyes, enjoying the cool, gentle breeze that blew off the river. They discussed the success of the dinner-dance, and how the money it made would benefit the hospital. For awhile their talk was relaxed and impersonal, the topics general and objective. But then Adriana's tone suddenly became quite personal.

"I couldn't help noticing that you and Connie disappeared toward the end, and you didn't come home until very, very late. Where'd you two go off to?"

Matt took a deep breath and let it out slowly. This was a side of his sister he could easily do without. He wasn't ready to analyze his personal life, let alone explain it to anyone else. For several seconds he didn't answer, then he opened his eyes and frowned at her.

"Aren't you the observant one? And nosy, too. Well, you can just go on wondering, because it's none of your business where Connie and I went!" He had no intention of revealing to his sister his actions of the night before.

However, he couldn't help smiling as his mind went back over the moonlight stroll along the river's edge at Briars Beach, Connie's hand held tightly in his. Or of the passionate hours that followed, their bodies entwined, twisting and rolling in the warm sand of the beach. That, followed by a dip in the river to wash away the sand before they could get dressed again. The scent of her body, the feel of her soft flesh, the taste of her kisses. They were all still fresh in his mind. It was an exciting, erotic night he'd never be able to forget. Which was exactly why he was having trouble sorting out his feelings this morning.

*Is it love?* he'd asked himself over and over again. *Or is it just lust?* He wished he knew the answer. The smile faded from his face as he pondered the question.

Adriana watched the play of emotions cross his face and had a strong sense of what he was going through. He was falling in love with Connie, but he was fighting it all the way.

"Well, at least tell me this. How do you feel about her? You've been seeing quite a lot of her these past few weeks, in spite of the tight schedule you're on. Are you two getting serious, or are you just friends?"

A tortured look crossed Matt's face as he looked at his sister. He wished he could answer that question. "I don't know," he mumbled. "That might sound crazy, but I really don't. I wish I did."

The ringing of the telephone interrupted their conversation.

"Saved by the bell," Adriana muttered as she jumped up and ran into the house to answer it. A few seconds later, she came hurrying back out. "It's Willy. He said it's urgent."

"Damn! What could be so urgent on my one day off?" Although Matt scowled and grumbled as he got up from his chaise, he was secretly grateful for the interruption of the much-too-personal questions that Adriana was throwing at him. Once in the house, he picked up the phone from the kitchen counter where Adriana had set it.

"What's up, Willy?"

"Sorry to bother you today, Matt, but we've got more trouble. I'm down at Briars Beach. There's been a double shooting down here. Chief Baxter thinks it might be related to the other murder cases we're working on, so he said it's our baby. Can you meet me down there right away?"

"I can be there in 30 minutes. I've been working out in the yard and I really need a quick shower, O.K.?"

"Sorry, Matt. No time for that. We'll have to take you the way you are. Things are a real mess down here."

"O.K., O.K. I'm on my way, then." Matt hung up the phone and rushed into his bedroom, stripping off his clothes as he went. He splashed warm water over his face, ran a wet washcloth over his arms and torso, brushed his teeth, combed his hair and put on fresh deodorant. It was a weak cover-up, but it would have to do. When he came out of his room five minutes later he was dressed and ready to go.

Adriana was in the kitchen, cleaning up from lunch. He explained briefly and asked her to call Connie and tell her he wouldn't be able to make their date to go swimming that afternoon, but that he would call her as soon as he could. Then he was out the door and gone.

Using his lights and siren, he raced through town and down the hill, made a quick stop at the bottom of the hill, and turned west on Highway 14. In five minutes he was pulling into the parking lot at Briars Beach, which was already crammed with police and sheriff cars, an ambulance, a rescue truck and various windsurfers' vehicles.

The temperature was climbing into the mid-80's. Not terribly hot, but the humidity was high and the combination created an oppressive, stifling effect that invaded everything. The strong breeze that had cooled them off all morning had died down. Now the air was still and heavy. By the time Matt had parked his car, he was once again covered with sweat.

People were milling around, talking and gesturing. From a quick glance around, it looked like there were about 25 bystanders and another 10 or 12 law-enforcement people there. Several officers were keeping the gathering crowd of curiosity-seekers back from the scene. The county sheriff assigned three deputies to question the eyewitnesses and the other people who were there at the time of the shootings. They were mostly windsurfers and reporters from both the Pine Crest Chronicle and the Hood River, Oregon newspapers.

Matt elbowed his way through the crowd until he came to the spot where Chief Baxter was conferring with a group of sheriff's deputies, city police, and state troopers. Willy spotted him and waved him over. In the center of the group, the two bodies still remained on the sand. One lay face-down, having been shot in the back and knocked flat. The other was crumpled in a heap, but face-up. His vacant, unseeing eyes gazed up at the sky. A clean, neat bullet hole stared unblinking out from the torso of each body. The ambulance crew was just picking up their equipment, unneeded and unused. The coroner stood by, waiting for the Chief to give him the OK to remove the bodies.

Willy brought Matt up to date on the events as he knew them. There were only about 15 windsurfers on the beach at the time of the shooting. A friend of the victims had called the police and reported the shooting. No one else had been shot, and it was uncertain how many shots had been fired. Neither of the victims had been carrying a gun. As far as they knew, no one on the beach carried any kind of weapon, but they were all being questioned. It appeared that the shots had come from somewhere else. Sniper fire.

"Luckily, there weren't too many people on the beach at the time. It could have been a real massacre."

Matt agreed with him. He thought of how crowded this beach would have been if a strong wind had been up and blowing as usual. They could have had bodies scattered from one end of the beach to the other. But today the strong wind hadn't materialized and what little breeze there was in the morning hours had died down after lunch. *Thank God for that*, he thought. He checked his watch. It was 2:25 p.m.

The afternoon was spent in fruitless search of nonexistent clues, and endless questions that were left unanswered. The press people started getting in the way and aggravating the authorities with innumerable inquiries. At least three television stations from Portland,

Oregon, had suddenly appeared. They converged at once on Chief Jess Baxter.

"Chief, can you tell us who the shooter was?"

"We don't know," the Chief answered.

"Do you have the gun?"

"No, we don't."

"Where were the shots fired from?"

"We're not sure."

"Have you found any clues?"

"Not yet."

"Are these shootings related to the other three killings?"

"We don't know."

"Do you have any suspects in those killings?"

"No, we don't."

"Are you any closer to solving those murders?"

"We're working on it."

"Why haven't you found the killer yet? Do you think it's a local man, or a stranger? Chief, we need some answers! The people have the right to know what you're doing about this wave of killings!"

The Chief was well known as a careful and patient man, but the long hours and frustrating events of the past few weeks had worn his composure down, and it was all he could do to keep from losing his temper.

Slowly reaching up, he carefully removed his sunglasses, folded them and slowly, but deliberately, put them into his shirt pocket. He looked at the reporter with cold, narrowed eyes. His grim expression emphasized his dark, rugged looks. Few men remained aggressive under that glare. No different from the rest, the reporter stepped back two paces. Baxter addressed the group of reporters in his strong, tightly controlled voice.

"This department is working around the clock every day on these murder cases. We are doing everything that can conceivably be done to solve them as quickly as possible. Every agency in the county and state is helping. Every viable connection is being checked out. My men are all working overtime. If there is anything to tie these cases together, we will find it. If there are clues, we will find them.

"We *will* solve these murders, but everything takes time. Somewhere along the line, we will find something that will lead us to our killer, or killers--whichever the case may be. I assure you ladies and gentlemen that this department is working at 100 percent capacity; and every man and woman is putting out 110 percent effort.

"That's all I can tell you. When we find out more, we'll let you know. Now, if you'll excuse us, we've got a lot of work to do. Thank you." Baxter turned on his heel and walked back toward the crime scene. Jerking his thumb at the group of press people, he gave this command to the first deputy he came to, "Get them out of here right now, and get this area cleared!"

Five minutes later the beach was clear. Yellow police tape marked the off-limits area. It would remain in place for the rest of the day and possibly the next. Matt and Willy helped take statements from people, but found nothing helpful. They went back to the police station to work on the case.

So far they had only one link between any of the killings --the fact that all the victims were windsurfers. To find other links, or to exclude that possibility, meant going through the same process, taking the same steps, they had with the other cases.

The first order of business was to re-check their short list of former suspects in the first three killings. Ed Roachea was working on a tug and 45 miles downriver at the time of the shootings. And Nick Truman, the dock worker from The Dalles, was out of town for the weekend, visiting relatives on the southern Oregon coast. The only connection between these two men was that they were friends who occasionally got together to share a few beers and tell long-winded lies to each other. Nothing in the files connected them to the two latest murders.

Who had killed Michael Sans, in the hit-and-run on Highway 14, remained a mystery. Although every law-enforcement agency in the states of Oregon and Washington was on the look-out for any small red sports cars, the search for the car had failed to turn up anything. One hundred and thirty-two such vehicles showed up on the computers as registered in the two states. Of those, all but fourteen of the owners had solid alibis, or were otherwise determined to be clean. The remaining fourteen were being checked out, but it was taking time. There was nothing to make Matt believe Sans' death had any connection to any of the other deaths.

## Chapter 22

Later the same evening, Marie Sanchez reclined in front of her TV set watching a re-run of one of her favorite shows. Having recently arrived home after a long and exhausting day at the hospital, she looked forward to a relaxing evening watching television. She'd stopped at the grocery store to pick up the week's supply of groceries, which had to be put away when she got home. Then she had to feed her dog, Max, a young stray female of medium build and mixed blood that had wondered in off the street the previous year, and had embedded herself firmly in Marie's life.

As soon as she'd finished those chores, she made herself a light meal of soup and a sandwich, which she carried into the front room and set on the small end table beside her easy chair. Kicking off her white hospital shoes, she lifted her tired, burning feet up onto the footstool and leaned back to rest. A scotch and soda fizzled in a frosted glass on the table beside her dinner. An overhead fan blew refreshing cool air down onto her, relieving the stuffiness of the small room.

Work had been unusually grueling. The patients, many of whom had been kept awake by the fireworks the night before, were tired, cranky and hard to please. She'd bumped into Victor Prescott when he came into work, late and in a terrible mood. Marie suspected he was suffering from a hangover. As the day wore on, he became even more cantankerous than some of her patients. Although, she reminded herself, when he'd gotten back from lunch he seemed to be in a little better mood.

She'd taken a late lunch herself, during which she'd done a few errands in town, then rushed home to grab a sandwich and put in a load of laundry. By two o'clock she was back in her car, headed back to work.

As she'd pulled away from her house, she noticed Victor's car parked down the road in front of the Morgan home and wondered what he was doing there. *He must be visiting Sam,* she decided. Just then, out of the corner of her eye, she saw Victor walking quickly up the overgrown driveway of the neighboring house. He was carrying something in a long, narrow case, but she couldn't tell for sure what it was and she didn't really care. She waved at him, but was in a hurry and had no time to stop and ask questions. She didn't even notice when Victor stopped and stared at her as she drove away. She turned up her stereo and listened to music on the local radio station while she drove back to the hospital.

The afternoon proved to be almost as bad as the morning, but she'd finally gotten through it and was gratified to be finished at last with this long day. By the time she left work, her back ached, her feet were killing her and she had a pounding headache.

It was wonderful to at last be able to relax and put up her poor feet. She sipped her scotch and soda and leaned back in her chair, closing her eyes. The aspirin she'd taken as soon as she'd arrived home was starting to take the edge off her headache, although she suspected that her state of relaxation had as much to do with the easing of her headache as anything else.

When she finished eating, she mixed another drink and returned to her easy chair in the living room. A short while later she thought she heard a car stop up on the roadway. *Now who could that be?* she thought. She hoped it wasn't someone coming to her house. The last thing she wanted tonight was unexpected company.

She heard a car door slam and a moment later her doorbell rang. *Maybe if I just ignore them, they'll go away,* she told herself. But the bell rang again, followed by a loud knocking. Marie sighed deeply and, groaning loudly, pulled herself out of her chair. The long workday combined with the scotch she'd had made her legs feel heavy and stiff.

When she reached her front door and looked out through the curtains, she recognized her visitor, even though his face was turned away from her. *Oh, Lord. Now what the hell does that fool want this time of night?* she asked herself. Reluctantly, she opened the door.

At the sound of the door opening, the man turned around. Marie's quick intake of breath was the only indication of her surprise. Stumbling forward, he pushed her back into the house ahead of him, stopping only long enough to secure the door once he was inside.

When he looked at her, his eyes were wide and slightly unfocused, looking beyond her. No, not beyond her, rather *through* her. *Yes, that's it,* she thought, *It's as if he's looking through me. Not seeing me at all. The fool is drunk out of his mind, and probably doesn't even know where he is!"* Her initial concern turned to anger as she faced her unwelcome visitor. She didn't appreciate being pushed around in her own home.

"Hey! What the hell do you think you're doing?" she demanded.

"Well, that's no way to welcome an old friend. I just stopped by t'say hello. Where's yer manners? Why don' you offer me a drink? I could use a drink." The man seized her by the arm and pushed her into the kitchen. "C'mon, let's have a lil' drink."

"No. You've apparently had enough to drink. I want you to get out of here. Go on. Go home."

The man looked down at her with determination in his eyes. Sweat rolled down his face. A large patch of dirty sun-bleached hair flopped across his forehead. It, too, was wet with sweat. The pale yellow shirt he wore had no doubt once been clean, but now was streaked with dirt. She had never seen him look or act like this, and it frightened her. She pushed away from him but he advance until he had her pinned against the kitchen table.

"Get me a drink!" he demanded.

Marie jumped at the force of his command. The sudden realization that he wasn't as drunk as she'd first thought came to her as she studied his dangerous posturing. Her senses began to reel. With shaky legs she edged past him and moved to the cupboard where she kept the alcohol, and poured two fingers of scotch into a glass. Her hands trembled as she set it before him on the table.

He picked up the drink, lifting the glass in a silent toast. She watched him drain the glass.

"O.K., you've had your drink. Now would you please leave?"

He looked at her and shook his head. "No, I don't wanna go home. I got some business to take care of." He sank into one of the kitchen chairs and slumped across the table, pointing his finger at her. "But right now, I'm kinda hungry. You got anything t'eat around here?"

Marie decided not to argue with him. *Maybe if I fix him a snack,* she thought, *he'll go away.* So she turned to the refrigerator and started pulling out some lunch meat, cheese and mayonnaise.

"How about a sandwich?" she asked.

"Is that all you got? I don't like sandwiches." He got up from the table and came over to where she was standing next to the open fridge. She firmly closed the door and turned to face him.

"Yes, that's all I have. I'm sorry. But, if you're hungry, you'll just have to settle for a sandwich. Now what kind do you want? I have bologna, cheese, or salami."

"Aw' right. I'll have salami and cheese. I'll help. What can I do?"

"Nothing. Really. Why don't you just go back and sit down."

"I don't want to sit down!" he said loudly.

Marie looked at him in exasperation. His expression had turned ugly. She wanted to tell him to get the hell out of her way and let her make the damned sandwich, but the look in his eyes silenced any protests before she could voice them.

Max started barking just outside the kitchen door. Marie wished she'd let the dog inside. She'd feel a little less vulnerable with Max, who'd become aggressively protective as she matured, in the house with her.

"Alright, fine. Just calm down, would you?" she said. "You know, I've changed my mind. You can help. Get me a butter knife out of that drawer."

The man walked over to a row of drawers and began looking through them. The second one he opened held the dinnerware, serving spoons and cutlery. He took out a butter knife, then spotted a large sharp carving knife in the drawer. He glanced quickly at Marie.

She had her back turned to him as she got tomatoes and pickles out of the fridge. He laid the butter knife next to the salami and cheese on the counter. The carving knife glittered in his hand.

She began making a couple of sandwiches as quickly as she could, not caring that she was making a big mess out of it. *If I can just get him talking,* she thought, *maybe he'll calm down and leave.* And so she tried desperately to strike up a conversation with him, speaking of work, of the weather, of mutual friends; but nothing seemed to work. He remained silent and brooding.

Indeed, he was thinking evil and dangerous thoughts.

*Keep talking, bitch. You always did talk too much. Always yakking. Carrying on about nothing. Just can't keep your mouth shut, can you? Drives me crazy. One of these days you'll talk to the wrong people...tell what you saw today. I know you will. Someday. Can't have that. No. Gonna have to fix that. Can't have any witnesses. That wouldn't do.*

She still had her back turned to him. The sandwiches were

finished. She slapped them onto a plate and reached for a napkin. Then she started to turn around.

He raised the carving knife high above his head.

Adriana drove up the road that led to Marie's house. On the car seat beside her, she'd placed the casserole dish Marie had left at the dinner-dance. *I don't know why I let myself get talked into being on the clean-up committee,* she thought. *Lord knows I've contributed more than my share of time and effort to the success of the event.* But, she'd committed to doing the work, so do it she must. *It would certainly help if people would remember to take home their dishes afterward.*

Matt had tried to talk her out of driving out to the bluff alone. He'd offered to go with her, even bluntly reminded her that at least one murderer could very well still be hanging around who knows where. He didn't like using scare tactics, and should have known they wouldn't work on his stubborn sister, but he had an uneasy feeling about her going out by herself.

Despite his obvious concern, Adriana had insisted on going alone. She valued her independence. Besides, he worried too much about her. She forgave him this "fault" because it made her feel good that he cared so much about her, although she wouldn't let him know that. Instead, she pointed out that she had been to visit Marie at least a dozen times and nothing had ever happened to her, and furthermore, she had no enemies, so why would anyone want to hurt her?

Matt had a hard time understanding that kind of logic, let alone arguing with it, so he watched helplessly as, ignoring his anxiety, she picked up her purse and the casserole dish and walked out the door.

Later, she wished she had allowed him to accompany her on her errand, and for years she wondered why her gift of insight hadn't warned her she was walking into danger.

She drove with her windows down, enjoying the cool evening air. The sun hovered near the horizon, resisted the call to surrender to nightfall for as long as it could, then sank gracefully down behind the mountains. Long shadows flooded the hillsides, bringing with them the soft, gentle breeze of early night.

Just before she pulled into Marie's driveway, Adriana noticed a small, red sports car parked along the road. *Who's car is that?* she wondered. It looked vaguely familiar, but she couldn't remember where she'd seen it before. She slowly drove past the car, looking inside. It was empty. *It's probably just someone out for an evening walk along the bluff,* she reasoned. *Or, it might be someone up to no-good.* Matt's words of warning echoed in her mind. Taking a small notebook out of her purse, she quickly jotted down the small car's license plate number. *Oh, God, I'm getting to be as paranoid as my brother.*

    Pulling her car down into the driveway alongside Marie's, she glanced around. Everything seemed normal. She set the parking brake, turned off the ignition, and dropped the keys into her purse. Picking up the casserole dish, she slid gracefully out of the car and walked toward the front door.

Inside the house, Marie turned and faced her visitor-turned-attacker. Her eyes widened in alarm. She opened her mouth to scream, but no sound emerged from her shocked vocal cords. Instinctively, she threw the plate of sandwiches up into his face, jumped backwards, and collided with a wall. Pressing herself up against the wall in an effort to get away from him, she could only watch in horror as he sprang toward her, chopping and swinging the stainless steel knife like a hatchet.

    Luckily for Marie, the drinks he'd had made him slow and uncoordinated, so that his blows fell short of his goal. She slid along the wall, trying to escape, but he moved to cut off her flight. He forced her back along the wall to the opposite corner. Now there was no escape!

    He advanced slowly until he towered over her. His eyes had that same vacant look as when she'd first opened the door to him. Her heart pounded wildly, as if trying to leap from her chest. Her breath came in huge, sucking gulps. She saw the man smile mercilessly and raise the knife high. Then, as if in slow motion, it descended.

    Marie threw up her arms to deflect the blows. The first one glanced off her shoulder, leaving a three-inch cut. Blood gushed down her arm. The sight of it made her sick. This wasn't just a bad dream. It was really happening to her!

    Opening her mouth, she finally found her voice. Primal screams tore from her throat. Scream after scream after scream. But there was no one to hear. Time and again, the man struck at her with the knife. She managed to block some of the blows, but not all. The front of her shirt was soon soaked with blood. All her strength drained from her body with the blood, and she began to realize the dreaded truth. She was going to die. Her attacker became a blur of motion and sound. Unconsciousness draped itself around her, threatening to smother her in a blanket of eternal darkness.

Adriana heard Marie's dog, Max, barking in the back yard. It was an anxious, almost frightened sort of barking that sent shivers down Adriana's back. She hesitated for a moment. *Oh, stop it,* she thought. *Now you're starting to scare yourself.*

    She walked the remaining few steps to Marie's front door, then reached down and pushed the doorbell, sending a wave of echoing chimes throughout the house. The small window in the door afforded a limited view of the inside of the house. She looked through it, hoping to get a glimpse of Marie. The front room was empty, but Adriana could see a light on and hear faint sounds of the TV. Looking toward the back, she saw the hallway that she knew led to the kitchen, bathroom and single bedroom. A light came from the kitchen doorway, which she could just make out. She reached down and pushed the doorbell again.

Through the pain and fear Marie heard a sound--Max barking frantically at the back door, scratching and digging to get in. But there was something else. Another sound trying to penetrate her foggy mind. And then she knew what it was. The doorbell. Someone was out there!

    Gathering her little remaining strength, she fought her way back from the state of semi-consciousness. One last chance presented itself. She screamed as loud as she could. Then she felt a hard blow to the side of her face. Stars exploded in her head, and everything turned black. She sank to the floor, unconscious and bleeding profusely.

    Her attacker also heard the doorbell. He knew he had to end this quickly. After he slugged Marie in the jaw, he thrust the knife once more into her, aiming for her heart. But his lack of coordination caused the blow to land too high, burying the knife in her shoulder. He raised his arm to stab her again. Then he heard someone yelling and beating on the front door. He jumped up and looked around. The back door offered the only escape. Stumbling over to it, he jerked it open, and stumbled down the back steps.

    Max was waiting. She didn't understand what was happening,

but she'd heard her mistress's screams and smelled the blood and the fear, and she instinctively knew that this stranger was evil. The strong impulse to protect her mistress overcame her own nervousness and fear. She lunged at the man, barking and snarling. As he ran past her, she jumped after him, catching him by the pant leg. He ran a few steps, dragging the dog, and trying to kick free. Max released her hold just long enough to get a better grip on the man's leg. Made contact with his hamstring. Clamped her young, strong jowls down hard.

    That brought the man down fast. His tall length slammed onto the hard ground, his arms flung forward. The knife flew from his hand and landed in the tall grass. Max remained firmly attached, snarling and glaring at the man, hatred in her eyes. A large, tight fist swung down and pounded the top of Max's head. She yelped, temporarily releasing her hold. The man's hand fell on a long stick. Gripping it tightly, he beat at the dog until she backed off.

    The man staggered to his feet and ran, limping, to the back fence, the dog close on his heels. The five-foot-high wooden fence barely slowed him down, but as he started up and over it, Max once more grabbed him by the ankle, biting down hard enough to make deep puncture wounds. The man yelled in pain. Kicking violently, he freed his leg, and scrambled over the fence.

Faint muffled sounds came to Adriana through the door. *Well, she must be home,* Adriana thought as she rang the doorbell again. *I hope she doesn't have company. I'd hate to interrupt an intimate date!* She heard more sounds from within and then what sounded like a scream. Pounding on the door, she yelled, "Hello! Marie? It's Adriana. Are you O.K.?" Grabbing the doorknob, she twisted and rattled it, to no avail. It was securely locked. She knocked loudly, again calling Marie's name. There was no answer. Listening closely, she heard the sound of a door slamming. The sound came from the back of the house. Someone had gone out the back door.

    On past visits, she had become acquainted with the outside, as well as the inside, of the house. A narrow path led around to the back, fenced yard. Nervously stepping off the front porch, she followed the path. Max's barking had suddenly become more aggressive, frantic and angry.

The high fence effectively blocked her view of the back yard. Adriana jumped up and down, trying to see over the high barrier. She got only a glimpse of the dog confronting someone, but she couldn't tell who. It wasn't Marie, she was sure of that.

Looking around, Adriana searched for something to stand on. A foot-tall tree stump afforded her a better view. Her heart throbbed madly within her chest, but she had to see what was going on. Without further thought, she stepped up on the stump. The descending darkness had created ghosts and shadows, but she could see well enough to witness Max chasing a tall, ragged figure of a man across the small back yard.

She watched in shocked terror Max's efforts to bring the man down, and the intruder's escape up and over the back fence.

Only a few seconds had passed, a minute at the most, but it seemed much longer. As if in slow motion, Adriana turned and looked back toward the front of the house, then back to where the man had escaped over the back fence. There was no sign of him, but Max was running back and forth along the fence, still barking. The realization came to Adriana that whoever the intruder was, he might have seen her and could easily circle around the fence and come after her. In a panic, she jumped down off the stump and raced back around the house to the front door.

She rang the doorbell again, then pounded on the door with her fist. There was no response from within. Looking around desperately for something to break the window, her eyes latched onto a large stone on the ground, a short distance from the door. She snatched it up and, shielding her face with one arm, swung the rock forcefully at the window. It cracked, but held firm. She tried again, but the glass was tempered and strong. Tears of frustration and fear blurred her vision. Time was running out.

Marie's attacker plowed a wide semi-circle through the heavy brush surrounding her yard, and made his way back to his car, unseen in the darkness.

Looking back toward the house, he saw a woman trying to break the window in the front door with a rock. She was going to find Marie and call the police. He was afraid she might have seen him, and he didn't want to leave any witnesses. Leaving his car, he crept quietly down the driveway.

Adriana imagined the intruder sneaking up behind her. Once again she drew back her arm. A short prayer flew through her mind, then she swung the stone with all her strength. The sound, exaggerated in her frightened mind, sounded like a thousand windows shattering, echoing in her ears as the window finally disintegrated under the force of the rock.

Before the attacker got halfway down the driveway, he saw the woman break the window, reach inside and unlock the door, then she was safely inside the house. Cursing his luck, he quickly considered his options. He could follow her into the house and kill her, but what if something went wrong. What if she'd already called the police. They could be here any second. He turned and ran back to his car, opened the door, and slid into the driver's seat, softly closing the door. The woman didn't see him. Starting up his car, he slapped it into gear, and careened down the road.

Chapter 23

Heedless of the broken glass still in the frame, Adriana reached a long, slender arm through the opening, felt around for the latch, and unlocked the door. Once inside, she re-locked the door, then grabbed a nearby chair and wedged it under the doorknob for added security. She knew it wouldn't stop anyone from getting in, but it would slow them down at least.

"Marie! Where are you?"

No reply. No sound within the house.

Outside, Max continued to bark aggressively. The man was still out there. The hair on the back of Adriana's neck tingled as a ball of cold, hard fear formed in her stomach.

She ran across the front room, down the short hall, and through the kitchen to the back door. It was slightly ajar. She pushed the door shut, then reached for the lock. The bolt slammed home with a loud clank. Shaky legs carried her backwards, away from the door, a hand over her heart to still it's clamoring. She came into contact with something behind her. Only then did she turn and look around. She had backed into the kitchen table.

But it was the discovery on the other side of the table that riveted her attention.

A scream caught in her throat, threatening to suffocate her, as she stared in horror at the sight before her. In the corner of the kitchen lay Marie, unconscious or dead, she wasn't sure which, and drenched in blood.

The scream finally escaped, growing louder and louder, until it threatened to shatter the windows, echoing throughout the house, before dying down to a helpless whimper. Realizing she had to do something, she walked as if in a trance over to where Marie lay. Bending down, she lifted her limp wrist with a trembling hand, and felt for a pulse.

This close, she could hear Marie's ragged breathing, and yes, there was a weak pulse! Scrambling to the phone hanging on the wall, she dialed the hospital's number and gave directions to Marie's house and asked the person she spoke with to call the police for her. Then she found some clean towels and began applying pressure to some of Marie's wounds.

Soon, the sirens of the ambulance and several police cars pierced the still night air, and Adriana felt a great relief. When they arrived at the house, she jumped up and unlocked the door. She directed the paramedics to the kitchen, then glanced up the road.

The red car was gone.

## Chapter 24

At the hospital, Adriana paced back and forth. The doctors had been with Marie for an hour, but there was still no word on her condition. Adriana held little hope that she would recover from the vicious attack. She'd been so pale and lifeless. There'd been so much blood.

For the past hour, Adriana had been going over and over the events of the evening with Matt and Willy. She had called Matt from Marie's as soon as the ambulance had departed. He'd promised to meet her at the hospital. Willy was already at the hospital when she arrived. He took over the investigation from the two police officers who'd responded to the initial call-out, gathering information from Adriana as well.

It was getting late. 1:15 a.m. Staring at the door to the emergency room, Adriana wondered what was keeping the doctor. He should have been done by now. One way or the other.

Reliving the events of the evening in her mind, she kept thinking there was something she could have done to prevent this from happening. Something. Somehow. But what? Maybe if she'd arrived at Marie's house a few minutes earlier, she would have scared off the intruder. Or maybe, if she hadn't gone around to see what was happening in the back yard, she would have discovered Marie sooner, and could have called the ambulance that much sooner. That might have made the difference between life and death. Or maybe...*Maybe what?* she asked herself. *Oh, I don't know. Something. Anything!* She resumed her pacing.

Matt watched his sister. He knew what she was going through, but there was nothing he could do to ease her anxiety. He, too, was concerned for Marie. But his relief that Adriana had not been harmed overshadowed his worry about the other girl. He shuddered to think of all that could have happened out there.

He'd been home watching television when the phone rang. Glancing at the clock as he reached for the phone, he saw it was almost

10 o'clock. Adriana had been gone less than an hour and probably wouldn't be back for another half hour or so. Picking up the phone, he wasn't expecting anything unusual. He sat in shocked silence as he listened to his sister's hysterical voice. For a few seconds he thought she was in danger, that the intruder was still close by.

When he realized that she was all right, that in fact the police were already there, he tried in vain to calm her down and promised to meet her at the hospital. As soon as he hung up the phone, it rang again. This time it was Chief Baxter, ordering him and Willy to investigate the attack on Marie.

Matt briefly explained his sister's presence on the scene. He heard the Chief swear quietly, then asked if Adriana was all right. Matt assured him she was only shook up a little.

"Good. I'm glad to hear that, Matt. Hang on a minute."

Matt waited several seconds, wondering what the Chief was doing. He was anxious to get to the hospital.

"Matt, since your sister's involved in this, I don't think it's a good idea for you to participate in the investigation. I'm going to assign someone else."

"Chief, please don't do that! I want in on this."

"You're too close to it, Matt. Too emotionally involved."

"But, Sir, this may be related to the recent murders we've had, and I'm already in it. I know these cases inside-out. If there's a connection, I'll be able to pick it up."

"Sorry, Matt, but my mind's made up. You sit this one out. Willy can handle it. That's an order."

"Yes, Sir," Matt responded, the disappointment evident in his voice. He hung up the phone, picked up a light-weight jacket, and left to meet Adriana.

Now he continued to watch her pace the floor, while he listened to Willy question the two other officers on their findings. Matt wanted to go out to Marie's with Willy and help with the investigation as soon as they were finished here, but he knew the Chief would have his hide if he disobeyed orders. All he could do was wait and let Willy do his job. He knew that when Willy was done, he would come and tell Matt everything he'd found out.

One of the doctors walked into the waiting room, drawing everyone's attention. The grave expression on his face left little hope that he brought good news.

Adriana, pale and silent, stood with clenched hands, waiting for him to speak. Matt walked to her side, and placed a supporting arm around her.

"Miss Sanchez is alive, but in very critical condition," the doctor reported. "We've had to operate, to stop all the bleeding and do some repair work. She made it through the surgery, but her chances of recovery are not very good. She lost a lot of blood. The next 12 to 24 hours are critical. If she makes it through that, maybe she'll survive. It will be at least 48 hours before we can offer any real hope. If you know of any next of kin, you should call them.

"I'm sorry I don't have any better news, but she took a severe beating. Quite truthfully, I'm surprised she's even alive. There's nothing more any of you can do here, so go home and get some rest."

"Doctor, can I go in and see her?" Adriana asked.

"No, I'm afraid not. She's still unconscious. And in her condition, I can only let immediate family in to see her. It's late. Go home."

Matt quietly thanked the doctor, nodded goodbye to Willy, then led Adriana out to her car and followed her home.

The doctor had talked briefly to Adriana about her own shocked condition and gave her a couple of tranquilizers in case she needed something to help her sleep that night.

When she got home, she called Connie and told her what had happened. Adriana was so upset Connie insisted on spending the night with her. Within fifteen minutes she'd packed a quick overnight bag and driven to Adriana's. Matt was relieved when Connie arrived safely.

They all three sat at the kitchen table drinking Chamomile tea and talking until 2:30 a.m. Finally, Matt talked Adriana into taking the pills the doctor had given her and going to bad. She took his advice. Within thirty minutes, the pills had taken affect and she was in a deep sleep for the rest of the night and most of the next day.

Matt and Connie talked for a while, then went to bed themselves. The events of the evening had a sobering effect on them, and instead of making love, they were content to lay quietly and hold each other, each contemplating the frailty of life long after they'd stopped talking. They laid awake for a long time, lost in their own thoughts, until they finally drifted off to sleep in the early hours of the morning.

Willy stayed at the hospital long enough to get a full report from the doctor, then ordered one of the police officers to stand guard at Marie's door, in case whoever had attacked her tried to come back and finish the job. Then he took three officers back out to Marie's house with him and they began what turned out to be a long night of investigating.

Marie's dog began barking as soon as Willy arrived at the house, but she was locked in the back yard and no threat to anyone for the moment. Willy knew that eventually, they would have to subdue the dog in order to look around the back of the house.

Willy ordered two of the officers to tape off a large area surrounding the house and yard.

They collected samples of blood, skin, hair, and clothing. Three good sets of fingerprints were lifted from the inside of the front door knob, a glass on the kitchen table and the table top itself. From the evidence in the kitchen - the glasses, the sandwich makings - Willy knew that either Marie had been in the middle of an evening snack or had made the sandwich for someone else. *Someone she knew,* he wondered?

Thinking hard, he considered all the different possibilities of how the attacker got into Marie's house. He went back out to the front door, scrutinizing it carefully. The only evidence of forced entry was the broken window, and Adriana had told him she broke that to get in. Maybe Marie opened the door voluntarily. Her attacker could have been someone she thought she could trust. Again, *someone she knew*? It had to be. Marie wasn't the type to invite a stranger into her home. He turned and scanned the front room. It was undisturbed, indicating the attack didn't occur until after they had moved into the kitchen. If the man came in through the front door, that is.

Maybe he had gotten in through the back door. But he would have had to go through the back yard, the dog's territory, to get to the back door. And the dog would have given Marie fair warning that an intruder was there. Maybe the man got inside before Marie got home from work. He could have been inside hiding. But, even so, Willy thought the dog would have continued to bark and would have caught Marie's attention when she did arrive home. He double checked the back door. No sign of forced entry there.

There was, however, blood on the inside of the back doorknob and on the door itself. Willy figured that was the way the attacker left. That followed Adriana's account of seeing someone run out through the back yard.

When they were almost finished inside the house, Willy ordered one of the officers, named Gene Stewart, to get a rope from his car and see if he could catch hold of the dog and tie her up safely out of their way.

Officer Stewart was of medium height and build, very mild mannered, and had a natural easy way with animals. Being an animal lover himself, he seldom failed to instill in them an immediate sense of trust. However, he knew this dog was under extreme duress, so he was extra cautious. He eased out the back door, speaking softly and moving slowly.

The overwrought dog went into a wild frenzy of barking that would make most men recoil in fear. Officer Stewart, however, felt only compassion and respect for the animal. He sat down on the step and continued to speak to the dog. After a few minutes his quiet manner and soft, reassuring voice worked their usual magic. The dog quieted down. Her mad barking became a troubled whine, and soon she began sniffing Officer Stewart's feet, then worked her way up his pant legs to his gentle, waiting hands.

The whining had ceased and her tail was slowly wagging in friendship. Officer Stewart slipped the rope through her collar, slowly rose to his feet, and led his new friend over to her doghouse, where he tied her securely. He patted her head and rubbed her ears for a couple of minutes, then went back to the house, got some fresh water and found the dog food and fed and watered Max. The dog wagged her tail in appreciation.

Willy stood watching out through the back window in wonder. He opened the door for Gene, shaking his head.

"I don't know how you did that, Gene," he said "but I'm sure glad you were here." He patted Gene on the back, then led his men outside to search the yard.

"Willy," Gene said, "I saw a knife on the ground about eight yards from the door." He showed Willy where it was. They took pictures, then picked it up and put it inside an evidence bag. They also collected more samples from some bloody hand prints on the fence, and took plaster casts of two of the footprints found in the dirt. After another hour, Willy decided they had everything they could find that night, and sent everyone back to Police Headquarters to file evidence and make out reports. By the time he got home, it was almost four in the morning.

Chapter 25

Connie spent Monday morning helping at the hospital. She saw Victor only a couple of times, from a distance. He seemed preoccupied and never seemed to notice her, much to her relief. Occupied with her own thoughts, she paid no attention to him and didn't notice the slight limp as he favored his right leg.

About 10:30, Connie was alone in the nurse's lounge taking her morning break when Victor walked in.

"Aha," he said, "just the person I've been looking for."

"You wanted to see me?" she asked.

"Well, of course I wanted to see you, Beautiful. I'm always wanting to see you, wishing you by my side. But, I've been rather preoccupied this morning. I hope you haven't felt ignored. How are things going?"

Connie gritted her teeth at the overt and unwanted flattery. Tiny sparks of anger danced in her eyes. She took a deep breath and tried to relax. *Don't let him get under your skin,* she told herself. *Let the remark pass. You've got enough to deal with today, so don't let this jerk get to you.*

"I've had better days, Victor, so take my advice and don't push your luck."

"Hey, I'm sorry. I was just trying to be friendly."

"Yes, but as usual, you're overdoing it."

"O.K., O.K. Again, I'm sorry. What seems to be the trouble? If you don't mind me asking."

Connie looked at him in amazement. She couldn't believe he hadn't heard about the attack on Marie, but he certainly acted as if he hadn't.

"Victor, surely you know that Marie Sanchez was attacked in her home last night and nearly killed."

"Oh, yes. Yes, I heard about that. A terrible thing. Just terrible."

"Then you also should know that Adriana went to her house and found her. It's very likely that she interrupted the attack as it was happening and scared off the attacker. She was lucky that he didn't come after her!"

"Adriana Goodell? Well, no. I didn't know that part. She must have been very frightened. Did she see who the attacker was?"

"Yes! I mean, no. Not exactly. She saw him run out the back of Marie's house, but it was too dark for her to get a real good look at him."

"I see. So, she wasn't able to give a description to the police?"

"No, not a precise one. She was really scared and upset. She called me after she got home last night, and I went over and spent the night with her. I didn't get much sleep."

"You must be terribly tired. I checked in on Marie earlier. They have a guard at her door."

"Yes, I know. They're afraid whoever attacked her will try to get in here and make sure she never wakes up. I've checked on her twice. She's still unconscious, but stable. She must be very strong. The doctors didn't think she would even make it through the night."

"The police will want to question her as soon as she wakes up. She'll be able to identify the man who beat her up. If he's smart, he'll be a long ways away from here by now." Victor looked thoughtful and stared out the window for a long time. Then he shook his head, as if to clear it of unwanted thoughts. He turned back around and looked at Connie with a strange, detached look in his eyes.

"You know, it makes you realize that life is short, and you shouldn't waste it, doesn't it?" He walked purposely back to Connie and sat down beside her on the couch.

"Did you get my flowers the other day?" he asked.

"They were delivered, yes. But I refused them. I don't want you sending me flowers, Victor. We don't have that kind of relationship."

"Hey, they were just flowers. What harm is there in that?"

"Look, Victor, I'm too tired to get into this with you today. Just don't be sending me any more flowers, okay?"

"Okay, fine, if that's the way you feel. I bet you wouldn't refuse flowers if your boyfriend sent them."

"That's none of your business!"

"So, how are things going with you and Matt, the Wonder Cop?"

Connie was instantly alert to the change in Victor. Her instincts warned her that something was different about him, something suppressed, yet not far below the surface. Anger or resentment, or maybe even danger. A strange tension filled the air. Victor's remark about her and Matt set her closer to the edge than she'd been all morning, her own anger building. Still, she tried to remain calm.

"That's none of your business, either," she said cautiously. "Let's not get into a discussion about my private life, Victor."

"But why not? We're friends, aren't we? And friends often talk about private maters. It's good. It's healthy. I just want to help you."

"Thank you, but we're not that good of friends, Victor. No offense. But I don't discuss my private life with anyone. Sorry." She moved further away from him, to the end of the couch. To her dismay, he also moved over until he was sitting very close to her, his right arm up along the back of the couch. His fingers played with a lock of her hair, twisting it around. He had her virtually pinned to the end of the couch, his thigh rubbing against hers.

"Well, now," he said in a deceivingly soft voice, "you see, that's just not healthy. You need to have someone to talk things over with. That way, you don't make so many mistakes in this life.

"Take you and Officer Goodell, for instance. Now, that's a bad match. Anyone can see that. Except you. So you need me to help straighten you out--keep you from making a big mistake."

The blood in her head pounded relentlessly. She began to tremble with suppressed anger. She turned to face him squarely, fighting to keep her voice calm.

"I am not making a big mistake! I'm in love with Matt." Her temper made her forget reason, forget that she wasn't going to discuss her private life with him. "If he wasn't right for me, if he wasn't everything I want in a man, I wouldn't have fallen in love with him. And neither you, nor anyone else, could ever convince me otherwise!"

"And I'm telling you, you're wrong," Victor shot back. He was prepared to fight for her love, even if that meant fighting Connie herself. "Matthew Goodell will never make you happy. He's no good for you. You deserve someone better. Someone like me. I could make you happy, Connie. We could make each other happy. You have to give me a chance!"

Connie eyed Victor warily, her pulse racing, and fought to regain her composure. She wanted to slap the self-important look off his face, but knew that wouldn't solve anything. And she was afraid of what he might do in retaliation. Lack of sleep last night had left her exhausted and vulnerable. Her head ached intolerably. She felt trapped and overwhelmed by Victor's domineering attitude. Close to panic, she realized she desperately needed to put some distance between them. His strange, aggressive behavior worried her.

She glanced around the room, stalling for time. The water cooler in the corner caught and held her attention.

"Look, Victor, I'm too tired to have this discussion." Rubbing her forehead with her hand, she quietly asked him to bring her a glass of water. He complied immediately, not suspecting any duplicity.

As soon as he stood up and walked across to the water cooler, she jumped up off the couch and rushed to the door. Victor heard her and whirled around, surprised.

"What are you doing?" he asked. "Where are you going?"

"Umm, I a..., I have to get back to work."

"What about your glass of water?" he asked grimly, the look on his face saying that he clearly understood he'd been tricked, and didn't like it.

"Sorry. I've changed my mind," she replied, and scooted out the door before he could stop her. Relieved to be out of his reach, Connie hurried to her next station of work, thankful that she wouldn't have to work with Victor that day.

She was supposed to meet Matt for lunch at noon, and couldn't wait to see him. She didn't want to admit it, but Victor was beginning to scare her, and she had the need of the strength and security she always felt around Matt.


Victor watched the lounge door close after her, seething with anger. The hand that held the paper cup of water trembled violently, splashing the cold liquid on his hand. He looked at it, then at the closed door, Connie's deception a painful blow to his male pride. He crushed the cup in his big fist, spilling water on the carpet, then threw it against the wall. *Damn you, Connie White. You won't get away with this. It's time you and I came to an understanding.* He was furious with himself for falling for such a simple trick. He'd not soon forget that she'd made a fool of him.

At noon, Matt met Connie at the High Tides Restaurant. From a distance, she looked gorgeous to him. *How can she look so good after the late night she had?* he wondered. But as she came closer, he could see that the strain and lack of sleep had taken their toll. Her eyes had the beginnings of dark circles around them. Fatigue showed plainly on her face. Parking beside her blue Toyota, he got out and gave her a quick kiss and a hug.

"You look tired. I'm sorry we kept you up so late last night," he said.

"That's alright. I wanted to be there."

He escorted her inside the restaurant and found a table in the corner, where they would have some privacy. He held out her chair as she sat down, then sat down across the small table from her, studying her closely.

"Rough morning?" he asked.

"No, not really. Just busy. I'm one of those gals who really needs her beauty sleep, and when I don't get it, it shows. I guess I look pretty awful." When she'd first seen Matt in the parking lot, relief had flooded her total being. Tears of joy and exhaustion had begun to flow, but she quickly brushed them away and got herself under control before he could notice.

"No, you don't. You look great," he reassured her. "But maybe you shouldn't work this afternoon. Why don't you go home and take a nap?"

"As good as that sounds, I really can't. I promised to do some work that can't be left for another day. But, don't worry, it's pretty easy. I'll be fine."

"So what did you do this morning that put you through the ringer? You shouldn't be this tired just from lack of sleep."

Connie knew there was no sense in trying to hide her difficulty with Victor from Matt. He was too astute, and she never was a good liar. He would see right through her if she tried to cover up the events of the morning. So she told him about her conversation with Victor, although she didn't go into details about exactly what was said. Only that he'd cornered her and asked her to go out with him again, and that he'd been acting kind of weird.

"I wish you didn't have to work along side of that guy. I don't like the way he treats you."

"It's not that bad, really. Most of the time, he just does his job and leaves me alone. It's just that lately, he seems to be obsessed with me."

"I don't trust Victor," Matt said. "And it scares me to think what he might do. I don't think you should trust him either."

"I *don't* trust him. Look, let's forget about him and just enjoy our lunch, O.K.?" She reached across the table and took both his hands in hers, gave them a friendly squeeze, and dazzled him with her smile.

He grinned sheepishly, and returned the squeeze and the smile. Her thumbs made slow, lazy circles across the back of his hands. It did funny things to his heart. When he looked into her eyes, he felt himself lost, the love he saw waiting for him there an unexpected, but surprisingly welcomed, surprise. He lifted one of her hands, drew it slowly to his lips, and gently kissed her soft palm as he watched her.

The caress made Connie gasp, and sent shivers up her arms and across her neck. As she gazed into Matt's eyes, her heart stopped for a second, then quickened. Her breathing became rapid and shallow. She swallowed hard, finally seeing her love returned in the depths of his eyes. She had waited a long time to see that look on his face.

"Excuse me. I hate to interrupt, but are you two ready to order?" The waitress stood beside their table, a pad and pencil in her hand, privately delighted to witness the obvious love and sudden passion of the young couple before her.

The spell was broken. They both pulled their hands away, embarrassed like a couple of school children, and quickly gave the woman their orders, neither one of them aware of what they ordered. When she'd left with their orders, Matt cleared his throat and tried to think of something to say.

"So, how did your morning go?" he asked, unconsciously repeating himself. "Did you get a chance to see Marie?"

"Yes. She made it through the night all right, but she still hasn't regained consciousness. I looked in on her right before lunch. I'm really afraid for her. But I talked with the doctor just before I left and he seems to be satisfied with her progress. He said her condition had stabilized, and that's good news."

"Then you should try not to worry. I'm sure the doctor knows what he's doing."

"I hope you're right," she replied, but she wasn't totally convinced that he was. However, excessive worry wouldn't help anyone, and would only make her more tired. All she could do was wait and hope.

While they waited for their food to arrive, she tried to relax and recapture the romantic mood. It felt so good to be in Matt's presence, and before long she was feeling her old, cheerful self.

They ate their lunch without really tasting the food, happy and content in each other's company. The hour passed too quickly, and before they knew it, it was time to get back to work.

Matt walked her out to her car, his hand protectively on her arm, and opened the door for her. Before she climbed in, she turned to him and kissed him quickly on the cheek.

"Thank you for lunch. It was really good to see you."

"You're welcome," he said, surprised and pleasured by the unexpected kiss. "When can I see you again?"

"Soon, I hope."

"Tonight?"

"Yes, I'd like that."

"Me, too. What time?"

"What time do you get off?"

"Six o'clock."

"Well, then, how about seven?"

"Seven's good."

"O.K. See you at seven."

"Yeah. Seven."

"`Bye, then." She turned to get into the car, but his hand held her back.

"Wait."

"Yes?" she turned around and found herself in his embrace, his hot lips crushing hers with a suddenness and urgency that thrilled her. He held her tightly for a moment, then released her quickly, embarrassed at his own impulsive actions.

She noticed a pink flush spread up his neck and face. It had been a long time since she had seen a grown man blush. It endeared him to her all the more.

"See you tonight," he mumbled, and turned and swiftly walked away.

She stood leaning against the side of her car, her heart beating rapidly. Her eyes followed him as he climbed into his car and drove away. Then she, too, got into her car and drove back to the hospital, thinking about him the whole way. Seven o'clock seemed a long ways off.

The afternoon went by in a daze, Connie's thoughts still on Matt and his passionate good-bye kiss. If asked to give an accurate account of what work she'd done, she probably couldn't do it. Luckily, it was only cleaning and restocking supplies. Important and necessary, but boring enough to let the mind wander a little.

Chapter 26

Meanwhile, Matt and Willy spent the afternoon pouring over the five murder cases they had going. The summer heat had abated slightly, and the janitor had finally fixed the air conditioner, so the office was reasonably comfortable. They studied the clues they'd found at the scene of the latest murders--the shooting of Jonathan Dewy and Don Suma on Sunday afternoon--to see if they were in any way linked to any or all of the other three deaths--Rusty McGreggor, Peter Bray or Michael Sans.

They found few similarities. Matt paced the floor as he listed off the facts on one hand.

"The first, and perhaps most significant, is the fact that all the victims were windsurfers. Reasonable conclusion: somebody had it in for windsurfers," he said. "Second: a hallucinogenic drug played a significant part in Rusty McGreggor's drowning, and a bottle of the same drug was found at the scene of Peter Bray's murder. Third: three of the five victims had black or dark brown hair. And last, all of the victims were male."

"What about Miss Sanchez?" Willy asked. "You think she figures in with this bunch?"

"The attack on Marie was a totally different MO except her attacker did use a knife, as in the Peter Bray case. However, she was the only female, the only non-sailor, and it appears that she may have known her attacker, may have let him into her house. Is there any connection? I think it's pretty far off the mark."

"I have to agree. There's nothing to tie her case to any of the other ones. But, if that's true, then why does my gut feeling keep telling me there's a connection?"

Matt looked at him without surprise. "Yours, too, huh? Mine's been saying the same thing. So what are we missing? What's the link?"

"I wish I knew."

By 4:30 p.m. they had exhausted every possibility. If there was a connection between Marie's attack and the five murders, they couldn't see it. The ringing of the phone interrupted their frustrated efforts. Willy answered it, spoke briefly, then hung up.

He looked up at Matt. "We just got a break. That was your sister. She just remembered something vital."

"What's that?"

"You remember she said she saw a small red sports car parked near Marie's place last night?"

"Yeah. What about it?"

"We have the license plate!"

"What?"

"That's right. When Adriana spotted that car last night, she wrote it down, thinking it might be important, then stuck it in her purse. In all the excitement, she forgot about it."

"Oh my God; that means we've got the dirty bastard. Come on, let's run it!"

"Hang on. That's just what I'm doing." Willy began punching numbers into the computer. Within a few minutes, they had the owner's name. Willy wrote it on a piece of paper and handed it to Matt.

"Victor Prescott?" Matt exclaimed. "Are you sure?"

"Yes."

"That doesn't make sense. There's gotta be a mistake. I mean, I don't like the guy, but he doesn't strike me as being violent. Adriana must have made a mistake."

"I don't know, Matt. We can't overlook it."

Just then the phone rang again. Willy answered it and spoke tersely, then hung up and looked at Matt. His expression spoke volumes.

"The gods are smiling on us. We just got another break. Marie Sanchez regained consciousness."

They grabbed their hats and headed out the door, stopping just long enough to ask the dispatcher to send a unit out to Victor's place to check on the license plate.

"I'll drive." Matt said as he headed for his car. Willy ran around to the passenger side and jumped in just as Matt jammed the car into reverse and tore out of the parking lot.

The hospital parking lot was full. Matt searched impatiently for a place to park. After driving down two full rows he spotted an empty space at the end of the third row. As they walked quickly toward the hospital entrance, they passed Connie's Toyota. In spite of his haste to see Marie, Matt lingered for a moment with his eyes on the blue car, remembering their luncheon date and anticipating this evening's dinner. He glanced down at his watch and saw that it was 4:45. Connie would be getting off work soon. Maybe he would get a chance to see her while he was there.

Willy noticed him looking at Connie's car and slapped him on the shoulder. "Come on, Romeo. Get your head out of the clouds. We've got work to do."

Together they hurried into the hospital. Matt glanced around, but didn't see Connie. He would check in the nurses' lounge when they were finished questioning Marie.

The elevator was busy, so they took the stairs two at a time and ran down the hall to the Intensive Care Unit.

The officer standing guard outside Marie's door saluted a wave to them.

Willy knocked quietly on the door and waited. After a few seconds a nurse opened it for him. In spite of their sense of excitement of at last getting to talk to Marie, they entered the room serenely.

Both men were shocked at Marie's condition. Her face was a mound of swollen, discolored flesh. Her nose was broken and swollen, her eyes small slits in the pulpy mass. The respirator had been removed, but there were still tubes that connected her to the oxygen, heart monitor and IV units.

The doctor had just finished checking her. He gave them three minutes to talk to her.

Matt stepped to her bedside and picked up her hand and held onto it. He said hello and asked her how she was feeling, then chastised himself for asking such a stupid question, but he couldn't think of anything else to say.

Willy, seeing Matt's discomfort and a little more experienced in dealing with attack victims, took charge of the interview.

"Hello, Marie. We feel really bad about what happened to you. Is there anything we can get for you?"

"No, thanks, Willy. I'm okay."

"We need to talk to you about what happened. Do you feel up to answering a couple of questions?"

"Yes," Marie replied, obviously in pain but willing to cooperate. Her lips were swollen and she could barely speak.

"Can you tell us what happened to you?"

In short, hesitant sentences, Marie told her story. After a few minutes she had exhausted her strength and become increasingly agitated. The attending nurse told them they would have to leave.

"Just one more question," Willy insisted. "Was the man who attacked you a friend or maybe an acquaintance?"

Marie turned even more pale, if that was possible, and began to cry. They both awaited her answer with heightened interest, but the nurse, seeing her distress, began to usher them out of the room.

"Wait," Marie choked, "it's alright."

The nurse hesitated a moment. Matt and Willy turned back to Marie, giving her their total attention.

"It was Victor," she said. "Victor Prescott."

That revelation hit both Matt and Willy like a rock. They stared at each other in shocked silence.

"Are you sure?" Matt asked. "Couldn't it have been someone else? Someone who looked like Victor?"

"No. I'm absolutely sure. He was in my house, for God's sake, as close as you and me are now. I've known him a long time. I'm not mistaken!"

"Alright, alright," Willy interjected. "Calm down. Matt didn't mean to imply you didn't know what you're talking about. We just didn't know if you got a good look at him. Now we do, and that's good that you did. Now we know who did this to you, and we're going to go get him. Thank you for your help."

The nurse insisted they leave and let Marie get some rest. Willy thanked her again and they moved out into the hallway. The officer was still on duty outside Marie's room. Willy stopped beside him. Matt went on across the hall to the nurses' station.

"Hank," Willy addressed the guard. "Has Victor Prescott been up here today?"

"Yes Sir, he was. He came by twice this morning and asked to go inside, but I wouldn't let him. Then he was by a couple of times this afternoon, but he didn't ask to go in. Just wanted to know if she'd regained consciousness."

"When was the last time he was here?"

"Just a little while ago. About 4:30, or so."

"Did he ask about her then?"

"Yes Sir, he did."

"And what did you tell him?"

"That she had woke up, and the doctor was with her."

"What was Victor's reaction to that, Hank?"

"Well, now that you mention it, he did act a little strange. I asked him if he was feeling all right, but he didn't say anything. Just took off down the hall. I thought he might have a touch of flu or something."

"It was `or something' all right. Ms. Sanchez says Victor's the one who attacked her last night. I want you to stay here and guard her door. Don't move from your post until your replacement comes, and repeat these instructions to him word for word. If Victor comes by, for God's sake don't let him into that room! Apprehend him and call us. Got that?"

"Yes Sir!"

Willy nodded to him and stepped across to the nurses' station. He called and reported their findings to Chief Baxter. Matt had called for the hospital security guards. While he waited for them to show up, he glanced up at the clock on the wall. The time was 5:00 p.m. He looked over at Matt and spoke.

"Well, I guess Adriana was right. It was Victor's car she saw."

Matt shook his head in wonder, "Yeah. People are full of surprises."

When the two security guards arrived, Matt asked them if they had seen Victor recently. One had seen him about four o'clock, the other not since morning. Willy tried having him paged, but there was no response, so the four men started a thorough search of the premises. The Chief was sending a backup team to help in the search.

Matt couldn't help thinking about Connie. She said she'd had a run-in with Victor that morning. Where was she now? She had to be in the hospital somewhere. Her car was still in the parking lot--he'd seen it himself. He had her paged. Several minutes ticked slowly by. There was no response. He asked every nurse and doctor he saw if they knew where she was. No one had seen her in the past 20 minutes. *This is crazy,* he thought. *Someone must have seen her since then. She couldn't just disappear into thin air!*

## Chapter 27

Connie had drug herself listlessly through the afternoon in spite of several members of the hospital staff telling her she should go home and go to bed. By 4:50 she had finished her work. Much to her relief, she hadn't seen Victor again. *I can't wait to get home,* she thought. *If I'm lucky, I'll get a short nap before Matt picks me up.*

Walking out to her car, she noticed that the temperature had really cooled down. After the past several days of unbearably hot weather she was ready for a change. Her car was still hot inside, however, from being locked up all afternoon, so the first thing she did was roll down the two front windows. The cool breeze swept through the hot interior. Connie leaned back against the headrest and closed her eyes. *Ahh...that feels good,* she thought.

The temptation to stay right there and give in to the overwhelming desire to sleep was almost too much to resist. But after a couple of minutes, she forced herself to sit up straight and ignore the temptation.

She retrieved her keys from her purse, inserted one into the ignition and turned it. A low, growling sound came from the engine. She checked to make sure she had the car in park, moved the gear-shift back and forth, and tried it again. This time the only result was a muffled, moaning sort of sound that she'd never heard before.

"Damn," she said. Getting out of the car, she walked to the front and lifted up the hood. Everything looked fine to her. *How would you know,* she asked herself, *You don't know a damned thing about cars!* She slumped over the fender and put her head down into her hands, closed her eyes, and tried to think. Although the temperature had cooled down, it was still hot enough that sweat began to trickle down her back and face. She heard a voice behind her. Startled, she jumped and banged her head against the opened hood.

"Having trouble?"

She whirled around, her heart pounding. Victor Prescott stood three feet behind her, a benign smile on his face.

"Victor!" she said, "You startled me."

"Oh, I'm sorry. I didn't mean to frighten you."

"That's alright. You didn't frighten me, just startled me. There's a big difference. I'm not afraid of you, Victor," she looked him in the eye with a confidence that she really didn't feel inside. He'd caught her off guard, and she didn't know what to expect. "I didn't hear you walking up, that's all," she said.

"Yes, of course," he replied. "So what's the problem? Won't your car start?" he asked innocently.

"No, it won't," she reached up to pull down the hood. "I'll just go in and call the garage. They can send out a mechanic."

But Victor had other ideas. "It's about five now," he said. "They're probably closed for the day, so it'll have to wait until tomorrow. But don't worry, it'll be safe here for the night."

Victor glanced quickly around the parking lot. So far they were the only ones there, but he knew that soon it would be full of people leaving for the day. He looked down at his watch. It was five o'clock. He wanted to hurry and get out of there before anyone else showed up, especially the cops. He'd seen Matt and Willy come into the hospital and knew that they were probably there to talk to Marie.

"Come on, I'll give you a lift home," he said. Victor's offer sent warning signals flashing in Connie's brain. She stepped away from him and shook her head.

"No, thanks," she said. "I don't want to put you to any trouble."

"Don't be silly," he replied. "It's no trouble at all."

He reached out and firmly took hold of her elbow, pulling her toward his car, which was parked directly behind hers.

Connie decided she was probably over-reacting, a result of her tiredness and worry over Marie. After all, Victor was a fellow worker. He was just trying to be nice and help her out. Besides, she was too tired to stand there and argue with him. He seemed to be over his earlier surliness. Soon there would be a surge of people in the parking lot, and she didn't want to be seen having a ridiculous argument in public. She didn't like Victor much, but felt that he was basically harmless, so she decided to give in and let him drive her home.

Thanking him, she allowed him to lead her to his car and help her in. She watched him hurry around and climb into the driver's seat.

"Buckle up," he said, flashing her a friendly smile. He buckled his own seatbelt. Unnoticed, he reached down and pushed the buttons that locked all four doors and windows.

Connie tried to relax. She looked around at the interior of Victor's car. It was beautiful. Blue leather interior, including the seats. And very comfortable. Tinted windows. Incredibly efficient air conditioning; it was already cooling her off nicely. Quiet music played on the obviously expensive stereo system. She made an effort to be cheerful and voiced her admiration of his car. He seemed to appreciate that.

After a few minutes, Connie's nervousness abated and she was glad she'd decided to let Victor drive her home.

Later she would regret that same decision.

After fifteen minutes of searching the hospital, Matt and Willy had to acknowledge that neither Connie nor Victor was in the building.

"I just checked outside, Willy. Connie's car is still here. I checked inside. The keys were in the ignition. She's not that careless. I'm afraid something's happened to her."

"Do you think she went somewhere with Victor?"

"No. At least, not willingly. She doesn't even like the guy. We had lunch together today and she told me she'd had an argument with him just this morning. He's still trying to get her to go out with him, and she doesn't want to have anything to do with him. Besides that, she and I had a date for this evening."

"Again?"

"Again what?"

"You have a date with her again tonight, after just having lunch with her today? You two are seeing a lot of each other all of a sudden."

"So? I happen to like her. A lot. And she's crazy about me."

"How do you know that?"

Matt shrugged his shoulders reservedly, wishing he hadn't said that. "My sister told me. She and Connie are best friends. And what's that got to do with anything, anyway?"

"Maybe a lot. Maybe nothin'. Come on. Let's go see if we can find Victor's car. One of the nurses told me he drives a late model Buick. Blue."

The parking lot had emptied out considerably since they had

arrived. Visiting hours were over, and the night shift had not yet arrived. It took them only a few minutes to determine that Victor's car was gone.

Victor thought Connie was coming around to his way of thinking at last. That's good, he told himself. That'll make the next few days easier. If she liked his car, she would really like all the other things he could give her.

"You know, you could have a car like this if you want. And nice clothes, and jewelry. I don't have a whole lot of money, but I do have a little. And I'd love to share it with you.

"I had a large insurance policy on my wife, and I've invested it wisely. In a few years I'll be able to travel all over the world and live in luxury. You could come with me, as my wife."

Connie looked at him in amazement. She couldn't believe what she was hearing. How could she have thought he'd changed any? She felt like the world's biggest fool.

"Victor, I'm flattered," she replied as calmly as she could. "Really I am. But it would never work out between us. We're too different. And, as I've told you before, I'm not in love with you. I'm sorry." She couldn't wait to get home and away from him. This was the last straw. As important as her volunteer work was to her, she knew she could no longer go on working in the same place as Victor.

"What is love, anyway? You will come to love me eventually, if you will just give me a chance to show you what kind of a man I am."

"Damn it, Victor! We've had this conversation before. You know I'm in love with someone else. Now let it go!"

"Yes, you have told me that before, but I don't believe you know what you're talking about!"

"Excuse me, but who the hell are you to decide what I know and what I don't know?" In her anger Connie failed to notice that they were not heading for her apartment, but in the direction of the bluff. "You are the most arrogant, self-centered, manipulative man I know! You think you can just waltz in to my life and take control, without any regard for my feelings or needs. You're crazy!"

"That's not true. I've taken everything into consideration. You should be grateful."

Connie turned and stared out the window, trying to regain control of her emotions and the situation. Suddenly she realized that they weren't anywhere near her place. Instead they were on a narrow country road. On one side were hills and trees, on the other a steeply sloping embankment. She spun around and glared at Victor.

"This isn't the way to my place! Where are you going?"

"I need to talk some sense into you, and it's obvious that I can't do that at the hospital or at your place. So I'm taking you on a retreat of sorts, away from any negative influences. Then maybe you'll finally come around."

Connie couldn't believe what she was hearing. She was being kidnapped!

The car slowed for a sharp corner. She reached down and pushed the release button of her seatbelt, at the same time jerking on the door handle. But the door was locked. She pushed the lever to unlock it, but it wouldn't work. Frantically, she tried the window lever, but it, too was locked.

"You son-of-a-bitch, stop this car! Do you hear me?"

"Sorry, I'm afraid I can't do that. You're coming with me, so you might as well accept it. Now settle down and put your seatbelt back on."

Instead, Connie reached over and started pounding on his arm and shoulder. Then she grabbed at the steering wheel. The car jerked to the right, careening off the road into the gravel, sending dust and rocks flying over the 35-foot drop off. Victor swore. In a squeal of tires, he just managed to maintain control of the vehicle.

When he had the car back onto the road, he slammed to a stop and turned on Connie. His face was red with rage. The whites of his eyes showed clearly around the pupil. Connie had never felt her life in danger as much as she did right now.

In a lightening flash, he lunged for her throat with both hands. She screamed and jumped back against the door. Victor's seatbelt prevented him from getting close enough to choke the life out of her, which at that moment is what he wanted to do. In his frustration and anger he drew his right arm back and struck her as hard as he could with the back of his hand. The blow snapped her head backwards; then she collapsed onto the seat.

Victor sat in his seat breathing hard, his heart pounding in his chest. From the way her head had jerked back, he was afraid he might have killed her. *Oh, God,* he thought, *what have I done now?*

He looked at Connie, then checked for a pulse. It was weak and rapid. But at least she wasn't dead. As he sat there staring at her, he suddenly couldn't decide if he was glad he hadn't killed her, or if it would be better to be rid of her. She was proving much more difficult to handle than he'd expected.

He was already committed to his plan, and all set up with the necessary supplies to hide out for two or three weeks if he needed to. Now that Marie had regained consciousness, he knew he couldn't return to either the hospital or his home.

Minutes ticked by as he wrestled with the decision of whether or not to let Connie live.

## Chapter 28

Back at the hospital parking lot, Matt and Willy, after discovering that neither Victor Prescott nor Connie White were anywhere on the hospital grounds, decided to drive to Connie's apartment in the hope that she would be there, even though her car was still at the hospital.

"Maybe she got a ride home with someone else," Matt said in desperation.

"Maybe. But why would she do that when she had her own car here?"

"I don't know! Maybe she went shopping with a girlfriend, or maybe her car wouldn't start and she called a taxi."

"Again, maybe. There's one way to find out," Willy replied. "Let's go on over there."

On the drive over to Connie's, Matt had a hard time keeping his thoughts off the negative. His fear that Connie and Victor were together overshadowed all other possibilities. If he was right, then Connie was in grave danger. And he was sure he was right.

It didn't make sense that she'd go shopping with another friend and leave her car at the hospital. She would have taken her own car and met her friend at the mall. And after the night she'd had last night, he didn't think she would even have the energy to go shopping.

They pulled into Connie's driveway and Matt jumped out and ran up to the door. The house was dark and quiet. He pushed the doorbell several times in quick succession, then pounded on the door. Please God, let her be home!

"Connie! Hello?" he shouted. But only silence greeted him. "Connie?" Reaching up over the door frame, he retrieved the spare key Connie kept there and opened the door. He ran through the small house, calling her name, but his only reply was the echo of his own voice. After a couple of minutes, he gave up and returned to the car, pale and shaken.

In the meantime, Willy had radioed headquarters. Two officers had gone out to Victor's house to check the license plate number of his car. The only car they found was a small red MG, and the license plate number matched the one Adriana had reported. The officers were staying at Victor's place, out of sight, in case he showed up there, but so far there was no sign of him. Willy passed this information on to Matt, which only served to increase his apprehension. The look on his face spoke volumes. They had better find Connie soon.

"Let's go over to your place and see if Connie's showed up there," Willy suggested.

Silent and withdrawn, Matt only nodded in response. A tight knot of fear in his stomach, which had started developing in the hospital, had grown into a full-blown volcano threatening to erupt. It took all of his self-control not to scream his fear at the top of his lungs. With trembling hands he fastened his seat belt. The buckle slipped out of his hands twice before he finally got it buckled. Sweat trickled down his face in spite of the cooler weather.

When they arrived at Adriana's, she met them at the front door. At first Matt thought she was sick, she was so quiet and pale. Grabbing her by the arms, he studied her face closely, and realized it wasn't illness that effected her, but fear.

"Adriana, what's wrong?" His eyes swept around the small house. Without waiting for an answer, he moved past her into the front room. "Connie!" he called. "Connie?" Running from room to room, he threw open doors so hard they banged against the walls, rattling in protest. Finally, he had to face the truth. Connie wasn't there. The rest of the house was empty. He rushed back to confront his sister, who was now seated.

"Tell me," he demanded.

"She's not here, Matt," Adriana replied in a shaky voice.

"I can see that!" Matt exploded. "Where is she? What has happened?"

"Take it easy Matt. Can't you see she's upset?"

Guilt flooded over Matt when he realized how visible shaken Adriana was and that his raving was only upsetting her more.

"I'm sorry," he said. "I'm just really worried about Connie." He reached down and kissed her on the cheek, then sat down beside her and took her hand in his. He quickly filled her in on the situation, and the fact that they'd already checked at Connie's apartment for her. The news made her even more upset, but he couldn't help it. She needed to be warned about Victor, and maybe she could help them find Connie.

"Oh, God," she said, "I knew something was terribly wrong, but I didn't know what. I thought you were the one in danger, Matt, but this afternoon I realized it wasn't you, but Connie. I didn't know what to do. I tried to call the hospital, but no one seemed to know where she was. And I called the police station, but you weren't there. I asked them to tell you to call me. Didn't you get my message?"

"No, I didn't. But we've been really busy. This whole thing was breaking wide open and things have been crazy."

"Matt, you don't think she's with Victor, do you?"

Matt could hear the panic in her voice and couldn't think of what to say. But she saw the fear in his eyes. When he didn't answer, she turned her question to his partner. "Willy?"

Being at a loss for words himself, Willy nevertheless knew that they had to tell her something, and she was too smart to be lied to. She'd already read the truth in their faces.

"We don't know that for certain. We don't want to assume anything, but we have to face the fact that she could be with him. It's a possibility. However, it's also possible that she got a ride with someone else, and maybe they decided to go somewhere for a cup of coffee or a glass of wine after work. We don't know for sure."

"Look at me, Willy. Look me in the eye," she demanded. Several seconds passed as she studied him. He felt like she had looked into his soul. She slowly nodded her head, and in a voice gone surprisingly calm, spoke with the wisdom beyond her years.

"You *know*, Willy. You know as sure as I do. I can see the truth in your eyes. Now the only question is, what are you going to do about it?"

Willy looked at Matt, who had also calmed down as if in acceptance of the inevitable.

"Well," he replied, "I guess now we have to get back to work."

"What's the next step?" Matt asked him.

"I think it's time we get our butts over to Victor's place and see what we can dig up."

"O.K. Listen, Sis, I want you to stay in the house and keep all the doors locked. And I don't want any arguments this time. Victor is a very dangerous man, so don't you be fooling around, you hear me? I want your promise.

"If anything happens, you call the station and they'll get hold of me. I promise. I'll tell them to be sure and give me any messages from you immediately. And if you think of anything that might help us, be sure to call right away, O.K.? I'll see you later."

Adriana stood up, calmer now but still trembling slightly, and promised she'd stay in the house. She saw them to the door, where they made a hurried exit and headed out to Victor's place down along the river.

The two officers assigned to Victor's residence were still there, their car hidden in the trees behind the garage. They came out when they saw Matt and Willy drive up.

Stepping out of the car, Willy asked them if they'd seen anything. They told him about the car in the garage. He gave them the latest instructions from headquarters.

"The Chief's sending out a unit to scour this place. They should be here soon, but we're going to go ahead and take a look around."

Matt was already at the garage. The garage looked big enough to house at least two cars and maybe a boat or camp trailer, and his curiosity led him to see what all was in there. A side door opened easily. Matt was surprised that it wasn't locked.

Apparently Victor's natural distrust of people was slipping, or else he had something on his mind that had totally distracted him from locking up his place.

Just inside the garage, nestled on a trailer against the near wall, was a short, wooden fishing boat. Only about 15 feet long, it looked like a nice little vessel, just right for fishing the small lakes up in the mountains. Something was parked on the other side of the boat that caught and held Matt's attention. His heart started to pound.

As if in a trance, he slowly walked around the end of the boat trailer to a small vehicle which was shrouded in a gray protective chamois cover. Reaching down, he slowly lifted the corner of the cover and looked under it.

*My, God. This is it!* He got a rush from seeing it. He turned and stepped over to the garage door.

"Willy!" he shouted, "Get in here!"

Willy came running, excited by the urgency in Matt's voice. Stepping through the doorway, he stopped cold in his tracks.

"What the hell? So this is it, huh?" He joined Matt in his examination of the vehicle.

"You bet it is!" With a quick flick of his wrist, Matt swept the cover off the rest of the car. "This is the small red sports car we've been looking for, the one that ran down Michael Sans, the same one that Adriana saw parked up at Marie's Sunday night. Check out the license plate. Look, I found some scratches on the front bumper. This is the car all right. A red MG. And it was right here under our noses the whole time. Damn!"

"Yeah, well the boys said it was here."

Matt kicked the tire in frustration, then stood with his hands on his hips and silently cursed his luck for not finding the car sooner. If he hadn't been tied up in traffic the other day when he'd seen this car drive by out on the highway, Marie would not have gotten almost killed and Connie wouldn't be in danger now. That fact was a hard one to swallow.

"O.K., O.K.," Willy said, "we got him for the attempted murder of Marie, but a red sports car with scratches on the bumper isn't enough to convict the guy of the hit on Sans. We'll need more evidence, something we can take to court. Let's keep looking."

The crime unit had arrived and began an intense search of every square inch of the garage, the house and the grounds. After half an hour, one of the team found a piece of yellow material in one of the trash cans and handed it over to Willy. Willy called Matt over.

"What color was the life jacket Michael Sans was wearing when he was hit by that car?"

"Yellow. Why? Did you find something?"

For an answer, Willy held up the piece of cloth for Matt to see. "I think this is the evidence we're looking for."

Matt nodded his head, but he knew that until they found Victor, all the evidence in the world wasn't going to do them any good. And they had looked everywhere. An all-points bulletin released earlier in the evening had produced nothing. Victor had, in effect, disappeared into thin air. And so had Connie. Were they together? Matt was sure of it.

As the crime unit continued their probe of the premises, Matt and Willy sat in the patrol car and tried to think of where Victor could be hiding. The radio crackled to life. There was a message for Matt; Adriana had called and wanted to talk to him right away. They decided to drive back into town and talk to her in person.

Adriana paced back and forth across the kitchen floor, waiting for Matt to return her call. Where was he? She was just reaching to pick up the phone and call the station again when she heard him pull into her driveway. Racing to the front door, she unlocked it and jerked it open just as Willy was reaching up to push the doorbell. His look of comic surprise went unnoticed.

"Well, it's about time!" she said tartly. "I was afraid you two hadn't gotten my message again." She literally pulled them into the living room as she spoke. "I may have something, but I'm not sure." Matt looked at her dubiously, a perplexed expression on his face.

"Have you heard from Connie?" he asked.

"No, I haven't. But I keep seeing Sam Morgan's face for some reason. I can't imagine why. What could he possibly have to do with Connie's disappearance?"

"I don't know," replied Matt. "He said that he was pretty good friends with Victor."

"I think you should go and talk to him," Adriana said. "I have a feeling he might be able to help."

"He might be able to tell us where Victor hangs out, or if he has a favorite get-away. Come on, Matt, let's go find out where this guy lives and have a talk with him."

"Wait," Adriana said. "I bet you guys haven't stopped to eat, and I made some spaghetti. Why don't you take a couple of minutes and have a bite?" It was the only thing she could think of to keep her brother in her site for a few more moments. She knew it wouldn't work, and it didn't.

"Sorry, Sis," Matt replied, "but not now."

"Thanks anyway, Adriana," Willy agreed, "but time is of the essence right now, as you know. We'll catch something later. Bye."

"Okay. Good luck. I pray you find them soon." She gave Matt a quick hug. "Be careful," she said.

## Chapter 29

After a few minutes Victor had calmed down and had come to his senses. He'd planned too long and worked too hard to throw it all away now. He knew Connie would come around to his way of thinking after a couple of weeks alone with him.

He looked at her closely. She was still unconscious. The road they were on was seldom used by anyone other than the few residents who lived at the end of it. However, he didn't want to take the chance of being seen by anyone, so he put the car into gear and continued on as quickly as the unimproved road would allow.

Five minutes later he passed Marie Sanchez's house. He never gave a thought about what had happened there the night before. That was over and done with and he had more important things to take care of now. So he continued on down the road for a short ways, then turned left down an overgrown driveway.

The empty house that Sam Morgan had first told him was for sale lay nestled among the trees and wild brush that had grown up in the absence of a steady inhabitant. Victor drove slowly down the overgrown drive, being careful not to break any branches or dislodge any rocks along the way. He didn't want to leave any evidence of his passing. A small lean-to in the back was just big enough to house his car, but first he had to get Connie inside and secured.

Victor was a large, strong man and had no trouble at all carrying someone of Connie's slight build. The side door he entered through opened into a small utility room, then into the kitchen and from there into the living room. A short hallway led to the bathroom and two small bedrooms. He walked past the first bedroom and the bathroom, then opened the door to the second bedroom.

After laying Connie gently on the bed in the middle of the room, he double-checked the window. It was securely locked and nailed shut. Returning to the bed, he checked Connie's pulse again. This time it was strong and steady. Then he left the room, locked the door behind him and pocketed the key.

As Victor quickly re-traced his steps back through the house, his eyes darted around continuously, checking and rechecking details. Everything looked fine, just as he'd left it. He hurried out to the car, started it up and cautiously drove it around and into the lean-to. Walking back around the house, he covered his tracks as best he could, pulling the grass back up, moving a couple of large branches across the path his car had made.

Then he walked out the driveway doing the same thing. He took a large bushy tree branch and swept it back and forth across the gravel where his tires had left tracks, obliterating any signs of recent use.

Inside the house, Connie slowly regained consciousness. As she lay on the bed trying to remember where she was, the events of the day gradually unfolded in her memory. The idea that she'd been kidnapped was incredible, ludicrous.

When she sat up on the bed, a sharp pain stabbed at the back of her head, causing her to wince. She closed her eyes and felt the lump on her head. Slow, deep breaths helped to alleviate the pain, and at the same time brought to her the smell of staleness and dust, like one would find in a storage room that had not been opened in many months.

She opened her eyes and looked around the small room. It was sparsely furnished with one chair and a dresser besides the bed on which she sat. Bright light filtered in through the one window. Sliding off the bed, she walked over to the window and tried to open it. It appeared to be stuck. Repeated efforts proved fruitless, and upon closer examination, she discovered it was nailed shut. Then she knew it was really true--Victor had indeed kidnapped her!

She ran to the door and tried to jerk it open, just to discover it was locked.

"Victor! Open this door!" Pounding on the door with her left fist, she rattled the doorknob with her other hand, but there was no response from without. Finally she stopped and rested her head against the door, listening for any sign of activity. Was Victor even out there? Or had he left her here alone?

Hot tears gathered and rolled down her cheeks. How was she going to get out of here? she wondered. Or was she going to die here? Where was "here", anyway? She had no idea.

Returning to the bed, she laid down and forced herself to think clearly. After a minute, sounds of a door opening and closing came from somewhere in the house. She sat up and listened carefully, her heart pounding wildly.

Only when Victor was completely satisfied that he'd erased his trail did he return to the house. He selected two small glasses from a cupboard and a bottle of bourbon from another, then got a plate of cold-cuts from the refrigerator and went to the door of the room where he'd locked Connie.

Retrieving the key from his pocket, he unlocked the door and slowly pushed it open. She sat on the edge of the bed. When he entered and closed the door behind him, she stood up and backed away, glaring at him, a mixture of hate and fear in her eyes. Tears of pain and frustration wet her cheeks and made her eyes look like big, gray-blue pools of water

His heart went out to her. She reminded him of a wild filly snared in a rancher's trap, scared but proud and spirited, and apparently untamable. Well, he'd soon subdue her and bend her will to his. The thought of that experience excited him more than he expected.

"Well," he said cheerfully, "I'm glad to see you're feeling better. I've brought us a drink to relax us, and something to eat. I imagine you're getting hungry." He set the tray on top of the dresser next to the bed. Reaching for a glass, he poured two fingers of bourbon and offered it to her. "Here, drink this. It'll make you feel better."

"No thank-you," she said emphatically, and disdainfully turned her back to him.

"Suit yourself," he replied. "Hungry?"

"No," she answered, refusing to look at him.

He felt his anger rising. Her stubbornness would try the patience of any man.

"You should eat something. Would you drink a soda? I have some in the refrigerator."

Connie wanted to refuse, but her throat was dry and parched and, she had to admit to herself, she was very hungry, the hallow feeling in her stomach making itself known. Looking around at the tray of food, she swallowed hard. Her saliva glands had suddenly become overly active. Be reasonable, she told herself. It'll do you no good to starve yourself. Glancing furtively at him, she nodded.

"Yes, I'd like a soda," she whispered.

"Good," he said. "I'll be right back." He left the room, locking the door.

As soon as he'd left, Connie walked over to the tray of food and made a quick meal of cheese, ham and crackers. Then she sipped on the bourbon Victor had poured. It was strong and burned her throat. She coughed hard and decided to wait for the soda he'd promised.

When Victor came back in, she was seated in the chair, looking out the window. She ignored him, acting as if she hadn't heard him come in.

He noticed the missing food. The fact that she'd eaten something pleased him greatly. Maybe she was going to cooperate with him after all. This called for a celebration.

"Here's your soda," he said, setting the can of pop on the table next to the food. His eyes locked on the glass of bourbon and he smiled. This was going to be easier than he thought.

Picking up the glass, he sniffed the contents appreciatively, then sipped the hot, fiery liquid. Aah, he thought, it is as good as I expected and well worth the money. When he'd drained the glass, he refilled it and just as slowly and contentedly emptied it again, as if he had all the time in the world.

The sound of him sipping his drink made Connie even thirstier, until she couldn't stand to ignore him any longer. With as much dignity as she could muster, she rose from the chair and crossed the room to the table.

The little she'd eaten while Victor had gone for her soda had only sharpened her appetite, causing her stomach to growl loudly in protest. She hoped desperately that Victor couldn't hear it as she sat on the edge of the bed and reached for the soda and more food. Much to her relief, he seemed absorbed in his own thoughts. She hoped he stayed that way the rest of the night, so she could concentrate on how to get away from him.

After she finished eating, she asked him if she could use the bathroom. He apologized for not thinking of that sooner, and, unlocking the bedroom door, pointed to the door across the hall.

"Freshen up if you like, or take a shower. Everything you need is in the closet just inside the door," he said.

Connie looked at him skeptically and wondered how the hell he could know what she needed and what she didn't. Much to her surprise, she found he was telling the truth. There were clean towels, washcloths, soap, shampoo and deodorant. There was even a woman's bathrobe hanging on the door, not brand new, but in good condition and clean. She was exhausted, hot and sweaty. A shower sounded marvelous.

Locking the door securely, she decided to take advantage of the opportunity. Stepping into the shower, she let the hot water pound her body until she felt the tension depart from her, leaving her feeling refreshed but still tired. Getting out of the shower, she dried herself off with a large, soft towel that felt wonderful and smelled of lilacs. She brushed her hair with a new, unopened hair brush she found on the counter. Next to that was a new toothbrush and toothpaste, so she cleaned her teeth. At last she felt almost like her regular self, until she thought of the madman waiting for her on the other side of the door.

When she walked out of the bathroom, Victor was there and led her back to the bedroom. She spent the next hour or so listening to him rattle on about his life and how much he admired her and how happy they were going to be together. At first she'd protested and argued, but then she decided it was mostly the bourbon talking and that Victor wasn't really listening to her. He was talking to himself, feeding his own fantasies. She began to ignore him, not even bothering to answer the occasional question he threw her way. He didn't seem to notice, so she once again concentrated on a way to escape.

By eight o'clock, Victor had downed his fifth glass of bourbon and was feeling the effects of the alcohol. His speech had become slurred and he was starting to stumble when he got up and walked around the room. The glazed look in his eyes led Connie to falsely believe he was no longer a danger to her.


When Matt and Willy got into Matt's car at Adrianna's house, Willy turned to Matt. "You'd better drop me off at the station so I can get my own car---and I think I'll pick up Jazz. We might be able to use him."

"O.K.," Matt replied curtly. His mind was racing ahead to the possibility that Sam held the key to finding Connie before Victor had a chance to harm her.

The drive out to Sam's would take about ten minutes. After Matt dropped off Willy at headquarters, he decided not to wait for Willy to get the dog. That would take only about five minutes, but Matt was too impatient to wait. Connie's safety was of utmost importance, and every minute counted.

As he drove past Marie Sanchez's house he was reminded of the events of the night before and wondered how she was doing. The doctor said she had a good chance of a full recovery, at least physically. Her emotional recovery would take a lot longer. His fear for Connie increased as he thought about Marie.

There was another driveway between Marie's house and where Sam Morgan lived with his brother, Tom. Matt could just barely see the roof and part of the house from the main road. Brush and trees hid the rest of the house. Matt wondered vaguely who owned it. Glancing down at the place as he drove by, he thought it looked empty, and the driveway showed no signs of recent use that he could tell.

Sam Morgan was home and answered Matt's questions as well as he could, but unfortunately wasn't much help. He hadn't seen Victor since early afternoon, and he didn't know any place where he might be hiding out. It seemed to Matt that Sam and Victor weren't really very close after all.

Matt, in his disappointment, was short-tempered. Sam became withdrawn and sulky. It was apparent that his feelings had been hurt, but Matt was beyond caring. He left strict orders for Sam to call the police station if he remembered anything that might help them find Victor, then turned around and walked quickly to his car. He backed his car around, spitting gravel and dust from the tires, and was heading out the driveway when Willy drove up. Matt stopped and talked to him for a minute, filling him in on what he'd gotten, or rather hadn't gotten, from Sam.

## Chapter 30

Connie looked out through the window. The light was fading quickly. The small bedroom had become stuffy and hot, and the smell of alcohol made her slightly nauseated. If only she could open the window a little and let in some fresh air.

Victor poured himself yet another drink. Connie lost count of how many this made, and she watched as he seemingly drank himself into a stupor, hoping that he would pass out. That would be her opportunity to escape. The minutes slowly ticked by, one by one. His speech became slurred. At one point he staggered to his feet and seemed to notice that night was coming.

"'ssgetting dark in here. 'xcuse me, I gotsa go pee. Then I'll get us'a candle. You like candles, doncha? No lights. Can't have light, ya' know. No light! Got that?"

"O.K. Victor. No lights. A candle will be fine."

"Dam' straight it will. Be right back. You stay here." He stumbled into the hall, leaving the bedroom door opened. Connie thought that might be her chance, but when he went into the bathroom, he left that door open, too, and kept his eye on her as he used to toilet. "Damnit!" she said, and turned and walked to the other side of the room, keeping her back turned to him.

When he'd finished, she heard him walk down the hall and into the kitchen and open a cupboard.

This was her chance. Looking down the hallway, she saw the way to the front door was clear. She slid along the wall until she reached the kitchen doorway. Victor was opening more drawers, cursing to himself as he searched for a match.

Connie calculated the distance to the door to be about fifteen feet. It seemed like fifty. She stepped back and closed her eyes and summoned all her courage. Taking a deep breath, she prepared to run as fast as she could across the floor. Just then a shadow fell across the kitchen doorway and Victor stepped into the hallway, blocking her escape.

"Going somewhere, Sweetheart?" he asked. He took her roughly by the shoulders and shook her hard. "Don't try any funny business or you'll be sorry!" He jerked her around and pushed her hard toward the bedroom, causing her to stumble and fall. Grabbing her roughly by the arm, he pulled her to her feet, then shoved her into the bedroom and locked the door behind her.

She was surprised at his strength. She'd have to be more careful, and much more clever, if she was to escape this place. She sat on the bed rubbing her arm where he'd grabbed her, and tried to think what to do.

Victor went back to the kitchen and in a few minutes returned to the bedroom and closed the door behind him. "Here," he growled. "Light this candle."

She got off the bed and walked over to where he stood holding a candle and box of matches. He definitely seemed to be more sober now. When she reached for the candle, he covered her hand with his and jerked her up against his chest. She gasped in surprise as she collided with him, his foul breath in her face. Turning her head away, she tried to pull the candle from his hands.

"Give me the candle, Victor."

"Forget the damned candle," he growled. "You know, you're more beautiful in this evening light... so soft and golden." He began to push her backwards toward the bed. "I think it's time we got to know each other better, and I'm in the mood for love."

"No, Victor. Don't!" She pushed against him, struggling to free herself. He easily forced her against the bed and began removing her clothes, ignoring her protests. Buttons popped and material ripped as he fumbled in frustrated incompetence.

"Victor, stop it! Please don't do this!" Connie's mind was racing. She knew she couldn't out-wrestle him, he was much too strong for her. All she could do was try to talk some sense into him. "If you have any feeling for me at all, Victor, you won't do this. Please, you don't want our relationship to begin this way. It isn't right!"

But Victor had become a man possessed. Connie's struggles excited him. He wanted her, and he wanted her now. He could feel his desire growing. It had been a long time since he had made love to a woman, and all the months of wanting Connie, the frustration of having to control his hunger for her had built up into an uncontrollable mountain of need, and rage. He no longer cared what she wanted. He had only this driving compulsion to take her and make her his, and to hell with the consequences. Now she lay on the bed, trembling and naked, tears rolling down her face, pleading for mercy.

With shaky fingers he ripped his own clothes off. "You're beautiful," he said. "So soft and vulnerable. You think you don't want me, but I know that's not true. Look at you. You're trembling with excitement and longing. Oh, yes. You want me as much as I want you. I can see it in your eyes."

Now standing undressed before her, it was plain for her to see his arousal. That both shocked and frightened her. She knew she had to do something quickly or suffer the consequences. If Victor was capable of kidnapping and rape, he might also be capable of murder. She didn't think it was possible to be more frightened, but suddenly she was. She knew she couldn't just lay there and not defend herself.

With renewed determination, she jerked both her legs to her chest, then thrust out at Victor's stomach with every once of strength she possessed. The bed gave her good leverage, and the blow struck home solidly, slamming the air out of his lungs with a loud "whoosh." He doubled over, the force of the strike sending him backwards several steps. His face turned white, his eyes bulged out, and the most surprised expression crossed his countenance. Then he began to wretch and, covering his mouth, made a desperate dash for the bathroom.

Connie jumped off the bed and stared at him, surprised at her own strength. The sound of his vomiting sickened her, but after a few seconds she realized that this was her chance to escape.

Her clothes were thrown about the room randomly, but she quickly retrieved her pants and top and threw them on, not bothering with her underclothes. Looking around frantically for her shoes, she finally spotted them on the other side of the room. It would take precious seconds to retrieve them, seconds she didn't have, so she left them and raced out into the hallway barefooted.

Victor was still in the bathroom. The vomiting sounds were less violent now, but still audible. Connie ran past the bathroom and through the front room to the door. But Victor wasn't stupid; he'd locked all the doors.

She struggled with the lock, a dead-bolt which required two hands to open. Precious seconds ticked by as she tried frantically to figure out how to do it. The thunderous pounding of her heart blocked out all other sound except that of her heavy, rasping breathing.

She had no idea what Victor was doing now. The temptation to turn around and look was great. It would take only a second, but that could be the second that saved her life, so she focused on the door lock. After what seemed like forever, it finally slid open.

With a shaky hand, she reached up and grabbed hold of the doorknob. Freedom lay just beyond the door, and all she had to do was jerk it open and run for her life.

After Matt and Willy left the Morgan residence, they stopped back by Connie's apartment in the vague hope that she'd returned home, but were not surprised to find the place empty. Willy took Jazz inside so he could get a good dose of Connie's scent, and picked up a piece of her clothing to take back to the hospital parking lot with him. There was a small possibility that she had walked or been dragged away on foot and he wanted to see if Jazz could track her. Since she hadn't turned up anywhere else yet, it was time to check out that possibility. After Jazz got a good taste of Connie's scent, Willy put him back in the car and headed back into town.

Matt followed in his car. It was starting to get dark. Where could she be, he wondered for the umpteenth time? He felt that this was all his fault somehow. He'd known that Victor was becoming obsessed with Connie and he'd not done anything to stop him. In spite of Connie's insisting that he let her handle the situation herself, he knew he should have stepped in and set Victor straight once and for all. He should have put an end to it before it got this far; before Victor became so fixated on her and the situation got to this point of madness.

They pulled up into the hospital parking lot and parked close to where Connie's car was still parked. They got out of their cars, then Willy let Jazz out of the back seat. The young dog jumped out and ran up to Matt, barking and wagging his tail. Matt scolded him and made him sit and stay.

"Pay attention. You've got some work to do," he said. Willy commanded the dog to his side, let him sniff the shirt he'd brought from Connie's place, and sent him on the search.

Jazz started sniffing the ground and wagging his tail, then followed a scent over to Connie's car. He started to wine and jumped up on the door and looked inside, then turned and looked at Willy.

"Keep looking, boy, she's not in there," he said. Jazz knew that already and jumped back down to the ground. Continuing to sniff the ground, he worked his way quickly around to the back of the car, then emitted a low growl and barked twice at Willy. He sniffed the air, then the ground, then walked around in circles trying to pick up the scent again, only to return to the spot where he'd lost it. He laid down with his paws out in front of him and put his head on his paws.

Matt and Willy had watched intently, hoping beyond hope that Jazz would find a trail for them to follow. The look of hopelessness on Matt's face was more than Willy could stand, so he looked away.

"Well, that's that," he said. "She obviously didn't walk away on foot. She had to have gotten into another car. We might as well go back to headquarters and see if anyone else has come up with anything. You can call Adriana again, too. And we'd better arrange for someone to come and take Connie's car home."

There was no response from Matt, and Willy was beginning to worry about him. He'd never seen him so withdrawn before, not even when Lisa broke up with him. *I hope to God that we find Connie alive and well*, he thought.

When they arrived back at headquarters, Matt went straight to the telephone and called Adriana. Unfortunately she wasn't any help. She'd neither seen nor heard from Connie all evening. She'd called several of Connie's acquaintances, but no one had talked to her.

No one at headquarters had heard or found out anything, either. Matt crossed his arms tightly and paced back and forth. He spoke to no one, wrapped up in his own fruitless thoughts, his mind numb with worry. It seemed they were at a dead end. There were no new clues to Connie's disappearance, and what little trail they had on Victor was getting colder by the minute.

## Chapter 31

With trembling hands, Connie turned the doorknob--she could hardly believe it--she was almost free--the horrible nightmare was over! This would all soon be behind her and she could get on with her life. Taking a deep breath, she pulled the door opened... the darkness beyond beckoned, offering safety. A soft scraping sound in the room behind her made her jump and look around.

Victor advanced on her---face flushed---eyes bulging. A strong arm shot past her---slammed the door shut! He grabbed her---threw her up against the wall---his hands on her shoulders in a biting grip that shot knife-sharp pains into her joints.

She thought her bones were sure to break under the excruciating pressure. She turned white... her eyes grew huge and round... her breath came in quick, shallow gulps.

Victor's expression was a blueprint of rage---lips tightly clamped---eyes now narrow slits of flashing light---the whole face red, like it would explode at any second.

"What the hell do you think you're doing, you sneaky, cheating little bitch?" he screamed at her. Then his voice dropped to a deadly whisper, "You trying to run out on me again? Huh? Answer me!" he ended in another angry shout, making her jump.

Connie's heart hammered in her chest. Her eyes darted around the room, looking frantically. But there was no way out. There was only Victor. She felt cold and clammy all over...the room began to spin...she started sliding down the wall, weak with fear. Only his grip on her arms held her up.

"No, Victor! No!" she whispered hoarsely. "I just wanted a little fresh air, that's all. Honest."

"LIAR!" he shouted. "You were trying to run away!" With a snap he jerked her against his chest, bringing her face within an inch of his own.

The strong stench of stale liquor mixed with vomit sickened Connie...her own stomach churned and buckled...the taste of bile erupted in her mouth. Her heart continued to pound violently. More frightened than she'd ever been in her life, she sought desperately for a way to reason with him. But, she thought, how do you reason with a madman? "Victor, I...I'm sorry," she stammered.

"Sorry?" he whispered...and the whispering was worse than the screaming... "Oh, you're going to be sorry, all right. You're going to pay for what you've done to me tonight. It's time you learned a lesson." In a flash, he pulled back his arm and slapped her hard--twice.

Hot, searing pain exploded inside her skull as her head snapped backward. The room spun around at a crazy angle while little flashes of colored lights danced across her vision.

Her knees buckled...she felt herself slump to the floor as if in slow motion, no longer feeling any pain. Oh, God, she thought, I'm going to pass out and he's going to kill me! I can't...stop...him. Get up...run...fight. Must stay awake... stay...awake... Finally unconsciousness kindly claimed her.

All evening Matt drove around searching for Connie every place he could think of, rechecking her apartment a dozen times.

Adriana called her house every half hour...and called Connie's friends in between to see if she'd shown up anywhere... even tried to bring up a vision of where she was. But no one had heard from her, no one had seen her, and no visions came. About 12:30 a.m. she fell asleep on the couch in front of the TV.

It was 1:30 a.m. when Matt got home. He woke up Adriana and sent her to bed, then took a long, hot shower and went to bed, but he couldn't sleep. His mind kept replaying the last few weeks when his relationship with Connie had developed far beyond what he ever thought it would. He'd fought it long and hard, but as he lay there thinking about it, he came to realize that he'd fallen in love with her in spite of his best efforts not to. When that knowledge came to him, and he thought he might never see her again, his whole being filled with an overwhelming, hollow emptiness like he'd never felt before.

The ache was so powerful he couldn't lie still any longer. He sat up and looked at his bedside clock. It was 3:00 a.m. Pulling on his clothes, he quietly let himself out of the house and got into his cruiser and drove around the back roads of the county until it was time to report to work.

By 8:00 a.m. that morning, Tuesday July 7th, Matt was at his desk in police headquarters studying the evidence they had gathered on Victor Prescott. A rifle had been recovered from Victor's residence. Tests proved it was the one used to kill Jonathan Dewy and Don Suma the past Sunday afternoon. Also, a bottle of knock-out pills found in the bathroom cabinet proved to be the same drug found in Rusty McGreggor's bloodstream after he drowned.

    Victor had no previous police record. His reputation in town was impeccable, and when the news got out that he was being charged with murder, the shock rocked the community. Calls came in from dozens of people who knew him and were enraged at the charges against him. But the evidence was in, and the facts spoke loudly.

    Pictures and descriptions of both Victor and Connie were faxed out in an all-points bulletin throughout the states of Washington, Oregon, Idaho, Nevada and California. In spite of the alert, neither could be found.

    Chief Baxter assigned two teams of men to continue the search while the rest of his men returned to their regular duties. He worked his own shift, then put in an additional four hours work a night on the case.

    Matt and Willy were one of the teams assigned to the case. Baxter didn't want Matt on the case, but Matt pleaded to be allowed to participate and Willy backed him up. Together they finally convinced the Chief that Matt could do the job. He looked at Matt and saw the worn, haggard look of him. But beneath that appearance, he could also see the fire and strength of a determined man. His experience told him that Matt would be all right.

    For his own part, Matt hoped the Chief's belief in him proved accurate. What Baxter didn't know was that Matt hadn't slept at all last night and he had no intention of wasting any time sleeping until he found Connie.

Morning sunlight streaming through the small window brightened the bedroom in which Connie slept. She'd regained consciousness sometime during the night, but had immediately fallen into a deep, exhausted sleep.

Victor had quietly unlocked the door and now stood watching her soft, easy breathing, satisfied that she'd recovered from the previous evening's clash with him. He hoped she'd learned her lesson. It gave him no pleasure to beat her, but she must learn to behave herself and if that took an occasional lesson, that's what he'd have to do. A little discipline never hurt anyone...it was, in fact, a necessary part of life. Life without discipline was chaotic and unproductive. It had taken his first wife five long years to learn not to cross him, but once she'd finally submitted to his rule, they had been much happier and life had become a pleasant and satisfying experience. He knew he was right. Connie would also learn to yield to his wishes.

As he watched her, she began to stir. The sunlight moved across the bed, rudely awakening her. She blinked and rolled away from the light. The movement caused her head to throb. She groaned and put her hands to her face and became immediately aware of her swollen eyes and bruised cheeks. What in the world? she wondered.

"Good morning sleepy-head."

The deep, male voice startled her--her eyes flew open, or at least as open as they could, and she saw Victor standing over her, a blurred, foggy vision.

"Where am I?" she asked.

"Why, you're in your new home, of course. Don't you remember?"

His soft, penetrating laughter sent chills down Connie's spine as her memory came flooding back. She pulled the covers up snugly around her shoulders and neck, a symbolic but futile barrier between herself and Victor. Licking her dry lips, she tasted blood, and remembered the grave danger she was in. Tears gathered in her eyes and spilled over onto her cheeks.

"What do you intend to do, Victor? Keep me here against my will forever?" she asked through swollen, cracked lips.

"I thought I told you..." he replied, a self-satisfied smile on his face. "I'm going to keep you here until you come to your senses and agree to marry me, then after we're married we'll move to Spain. I have a small villa there. You'll like it."

She looked at him aghast. My God, he really believes that's going to happen, she thought.

"Victor, are you crazy?" she asked, her voice choked and hoarse.

"You'd better get something straight right now. I don't love you--there's no way I'll ever marry you--and I'd rather die than be forced to spend my life with you!"

The smile faded from Victor's face. He looked at her down his long nose, his eyes narrowing at her words. It was a long moment before he spoke.

"Well, then. It seems we've come to an impasse. Perhaps you need some time alone to think over your foolishness." He turned to leave the room.

Connie saw he was going to lock her in again. "Wait!" she demanded, glaring at him.

"Yes?"

Her pride fought with reality for several seconds, but she hadn't used the bathroom since the evening before. She glared at him for several moments. Reality finally won out. She lowered her eyes and spoke softly.

"I'd like to use the bathroom. Please."

Victor seemed pleased that she was acting rational again. It gave him hope. He smiled and agreed to let her go to the bathroom. While she was in there he made her a light breakfast of fresh fruit and juice. He'd planned well and they would get by fine on the provisions he'd stocked. When Connie finished in the bathroom she felt much better. She returned to the bedroom with trepidation, wondering what Victor would try next.

But Victor had decided to give her time alone to think. He put her breakfast and a bottle of water in her room and locked her inside. He said the solitude would do her good. She agreed. Anything was better than having to put up with him in the same room. He had slipped beyond the bounds of reason and she needed time to think of a way out of her situation.

She spent the next 36 hours in relative solitude. He allowed her out to use the bathroom when she needed to, but otherwise kept her locked inside the bedroom. Little changed. She still refused to see things his way.

Becoming frustrated and angry after almost two days, he decided it was time to try another tactic.

## Chapter 32

At 8:45 p.m. Wednesday evening, Lt. Willy Wilson sat at his desk at police headquarters writing up a report of the day's activities. He glanced up as the door opened and watched Matt Goodell walk in. Although Matt's clothes were clean and he looked well groomed, upon closer examination Willy could see lines of stress around blood-shot eyes shadowed by dark circles. He shook his head.

"You look like hell. I thought I told you to get some sleep."

"I tried," Matt responded, "but I couldn't sleep. I just keep thinking that I've failed her. I should be able to find her, but I can't. There's a part of the puzzle missing. It's right here in front of us, but we can't see it. I keep thinking I've almost got it figured out, then everything gets fuzzy, you know what I mean?" It was a rhetorical question and he continued without waiting for an answer, "I know what you're gonna say... 'If I would get some sleep, I could think more clearly. I'd be able to see what that missing piece is.' You're right. The trouble is, as soon as I lay down and close my eyes, my brain kicks into gear and starts going over everything again---only dammit, I'm not coming up with any answers."

Willy knew there was no use in pretending he didn't know who "she" was that Matt kept referring to. "How long has it been since you had more than an hour's sleep?"

"I don't know. About three days I guess."

"Maybe you should see a doctor about some sleeping pills."

"No. I don't need a doctor. And I sure as hell don't need to get pumped full of sleeping pills. I'd be worse off than I am now."

"Well, you're sure as hell not much good like this. If the boss sees you, he's going to kick you out on your ass."

"Oh, yeah? Well, then I guess I'd better not let him see me."

"Whatever. By the way, I stopped by the hospital earlier to check on Marie Sanchez. She's doing much better. The doc says she'll make a complete recovery. And she's ready to testify against Victor. Actually, she's mad as hell."

"Yeah, Adriana told me the same thing. That's good news. I'm glad she's going to be O.K. I can't wait to get my hands on that son-of-a-bitch myself."

At her apartment in town, Adriana paced back and forth between her kitchen window and the front door. She'd tried to watch TV, but found she couldn't focus on the program. Picking up a romance novel she'd started, she'd tried to lose herself in the story but the words just blurred together, so she gave up and proceeded to pace.

Why couldn't she help Matt find Connie? She'd tried so hard to bring up a vision of where Connie might be, but all she drew was a blank cloud of fuzzy images of some stupid little house in the middle of nowhere, surrounded by trees and brush. She could vaguely hear muffled voices, but nothing clear. She assumed it was a childhood memory of one of their summer camping trips in the mountains. They'd often visited a small cabin belonging to one of her uncles. That must be what she was seeing.

What good was this gift of clairvoyance if she couldn't call upon it when she needed it, she asked herself. It wasn't a gift after all, she thought, but a curse.

As she passed by the kitchen table she picked up a sweater that lay there and hugged it to her breast. It belonged to Connie. She'd recently worn it on a date with Matt. He'd brought it over hoping Adriana could pick up on Connie's energy from it and get a psychic reading to help them locate her. But so far it hadn't helped.

She stopped pacing and stood at the kitchen window, staring out into the gathering dusk, still clutching Connie's sweater. Storm clouds that had been gathering all evening darkened the sky prematurely, creating an eerie and ominous atmosphere. As she watched the storm come, her heart became heavy and sad.

A loud clap of thunder suddenly rumbled through the house, followed almost immediately by a blinding flash that split the sky from north to south. Mesmerized by the thunder and lightning, she never even flinched, but stood staring into the oncoming storm as if hypnotized. Crackling with heat and energy, it seemed to come alive, to become a separate entity, to pulsate and throb of it's own accord. And that's when she saw it. Her vision. The one she'd been waiting for. The one she'd prayed for. The one she hoped would help Matt find Connie.

*Darkness made it almost impossible to distinguish faces. She heard thunder, then a flash of light and she saw vague images of Matt and Willy talking to someone...the person had his back to her. She saw a small, dark house...then Connie's face. She was scared...and crying, and her face was bruised. There was a lot of yelling--and gunfire--and someone screaming--more gunfire--a dog barking--and Matt's face... someone shot--she couldn't see who...and then silence...and darkness...then another clap of thunder followed immediately by lightening--the man talking to Matt and Willy turned around--she recognized Sam Morgan...*

The vision went as quickly as it had come, leaving her weak and shaky. Closing her eyes, she tried to bring it back...but she couldn't. What did it mean, she wondered? Sam couldn't be involved in this...it didn't fit. But whatever his connection, she had to let Matt know.

Matt and Willy hovered over Willy's desk, brainstorming for ideas on the case when the ringing of the phone interrupted them. Willy reached across his desk and picked up the receiver. He spoke briefly to the person on the other end of the line, then handed the phone to Matt.

"It's your sister."

Eagerly taking the phone from him, Matt spoke anxiously into the receiver, "Did you find her? Has she called?" The disappointment on his face told Willy the answer.

As briefly as she could, Adriana told Matt about her vision. "I don't know what it means, Matt. I'm sorry it wasn't any clearer."

"That's O.K. I'll take a drive out there and talk to Sam. Maybe something will come of it this time. `Bye." He slowly replaced the receiver as he tried in vain to make a connection between Sam Morgan and Victor.

"What the hell was that about?" Willy asked, not liking the expression on Matt's face.

Matt explained briefly, then said, "I'm going to take a run out there and see Sam. You wanna go?"

Willy made a quick decision. "You'd better ride with me; you're in no shape to be behind the wheel of a moving vehicle."

Before they could get out of the police station, the phone rang again. Willy grabbed up the receiver and spoke briefly to the person on the other end of the line. Matt watched him impatiently, the words floating by him in a dazed jumble.

After a few seconds, Willy replaced the receiver then looked up at Matt with a funny expression on his face.

"That was Sam Morgan," he said. "He said he might have something for us...come on, I'll fill you in on the way out to his place." He was relieved to see a spark of life come into Matt's eyes.

Outside, darkness was coming fast. Storm clouds had been gathering all afternoon and evening, bounced around by the wind as it gusted and kicked about. The temperature had dropped considerably, bringing relief from the earlier 95-degree heat. Thunder echoed back and forth through the mountains, getting closer with each passing minute.

Matt slid into the passenger side of Willy's car. Willy jogged over to the dog kennel, retrieved the police dog Jazz and put him into the back of the car, then walked around and got in behind the wheel. As he started the car, he turned toward Matt and gave him a worried look.

"You O.K.?"

"Yeah, I'm fine. What's up?"

"Sammy Morgan said something kind of strange. It seems there's a house next to his that's been vacant for awhile, and that about three weeks or so ago he showed it to Victor. You remember, Sammy told us that at the dance. Well, last Sunday Victor was interested in looking at it again. Sammy had a bad case of the flu at the time and was too sick to take Victor down and show him. So Sammy gave Victor the spare key that the owners had given him for emergencies, and Victor was going to go down and take a look at it."

"What's so strange about that?"

"Victor never returned the key."

Matt sat up straight as Willy's words sank into his brain, adrenaline bringing him wide-awake. "Sweet Jesus --that's it --that's why we haven't been able to find them! They're not traveling across country...they're hiding out. Right here under our noses! That clever bastard." He pounded his fist on the car dash. "What are 'ya waitin' for? Let's go!"

Willy was glad to see Matt come alive. "Alright, alright... calm down. You may be right--this could be our lucky break. And you may be wrong. It could be just another dead end. But whatever we find, or don't find, let's do this by the book. We don't want to mess anything up,

O.K.?"

"Yeah, sure. Of course. But this is it, Willy. I can feel it."

They made the ten-minute drive out to the Morgan place in about seven minutes. Matt fidgeted, urging Willy to drive faster. His heart was racing with anticipation, his mind now tack-sharp. If gut feelings were anything to go by, this was the break he'd been praying for. He knew it as sure as he knew his mother's name.

Willy glanced at Matt, worried. If this turned out to be another false lead, he didn't think Matt could handle the disappointment.

And if it turned out to be Victor's hiding place, he wondered how Matt would handle that, too. Would he be able to trust Matt to remain in control of his emotions? Willy didn't know for sure how important Connie had become to Matt---he wasn't sure Matt even knew---but he could make a pretty good guess...it was the same way Willy felt about his wife---and he was crazy about her. He'd kill anyone who tried to harm her.

Looking at Matt now, Willy tried to read his thoughts but found it impossible. He saw only the wild look of a desperate man on Matt's face.

## Chapter 33

Down in the vacant house on the bluff, Victor decided it was time to move Connie to a new location. If he got her away from Pine Crest for a while, maybe she'd be easier to reason with. He looked out the window. The sun was going behind some gathering storm clouds. The gathering clouds would bring an early dusk.

They could leave as soon as it got dark and be over at the coast by 1 a.m. Nestled in the mountains of the coastal range was the cabin of an old hunting friend of his. Surrounded by lush trees and bushes, it was the perfect hideaway...isolated and unused most of the year, and accessible only by the track of an old road barely visible through thick, wild grasses and weeds.

He quickly made preparations to leave, throwing together all the food he had in the house into a box. Picking up the box, he carried it out to the car and stored it in the trunk. He didn't want to move the car out of the lean-to until it was time to go. No sense in taking a chance on someone spotting it from the road. He reached into the car and unlocked the glove compartment and pulled out something wrapped in a cloth.

It was a high-powered Browning 9mm pistol. He liked it for it's accuracy, balance and size. He checked the 13-round clip, then stuck the gun in the back waistband of his pants. Glancing around, he hurried back into the house. He wanted to move quickly. In his haste, he forgot to lock the front door.


The Morgan place was around the next corner and at the end of a short, straight stretch of road. Matt fidgeted constantly, his breath coming in short, rapid spurts. He strained to see ahead, but the corner blocked his view. As they rounded the offending corner he could see Marie Sanchez's house about a quarter of a mile away. Another quarter of a mile beyond that sat the Morgan home.

As they approached Marie's house, Willy slowed down and

turned off his headlights, leaving only the parking lights to see by. After they drove past her house, Willy stopped and they both looked for the driveway leading to the vacant house Sam referred to. When they spotted it, about halfway between the two houses, Willy looked closely for signs of recent use, but it was too dark by then to see anything.

"It doesn't look like there has been a car down this road in months," he said. "Sam must be mistaken."

"No, I don't think so."

"We're grabbing at straws here. Wasting our time."

"Dammit Will, you don't know that! They're here--I know it. I can feel it."

Wilson looked at Matt with raised eyebrows. "I think you're wrong, buddy."

Matt frowned at him, lips compressed and silent.

They pulled into the Morgan driveway, got out of the car and quietly closed the doors. The wind howled through the trees, breaking off small pieces of limbs and sending them flying through the air. Thunder continually reverberated back and forth between the mountains, quickly followed by bright flashes of lightening.

Jazz whined from the back seat, obviously not wanting to be left in the car. Willy spoke sharply to him through the partly open window.

Sam Morgan met them at the door. He turned on the outside light, flooding the small back yard and illuminating everything within its range, including Willy's cruiser.

"Sam, turn off that light!" Matt ordered, his heart in his throat. He felt like a duck on a target range.

"What for?" Sam asked, but quickly responded to the demanding tone of Matt's voice. The yard was once again blanketed in darkness.

"Because, dammit--if Victor is down in that house, we don't want him to know we're here!" Matt scolded him.

"Take it easy, Matt. He didn't know any better."

Matt just scowled and clenched his teeth, biting back more sharp words. Connie and Victor were down in that house. There was no doubt in his mind. Adriana's visions were many things... surprising, wild, unexplainable, mysterious. But one thing they never were.

They were never wrong.

Willy studied him for a few moments, then nodded. Turning to Sam, he gave him strict orders to stay in his house and not come out until it was all over. Sam's mouth fell open and he started to protest, but found himself speaking into the empty darkness.

Matt and Willy hurried back to the car. Matt reached for a flashlight while Willy put a leash on Jazz and let him out of the back seat. The dog wagged his tail and jumped around, but quickly came to heel on command.

They ran back to the driveway leading down to the vacant house, then down the driveway toward the house. Jazz became more excited and began emitting low growls. The hair on his back raised up and he strained forward against his leash, ignoring Wilson's repeated commands to heel. Willy finally gave up and released the dog, knowing that he would stay close.

Jazz immediately ran ahead of them, then stopped dead when he ran across a fresh scent trail, and began running back and forth trying to find the source. Willy watched him and knew he was onto something hot. Jazz ran around behind the house to a small lean-to shed, then back around to the front door.

When Willy and Matt reached the house, they looked in through a small window. A candle burned brightly on top of a cardboard box in the small frontroom. Dim light filtered down the hallway that Matt thought must lead to the back of the house and possibly the bedrooms and bath.

"There's someone in there. It's gotta be them. Let's break down this door and get in there now!"

"Hold your horses, Matt. It could be anyone. It might even be the owners. They could be having a romantic evening and enjoying the storm. We can't just bust in for no good reason!"

"Oh, hell, Willy. What are you waiting for? It's them and you know it! Even Jazz knows it."

Willy jerked around and came face to face with Matt. "You're losing your perspective, Officer. Don't get stupid on me or I'll kick your butt out of here, you got that?" he hissed the words out. "As for that dog, he's just a young pup still learning the ropes. Like a rookie, he sometimes makes mistakes. So don't put too much store by his behavior. I don't. Now...are you gonna do this by the book, or do I have to wait for your replacement to show up?"

Blood rushed to Matt's face. He clenched his teeth and held back the angry retort that begged to be shouted. After several seconds, his eyes dropped from Lt. Wilson's and he slowly exhaled.

"O.K. You're right. I'm sorry."

Wilson studied him for a moment, concluded that he had managed to calm the young man down, and decided he would be all right.

"O.K. That's better. I have to be able to rely on you, Matt. Can I do that?"

Matt's head jerked back up. He lifted his chin slightly, looked Lt. Wilson in the eye and firmly replied, "Yes, Sir. You know you can."

Wilson nodded. "Good. Now let's see if anyone's home," he said, and turned around and knocked on the front door.

## Chapter 34

Once back inside the bedroom, Victor poured Connie and himself a glass of wine. He set the two glasses on a small tray and carried it into the bedroom. There, he set the tray on the dresser. Handing a glass to her, he told her of his plans.

"We're going to take a little trip. I've decided you would benefit by spending some time away from here. I have a friend who has a cabin that he never uses, over in the coastal mountains. I'm convinced it'll do you a world of good to spend some time there." As he spoke, he turned and reached for his own glass of wine.

Connie watched him turn around, then gasped, her eyes widening in shock when she spotted the gun in his back waistband. She started to shake uncontrollably, her breath coming in sharp, little gulps. The glass dropped from her hand, shattering on the floor.

"What's wrong?" Vicktor asked, looking at her.

With a trembling hand, she pointed to him and stammered.

"You... you have a g-g-gun! Wh...what are you doing with a gun? My God, Victor!"

"Oh, this?" he asked, pulling the weapon out of his waistband and holding it out for her to see. "Just a little self-protection."

She'd seen and even handled guns before. Matt carried a gun and she wasn't afraid of that. But the idea of Victor having a gun frightened her more than she wanted to admit.

"Don't worry about it, it's harmless." He put the gun back into his waistband. "Let's just forget about it, O.K.?

"Now, let me tell you about this trip. I want to leave right away, so we don't have much time..." and he proceeded to talk. She tried to reason with him but he turned a deaf ear to her, so she finally gave up and began pacing across the floor, her hands over her ears. Outside, darkness had fallen. The wind had picked up and the thunderstorm that had been threatening for the past hour finally erupted. She stood by the window and focused on the storm as lightening streaked across the sky and thunder rumbled throughout the gorge.

Outside, Matt waited impatiently for someone to answer Willy's knock on the door. As Willy raised his hand to knock again, thunder rolled through the surrounding mountains, followed by a short flash of lightening and immediately another clap of thunder, closer this time. Matt saw something move out of the corner of his eye.

He jerked his gun from the holster, swung around, pulling the hammer back as he moved, took aim at the man standing ten feet behind him and squeezed the trigger just as a bolt of lightning blasted the sky. Something made him shift his aim just as he fired. Another crack of thunder exploded on the heels of the first, deafening the sound of the gunfire. It was followed instantly by another long, bright flare of lightning to reveal the man as Sammy Morgan.

As Victor spoke, Connie closed her eyes tight as if she could block out all sight and sound of him. But he continued to ramble on. She was thankful for the noise of the storm that drowned out a lot of his drivel. The man was a lunatic—absolutely and completely out of his freakin' mind! Dear God, how was she ever going to get away from him?

"Connie, dearest, you're not being reasonable. I'm telling you, this is going to be the best thing for us. You'll love this little place on the coast.

"It's secluded and quiet...really restful. There are deer and squirrels and birds. It's great. Kind of rustic, but romantic. The winters are mild compared to here -- we could stay all winter if you like. I know you're going to like it there, just wait and see..." and he babbled on and on.

Matt stared in disbelief at Sam Morgan standing before him, pale and shaken, but unharmed. Overcome with relief, Matt sagged against the side of the house, his gun dangling from his limp arm. Willy stood watching them and shook his head in wonder.

"Good God, Sam... What the hell are you doing here? Trying

to get yourself killed, you damned fool?"

"N-n-no, s-Sir. I just wanted to watch. I'm s-s-sorry." The color slowly came back into his face, the excitement of the unfolding events overshadowing his fear. Jazz ran over to him and began licking his hand, his tail wagging.

Lt. Wilson looked at Matt and raised his eyebrows in silent question. Matt had holstered his weapon, but was still shaken by his near-fatal mistake. Wilson could see the pressure was getting to him. The signs were unmistakable. He considered sending Matt back, but knew he'd have a fight on his hands if he tried to do that. Instead he talked to Matt for a couple of minutes to calm him down, and hoped to God that would be enough.

Lt. Wilson walked over to Sam. Reaching down, he scratched Jazz behind the ears and ordered him to heel. The dog responded immediately. Then Lt. Wilson looked up at Sam.

"Sam, you almost got shot here tonight," he whispered harshly. "You know that, don't you?"

Sam's eyes widened as he finally realized his close call with death. "Yes, Sir."

"O.K. then. We don't want that to happen, right?"

"No, Sir, we sure don't."

"Right. Now, I don't know what's going to happen here, but I don't want you anywhere near here. You understand? I want you to go back up to the house until we're done, O.K.?"

"Yes, Sir. O.K."

"O.K. We'll come up and talk to you later, when we're done here. I promise. Now get going."


Connie concentrated on listening to the wind howl outside and the thunder rumble. She thought she heard a knocking at the door, but couldn't be sure. She stopped pacing, opened her eyes, moved her hands away from her ears and listened carefully.

Victor grabbed her by the shoulders and shook her hard.

"Stop ignoring me!" he shouted. Then he twisted her arms around behind her back and pushed her against the wall. Bending his head, he kissed her roughly on the lips, then trailed hard, vicious kisses down her neck. His body pressing up against hers was hard and unyielding.

Adrenaline raced through her veins. As soon as her mouth was free, she emitted an ear-splitting scream that made the thunder seem quiet.


Willy had turned and walked back to the door and knocked again, louder this time. A few seconds of silence passed. Even the storm seemed to be holding its breath.

Then a loud, piercing scream split through the night, breaking the silence. Jazz jumped, barked once, than stood leaning against Willy's leg, trembling with excitement.

Willy looked at Matt and nodded once. Then, drawing his gun, Willy reached for the door handle, twisted it carefully, and slowly pushed open the door. Jazz was beside him, with Matt following closely behind, his gun also in his hand.

They heard sounds of a struggle coming from the other room, where dim candlelight flickered, and quickly headed in that direction.

Jazz stuck to Willy's leg as if glued there, emitting a low, almost constant growl, ears back but no longer afraid, eager now to do his job.

They moved through the house quickly, unheard over the sounds of the storm. It took maybe six seconds to reach the bedroom door. Matt reached out a hand and touched Willy on the shoulder. Willy froze in mid-step, jerking his head around at Matt in question. Matt wanted to take the lead.

Shaking his head, Will indicated that Matt should stay behind him, then turned back around and carefully peered in through the open doorway. He signaled to Matt and they both stepped into the bedroom, guns pointed at Victor, who had his back to them as he continued to force himself on Connie, ripping at her clothing.

Shaking with uncontrollable rage at the scene before him, Matt shoved his pistol back into his holster as he lunged across the room. The bed standing between him and the two struggling against the far wall was no obstacle.

"Victor!" he bellowed as he leaped onto the bed and flew through the air at Victor.

Startled, Victor released Connie, who jumped to one side as

Victor pivoted around. Matt landed on him, slamming him into the wall---the same wall he'd just had Connie pinned against. Caught completely by surprise, Victor had no chance to draw his own gun.

Matt doubled up his fists and hammered Victor with a barrage of vicious blows until Willy grabbed him with both hands and pulled him off.

"That's enough," Willy shouted, turning and putting himself between Matt and Victor. Facing Matt, he pushed him back to the edge of the bed. "Get hold of yourself, Matt!"

Victor, having quickly recovered from Matt's attack, reached behind his back, pulled out his gun, and aimed it at Willy's back.

"Look out---he's got a gun!" Connie screamed.

But Matt was ready. Glaring at Victor even as Willy pushed him back against the bed he saw Victor pull out the gun. He pulled out his own weapon---as Victor aimed his gun at them---and Matt pushed Willy aside just as Victor fired.

A hot searing pain shot through Matt's left shoulder. He fired three quick shots--and one more just to be sure. It wasn't needed. Out of the corner of his eye he saw Jazz lunging for Victor as Matt fired off his last shot. The dog clamped his young, strong jaws around Victor's gun arm in a vicious, bone-crushing attack, snarling and shaking Victor's arm with all the energy and hate he could muster. Matt's last shot hit the dog, slightly grazing him across the shoulders. Jazz whined, but hung on to Victor's arm and went down to the floor with Victor as he fell.

Matt's first bullet hit Victor in the side. The next two went straight through his heart. He was dead before the fourth shot was fired.

Willy raised himself off the bed where Matt had flung him and called off his dog. Jazz was silent and obedient in spite of all the excitement, proving himself to be the trooper he was trained to be. It all happened so fast, there was no time for comprehension, only instinct, training and gut reaction. Matt, Willy and Connie stood and stared in disbelief at the man on the floor whose life had ended so violently.

Gun smoke and shocked silence filled the room.

x x x x x

Made in the USA
Lexington, KY
17 May 2010